THE MYSTERY OF
YAMASHITA'S MAP

THE MYSTERY OF YAMASHITA'S MAP

James Mckenzie

James Mckenzie

Book Guild Publishing
Sussex, England

First published in Great Britain in 2006 by
Book Guild Publishing
Pavilion View
19 New Road
Brighton, East Sussex
BN1 1UF

Typesetting in Baskerville by
Keyboard Services, Luton, Bedfordshire

Printed in Great Britain by
Antony Rowe Ltd, Chippenham, Wiltshire

A catalogue record for this book is available from
The British Library

ISBN 978 1 84624 098 0

To Mum and Dad, my family, and to all the branches in our tree. A special thanks to my wife Helen, and to my children Steven and Ian, for their patience and forebearance.

Acknowledgements

To Nards Jebulan for giving me the inspiration, Paul Elliott for burning the midnight oil researching and documenting, and to the Filipinos who welcomed me into their culture, teaching me to believe the unbelievable. My thanks also go to Carol and her team of super heroes for bringing this story to print.

Prologue

The Philippines, 1945

The broken bodies lay like hideous eruptions on the surface of the dried earth, their dull skin reflecting no light from the sun that beat down relentlessly in the midday. Of the living, there were two kinds: those that had guns, and those that had spades. Those that had guns stood on the high ground or under the shade of small beige tents which were flecked with fly droppings and particles of mud thrown up over time, time that had been harsh and unyielding. Those that had spades dug on and in the ground or occasionally, with backs bent, carried wooden boxes which weighed much more than their undernourished frames could manage.

Every few minutes another body would lose its will to cling on to what little life it was allowed to have and fall to the ground where it was first beaten, to make sure of its lifelessness, and then dragged away from the mass of people to the makeshift open grave at the edge of the encampment. Those with guns knew that time was running out: they knew that the war was coming to end and things had to be taken care of before it did. This was why their guns were seldom in their holsters; this was why their

1

whips had more ferocity these days. This was why their beatings aimed to kill rather than to reprimand. A dead worker here was better than a sick one and so the transition from one to the other was undertaken swiftly and with precision.

The flies made their home in the bodies that were left for the animals and the sun to pick over. The mounds of tanned leather human skin were a testament to the worthlessness of the lives of those who once inhabited this area but had now fallen victim to slavery or greed. You might, if you glimpsed a slight percentage of this picture, think that it was, perhaps, a vision of hell, that the faces of those who dug and carried and sweated and died were those of the dammed, forever doomed to carry on as they were now for all eternity; that the relief of death would never come. Here though those who keep guard are all too human.

In one of the tents, at midday, General Tomoyuki Yamashita sits and eats. The rice bowl he holds in his lap has been with him all through the war and before that was his father's. He is a man who likes to do things correctly, with little or no fuss. Gently, he lifts the bowl to his lips and, with his fingers slightly bent, scoops the rice into his mouth, letting the pale brown sauce fall over his lips and run down his chin.

His light brown uniform is stained slightly with sweat and dust but, unlike most of those around him, is in near perfect condition. He places the bowl on the small side table, pours some tea into a cup and drinks. With thought, he shouts to his second in command who has been standing outside the tent waiting for just such a call.

'Amichi!'

The flaps of the tent open and a young officer shuffles in apologetically. He knows also that time is running out; he knows that soon the Americans or the British will be

2

coming through and that the questions they will ask will be hard for him to answer. This is the time, he thinks to himself, that one becomes a man again instead of a soldier; these are the times when one has to answer to oneself. He can barely believe he is thinking such things and, quickly, checks about him to make sure no one has been reading his thoughts.

Trying to avoid eye contact, he watches Yamashita slap his open palms on to his knees..

'How is the tunnelling?'

Amichi bows. 'Very well, General. We have eighty percent of the gold stored already, a little more to go.'

'Good, good. What about the jungle, how long will it take to cover the ground?'

'Not long at all, General, perhaps a year at the most. The growth around here is tremendous. They say if you stand still for an hour you will become part of the jungle.'

Yamashita laughed, exposing his shining white teeth and blood red tongue. 'Good, but I don't intend to become part of the jungle. As soon as this is done I am returning to Tokyo. I have done with this place.'

'Yes, General.'

'However, I need you to do something. I want you to map the area. Once the jungle reclaims this land you won't be able to tell this place from thousands of others.'

'Yes, General.'

There was a pause between the two men; a question that remained unasked seemed to disturb them both. The tunnels that hid the gold, that were being dug day and night by the Filipino workers, would surely pinpoint the location even after the jungle had grown back. The entrances to the network of underground safes would be visible from the ground. All they had to do was come back to the same area and there they would be. Amichi hesitated but Yamashita waved him away with a magisterial movement of the hand.

Outside, the air was hotter than he had remembered and Amichi felt it hit his skin. The sun was so bright now it hurt his eyes to look at the dry ground that would be watered by the rains of the rainy season and spring to life again. He called to a foot soldier to bring him a pencil and paper and began to scout the ground.

Mapping the area was going to be difficult, it all looked so similar, but eventually he found local landmarks: the river, the hill, the pile of earth where last week's dead were buried. After he had completed it, he had it sent to Yamashita.

Hour after hour, day after day the trucks kept coming with gold. Most of it had been looted from temples and rich homes across almost the whole of South East Asia. It had been one of those spoils of war that is broken and invested by the winner but hidden and longed for by the loser. Amichi thought that, in a war, very rarely do those who own the riches ever get to keep them – eventually they will always be taken either by the victor or the vanquished. His thoughts turned to his own two daughters at home and, not for the first time that week, he wished he could see them again.

Suddenly, one of the guards of the tunnel entrances rushed up to him, bringing him out of his dream with a jolt.

'The tunnel,' he shouted. 'The tunnel is down.'

Amichi weighed up the situation. He knew in these moments there was protocol to be followed. He had been given orders for such occasions and these had to be adhered to, whatever the moral implications.

He examined the mouth of the tunnel. 'Any Japanese in there?' he asked.

'Yes, Captain.'

4

'How many?'

'Six, Captain.'

'How many Filipinos?'

'Thirty-eight, Captain.'

Amichi thought a moment. There were enough Japanese to warrant digging them out; no amount of Filipinos however could justify the spending of time and the endangering of Japanese lives. If the ratio was a little higher, the tunnel would just be closed up and work begun somewhere else. He ordered the tunnel to be dug out and made his way to the general's tent.

In his tent, Yamashita studied the map. He liked its thoroughness and its complexity. He had thought very little of Amichi since he joined his unit: there was something weak about him, something untrustworthy. Yamashita decided that after this spell he would have Amichi sent to the units in Malaya, where the jungle is likely to swallow up young, irresponsible captains who look and listen too much.

He examined the map again. He recognised its contours and its landmarks. He carefully folded it up, flattening the folds with his strong stubby fingers. He leaned across his desk and picked up a small leather volume concerning the Buddhist temples of China; he smiled to himself at the aptness of his choice. Taking the folded piece of paper he eased it gently into the space between the spine and the binding, making sure it could not be seen from the outside. He opened and closed the book a few times to make sure it was safe and then replaced the book back on the shelf where it belonged.

For all his military history, for all his pride, for all his ruthlessness, Yamashita was a lacklustre man. Throughout all this his heart and mind raced with the thought of returning after the war and opening up the tunnels to find the gold that was waiting for him. One could live easily on a general's salary, but easy only. He had felt to himself that he was owed greater things by the Empire – the Empire that had taken his father and his grandfather, that had harried him round from place to place, never letting him rest, never allowing him any peace.

He thought about the time in the future when he could afford the lifestyle he knew he was born for. He thought of the faces of those who had ridiculed him in the past. He thought of their jealousy and of their hatred for him. In fact, he thought so hard of these things that he failed to notice, across the other side of the tent through a hole in the fabric, the eyes that had been staring at him for the last five minutes. The eyes of Amichi, which blinked once and then disappeared.

In one of the sweltering tunnels Bayani sat with his back against the cool wall of earth. He had been digging all day and the blisters on his palms began to ache with the pressure. The scarf tied tightly around his forehead was soaked with sweat and with the blood that dripped from the wound in his head. But he was a strong one; he had been born nearby and only just been captured by the Japanese. He could stand more of this; he could stand more than they could ever give out.

He glanced over and saw an old man he recognised from that morning. The old man looked in trouble – he was breathing heavily and his eyes were closed. Bayani noticed that there was a thin stream of spittle running from his lip, almost ready to hit the ground. The old man had been carrying boxes all day and was already broken by the weight. Someone, somewhere, thought Bayani to himself, must know about the things that are going on here. Someone must be able to help.

He slowly stood up and crossed the tunnel to where

the old man sat. He put his arm around the old man's shoulders and wiped his mouth with his shirt. The man rested his head on Bayani's shoulder and, as he gently stroked his head he felt the old man weeping.

Suddenly, there was a noise; a Japanese guard was pushing through the bodies in the tunnel. He reached the spot where the two sat and prodded Bayani with his rifle. Bayani did nothing, just continued to look after the old man. Again the guard pushed his rifle into the ribs of Bayani but again he did nothing. Quickly the guard raised his rifle as far as he could in the tunnel and brought it down squarely on the head of the old man, splitting it open and causing the blood to gush out over Bayani's chest. The old man fell forward and lay in the dust and the earth of the tunnel floor.

Bayani shot up and stood facing the Japanese guard. For a moment there was silence: all digging stopped, all movement ceased. The Japanese guard was shaking slightly, with fear or with anger, neither were really sure. Bayani picked up his spade and the guard flinched, holding and cocking his rifle at Bayani. For the briefest of moments the tunnel seemed to fill up with the breathing of the two men. There was nothing to choose between them; Bayani knew he had death on his side – here in the hell of the tunnel he owned death. He had no family to speak of now, no home to miss, no position to think of. Here, in this tunnel, he had all that he would ever have.

Bayani swung the shovel and felt it come crashing down into the wall of the tunnel. He began digging as he had that morning and all the others like it since he had been taken captive. The Japanese guard smiled slightly and lowered his gun. Deep inside him he knew he had had a lucky escape; there is a fear that only an oppressor can feel – it is the fear of knowing you are pushing someone who has nowhere else to go.

7

Outside, Amichi was overseeing the digging of the collapsed tunnel. Diligently he ordered the earth to be removed with hands rather than spades to avoid further collapse. As the tunnel was freed, men clambered out with their faces and bodies covered in black dusty earth. They looked for all the world as if they were crawling from their graves on judgement day – their eyes blinking in the sun as they crawled through the ever-widening gap that had been opened up in the side of the mound.

From the tunnel he worked in Bayani could hear the commotion. He had felt the tunnel implode and guessed it was only a few hundred feet away, perhaps even the tunnel next to the one where he was working. He had got used to collapses, either of his tunnel or the surrounding ones. Some days there would be as many as three or four right after each other. The earth would shake and rumble and then there would be silence. The awful silence of men trapped.

Amichi dragged a comrade out of the hole in the ground. The man coughed and spluttered and his spittle made dark patches around his mouth. Amichi cleared his throat and poured some water over his face to wash it. He could see the fear on the man's face. Whoever works underground, whether they are miners or tunnel diggers or those who oversee them, gradually comes to accept the danger, but it is ever present. There is a constant fear of a collapse, a constant notion that the walls are beginning to move and the roof is beginning to cave in. Amichi himself had had friends who had entered the mouth of the tunnel in the morning and not come out again.

The tunnels were freezing cold in the morning, but as the day and the bodies in them heated up they became ovens which slowly cooked those inside until they thought they would rather die than last another day. All the time, there was the moving of the boxes, all the same size, all made of strong Japanese oak, each one containing gold, stolen and melted down into perfectly-sized ingots, for after the war.

Of course, Amichi knew that the Filipinos knew nothing about the gold. They were merely told to dig and carry and they dug and carried. They were expendable in this operation and they were the one commodity that was cheaper during war than at any other time.

Slowly, all of the Japanese were removed from the tunnel and, one by one most of the diggers came out also. Had there been a head count, it would have revealed that six were missing, lying dead by the portion of the tunnel which had seen the heaviest collapse. But there were no head counts any more; there was not the time and besides, one never counts that which is useless.

In his tent Yamashita was writing his report. This whole operation, of course, was sanctioned by the Imperial Army and, because of that, he had to document everything. Of course, what was the harm if a few details here and there went missing, like the location of a certain tunnel, the full map of the area, the number of boxes stored or the exact contents of each box?

Yamashita smiled at his creativity as he managed to weave all four of these lies into his report, which concluded that a great many of the Filipino captives were, even now, cheating the Imperial Army out of many of the gold bars by storing them in tunnels dug under the cover of darkness. He wrote of his suspicions regarding Captain Amichi, thinking that perhaps the young officer would be better utilised if he were to be offered a desk job in Manila, ordering supplies or seeing to everyday logistics. He thought that he should be sent word of his family and wished for leave to see them.

Sealing the paper he placed it in his case and poured

9

more tea for himself. He did not mind the heat here – the heat was something that one could regard as rather pleasant after a time – but he hated the flies. They crawled over your skin and on your eyes as you slept; they buzzed around your face and caused a gentle breeze to blow eerily across your skin. Once again, he swatted one but it evaded him and flew out of the tent. Yamashita arose, crossed the tent and lay on his small mattress. He sighed to himself. These days of war were torture for a man of his sensibilities.

With a groan he eased himself down and lay, gazing up at the ceiling of the tent, where the sun illuminated it. His eyes closed and he heard the faint sound of the men as they worked. He could feel himself drifting off to sleep.

He awoke with a start, realising there was someone next to his bed. He sat up and quickly grabbed the gun that he kept beside him. As his eyes opened, however, he realised it was only Amichi.

'Yes?' he said, angrily.

Amichi held a piece of paper in his hands. He nervously fidgeted with it, rolling it over in his fingers, creasing its edges.

'This came, sir.'

'What is it?'

Amichi held it out before him. 'I think you should read it.'

Yamashita rose and took the paper. He crossed the tent and picked up his reading glasses from the small desk. The script was hastily written with a pencil that needed sharpening. It said that the time was nearly up, that the Americans had killed hundreds of thousands in one day, and that he had to return to Manila and then go on to Tokyo.

Yamashita slowly sank down into his chair. He thought

to himself for a moment. He knew what this meant. In war, you do what you can, you survive for that day only, you are happy when it ends and you can say to yourself, 'I have made it for another day'. You sleep and then the next day it begins all over again. This strategy only works, however, if either the war continues or you win. In war the loser loses everything.

Amichi hovered over the general's shoulder. He knew too what the letter meant. He knew that the dead in the hills and the gold could not be found. He knew that nothing of what they had done here could ever get out to the Americans or the world that they represented. The new world that was coming closer and closer with each day. Amichi leaned closer, until his breathed flecked the side of the general's face. 'General?'

Yamashita was silent.

'General? What will we do? General?'

Slowly, the general turned. His face was splashed with beads of sickly sweat that emanated not so much from the heat as from the situation. Again Amichi spoke.

'General? We can't leave the tunnels as they are. We can't leave the area like this for...' He stopped briefly. 'The Americans.'

The general looked again at the paper he held in his hands and brought his face up to the level of Amichi. Avoiding his gaze and staring straight ahead he whispered, 'Blow up the tunnels.'

Amichi had feared this moment. He recoiled. He had lived this moment for the last few months. He knew that there would come a time when the choice would be made, but there was nothing to say now.

'Make preparations, Amichi.'

Amichi left the tent and crossed the small patch of land to the tunnel entrances in a daze. He knew what this meant. For there to be no sign of what they had done here, for there to be no record, those who had worked the tunnels day and night for a year or more would have to buried with them. He just didn't know yet if he was to be one of them. The day seemed darker now, the sun a little dimmer, the flies a little closer. He found it hard to breathe as he surveyed the tiny holes cut into the side of the hill, out of which small men like ants constantly appeared.

He called a sergeant over and ordered all the dynamite they had to be brought up to where he stood. From where he was he could see the rest of the jungle. It seemed so peaceful, so serene and so still. Somewhere he heard the striking of shovel or pick on hard earth and it seemed to sound on forever. This was a sound he had heard every day for longer than he cared to remember. He knew what was happening here. He knew that this was merely the outcome of one man's ego. He knew that all these deaths were avoidable, that they were a product of a mind that had become diseased and removed from reality. He knew that there would be nothing for him unless he took it and made it his own.

Quickly he ordered the explosives to be piled high in the tunnel entrance. These were good soldiers of the Empire – they acted without thinking, without question- ing. When it had been done he walked to Yamashita's tent.

'The tunnels are primed, sir,' he said.

Yamashita was sitting in his chair, head bowed in a strange intensity which seemed to transcend the tiny surroundings. He was silent and his eyes were closed. Amichi moved over and stood beside him. Still the older man said nothing.

'The tunnels, sir...'

Yamashita raised a hand to stop the other from talking. Quietly, he lowered it again and placed it on his knee.

The two men stood together in a silence that lasted for minutes.

Suddenly, Yamashita opened his eyes and stood. 'Shall we prepare?' he said, and walked out. Amichi, thinking that his time was ripe, reached a hand out and grabbed the small book where he had seen Yamashita hide the map of the tunnels. Quickly he placed it inside his shirt and followed his general outside to the heat of the day.

Yamashita stared at the tunnel entrances. 'Is there enough?' he asked, nodding at the explosives.

'Enough to blow five times as much,' Amichi said.

'And the captives?'

'All but a handful still digging inside.'

'What about Japanese?'

Amichi looked around him, quickly counting in his head. 'About thirty.'

Yamashita bowed, Amichi did not know whether in prayer or in guilt.

'Give the order,' Yamashita said and Amichi raised his hand.

In the tunnel Bayani first heard the explosion then felt the shockwave as it blew through him and the others. At first, of course, he thought that it was collapsing but pretty soon he realised that no collapse was ever so strong or so violent. He felt the bodies of those around him falling; he could hear the breath being torn from their chests and could sense the fear in the air.

Suddenly, someone said that the tunnel had been blown and that there were dead men by the entrance, so he pushed his way to the front. He could smell the rich smell of blood as his fingers scrambled over rocks and bodies and the remains of the wooden boxes. Behind him someone lit a match but was told to put it out quickly. Above the sound of panic he heard clearly the voices of the Japanese soldiers attempting to calm each other down and assure themselves that it must have been some kind of accident. They will be digging, they said to each other, they will be digging us out even now.

Bayani knew, however, that never did the entrance of the tunnel collapse: the entrance was shored by thick wooden beams; there was no chance on earth they would have collapsed. He knew that for some reason it had been blown.

He dug with his hands at the wall of solid earth that stood before him but after a few minutes gave up. The fallen beams and the earth had formed a thick wall which completely covered the inside of the tunnel. There was no way out. He slumped down onto the floor and placed his head in his hands.

To his right a fight started out. Two Japanese guards had been arguing over what to do next and voices were raised. The air in the tunnel got thicker as they screamed and screeched at each other, pulling at each other's clothing. One of the guards pulled a gun and fired. The noise reverberated around the tunnel and caused clods of earth to fall from the roof. Bayani jumped up and made a lunge at the guards in the darkness. He found the gun, wrenched it from the hand of the guard, then made his way to end of the corridor, where he sat again.

All about him men were moaning, in pain and in fear, their voices – some in Japanese, some in Chinese, some Filipino, some in dialects he could not understand – had a strange eerie quality about them. The panic had receded now and all that was left was the dim roar of humans trapped like animals.

For hours, they waited for the digging but no one came.

Bayani, coughing with lack of air, crawled through the tunnel to where he had stood as the explosion happened. The voices were less now, there was less movement. As he made his way across the bodies that now seemed stacked almost to the roof, there was very little resistance. He felt each one as he passed and realised they were dead, either from their wounds or from suffocation. He reached the area of the tunnel that was clearer and sat, gently rocking. The guards who had been desperately trying to find a way out had stopped now; mostly he could hear them gently crying in the dark or talking to loved ones or saying nothing at all, just breathing deeply as the air became thinner and their heads became lighter.

When he could hear no more, Bayani reached for the gun and lifted it to his head. He closed his eyes. Outside nothing was disturbed by the single gunshot that came from deep within the tunnel. All the soldiers had gone now, moved out in the past six hours. All the captives had been killed or else had escaped back into the jungle. The sun was down and only the empty tents fluttered slightly in the evening breeze giving signs that the life that had been here was here no longer.

Manila 1946

The trial had ended and the verdict was in. Anyone who watched it was in no doubt as to the outcome: these were some of the worst crimes of the Second World War. The litany of inhumanity seemed to stretch on forever and no one really knew how many had died on the various missions of General Tomoyuki Yamashita. The General was taken into the holding cell to wait for his time.

Outside in the street people were smiling as they heard the news. They had followed the trial ever since his capture and were glad that it was finally over. Most people knew someone or had heard of someone who had been killed by Yamashita's troops and now they were satisfied that the justice that had been promised to them was coming. Only a few mumbled and moaned about the paucity of real justice, the imbalance – one's man's life for thousands.

Most, however, smiled and slapped each other's backs, thinking the war had finally delivered its last victory and it was theirs.

In the morning they took the general, who had freshly shaved, and led him to the gallows. The day was bright and hot as many days are in Manila. They led him up the stairs to the platform and placed a rope around his neck. There was a small crowd gathered outside the prison where the execution was being carried out; men and women jostled for position, straining to hear anything from inside the walls, but it was impossible. A seller of fruit wandered among them, lifting the atmosphere to one of market day or carnival and the look on the faces of each of those attending was of quiet joy, tinged perhaps with anxiety that all should go well.

Inside, they pulled the lever and the general fell.

The gates were opened and a guard let the crowd see the body, gently swinging in the sunlight. The crowd cheered, some women hugged each other, men pushed and shoved so that they could get a better view, desperately wanting to make sure it was him, that it was Yamashita and that he was finally dead.

Towards the back of the crowd, a man with a large head scarf stood quietly contemplating the scene. In his hand he held a book close to his chest and in the book a map was concealed. On the back of the map he had written his name, Amichi, so that history would know his own culpability, his own guilt.

1

Hong Kong, present day

Professor Okada sat at one of the long desks that faced towards the window. The sun was just dipping below the line of the harbour and it threw startling patterns of light on the wall. He raised a prism-like geodesic crystal to the window and watched as the light refracted and sent spectral shafts of different colours around the room. No matter how many times he did this it still delighted him as much as it had when he was a little boy. He was fifty, balding, and had been a Reader in Geology at Hong Kong University for almost twenty years, but it was the simple things still that kept him going.

Classes were almost over for the summer and he was looking forward to the fishing trip he had planned. Fishing was never really his thing; he liked to sit and watch the water. Often he would forget to bait the line specifically to avoid the accidental catching of a fish that he found so ugly and unwholesome. He looked forward to spending some time at his cabin by the river, where he could collect samples from the local rock formations and sit and watch the water for most of the day, seeing in its brightness something that was lacking for most of the year spent in the big city.

He carefully placed the sample back into its case and brushed off the dust that had gathered on its top. Then he replaced the whole thing back in the drawer and hopped from the tall lab stool he had been sitting on. Really, one of these days he should start that diet he was always meaning to go on. Really, one of these days he should start looking after himself a little.

The door to the lab swung open suddenly and a bright young Japanese girl danced in.

'Lisa,' the professor exclaimed.

'Hello, uncle,' she replied. 'I've come to take you home. You will be here all evening if I don't drag you away.'

The professor smiled and touched his nose with his index finger. 'You know me too well. But I must just finish up a few things.'

'Uncle...'

'Just a few things.'

As he pottered about with slides and charts that meant nothing to Lisa she idly looked around the room.

'What are these rocks?'

'They are samples. Some I collected myself, others were donated, others have been here for years. As long as I can remember, anyway – longer than twenty.'

'Some only look like rock.'

The professor laughed.

'Some only are rock. Geology is ninety per cent rock, nine per cent volcano and one per cent gold.'

'You have gold here?'

'Yes, a piece somewhere, but it's unprocessed. It would leave you highly unimpressed.'

'That's life, I suppose.'

'Well,' the professor said. 'That's geology anyway.'

Lisa picked up a stick of chalk and started signing her name across the blackboard. The professor winced as the chalk scraped and whistled its way across the surface.

'I may be some time yet,' he said. 'Why don't you go

20

to the machine down the corridor and get us both some coffee?'

He handed Lisa some change and set about arranging charts and books, depositing some into his briefcase, dropping most on the floor.

At the coffee machine Lisa hesitated for a while, making the momentous choice of tea or chocolate. From the corridor on the fifth floor you could see right into the heart of Hong Kong. She liked to watch the bustle and the business of the streets at this time, when it was at its busiest. Down in the street, however, today, something caught her eye. In amongst the thousands of people milling to and fro was a young woman, dressed in bright red, running. Lisa moved over, nearer to the window and leaned her forehead on it. Squinting, she could clearly make out the face of the girl – she looked Japanese and was clearly running for all she was worth.

Lisa adjusted her glance along the street and saw she was indeed being chased by four men dressed in smart but plain clothes. The first of the four men wore sunglasses and had a shock of dark black hair. His hand was permanently placed inside his jacket as if concealing something – perhaps, Lisa thought to herself, a gun.

She shook herself. How ridiculous, she thought, the girl was running away from the police, or she was running to catch a taxi, or else she was running from a jealous boyfriend. These things happen all the time in a big city like this. She had, after all, been told many times that she could be obsessive and compulsive and that some day her imagination was going to get the better of her.

She took the cups from the machine and made her way back to the classroom where the professor was clearing up. Something, however, made her stop; something made her put the cups down on the ground and make her way back over to the window. Something made her press her nose up against the glass again and look downward to the street below where she saw the girl in red enter the University by the front door, leaving the men chasing her at the entrance unsure of whether they could chance going in.

Lisa once again shook herself. There was, she reasoned, nothing to be concerned about: it was a student late for an appointment, a date at the library or cafeteria, or with an important deadline to meet. She bent down and picked up the cups again then made her way to the classroom of her uncle and kicked open the door.

Inside the professor was slumped over the desk. Lisa felt her heart leap; she slammed the cups down on the desk beside her and rushed over to where her uncle's body lay, seemingly lifeless, across the table. Slowly she leaned over. She could hear the sound of her blood rushing through her ears and feel the beat of her heart on her ribcage. Her hand touched his shoulder but he did not stir. She walked over to stand beside him but his head was turned away from her.

'Uncle?' she whispered. 'Uncle?'

She rose and walked round to the other side of the desk where she saw his face, eyes wide open staring at the desk with intense concentration. As he saw her, his face lit up slightly in a smile. 'Diamonds!' he said.

'What?'

'A diamond, around here somewhere – if you see it, grab it.'

Lisa began to look on the table. 'Is it small?' she asked.

'Not too small, but it's clear, few facets, very unreflective … was very cheap, hardly worth bothering about.'

Lisa patted the desk with her hands. 'Sample?' she asked.

Her uncle looked up. 'A sample of what?'

'Was the diamond a sample … for the lab?'

The professor smiled. 'My cufflink,' he said, and showed her the space where once a small, evidently cheap diamond had sat. Suddenly there was a crash and a rush of air as the door to the classroom flew open. Both Lisa and the professor turned around with a start and Lisa recognised the girl who ran in as the same one she had seen in the street below only moments earlier. The girl looked half dead. She was about twenty and had long black hair tied in a ponytail behind her head. She wore a distinctive red coat, the type they used to wear in the country years ago but which was very seldom seen these days. Her brown eyes flashed wildly as she crossed the room. 'Okada San?' she said, barely able to speak through either fear or exhaustion.

The professor replied that he was.

'I have something for you,' the girl said, and brought out a small book, bound in brown leather. She looked at it lovingly before thrusting it in the professor's arms. There was a brief moment of silence that was broken only by the sound of further footsteps in the corridor outside. The girl looked terrified and ran over to the window. Finding nothing there she opened the door and ran out, crashing it behind her.

She knew that Tanaka and his gang had come from Japan and that they were after her. They would probably catch her and she knew they must not get the book. She had been lonely in Hong Kong. There were very few Japanese, but she had read articles in the newspaper written by a Professor Okada, he seemed intelligent, he seemed kind, he seemed honourable.

The professor and Lisa looked at each other barely able to speak. Lisa pointed at the book. 'What is it?'

Her uncle opened the cover and read a little. 'It's about Buddhist temples in China. How odd. I have never heard of the author. A European by all accounts, but it's in Japanese. A fair mix of races, wouldn't you say?'

'Is there anything written in it?'

'Yes, hundreds of things.'

'No, anything written for you.'

The professor leafed through. 'No, no pencil or pen marks, just the printed word.'

'Perhaps she had heard of the renovation projects you have carried out, uncle. Perhaps she wants you to carry out some work.'

'She could have asked. I would probably have said yes,' he said with a smile. 'Perhaps it's late at the library and she didn't want to pay the fine,' the professor said and laughed to himself. 'Anyway, whatever it is, I need to find that diamond before I go home or I will never be able to speak to your father again.'

Lisa bent and started patting the floor with her hand but only succeeding in finding dirt.

Later that evening back at his small apartment, Professor Okada ran a bath. As he eased himself into the hot water he opened the book. There was something about it that puzzled him – nothing he could put his finger on, just something that did not seem right. Not with the writing but with the book itself. It did not feel right; it was stiff and would not close properly.

Gently he lay back and let the water flow over him. He raised the book to his eyeline but could see nothing. He assumed it must be the book's age – sometimes when the leather had got damp and then dried quickly it shrank, either splitting or making it hard to close. Sometimes, the binder would use too much glue or too little and this would manifest itself in inconsistencies later in life. He shook the book but nothing came out. It was definitely there though – something about it was not quite correct.

Suddenly he noticed something. It was the spine, the

24

spine was stiff. He had had a book like it once – the paper that made up the thick binding had come loose and he had to get it rebound because it wouldn't close. He turned the book sideways and held it up to the light. Was there something there? Some dislodged piece of paper?

The telephone rang.

The professor sighed. Of course it's a cliché, he thought to himself, but it also happens to be true that just when one is in the bath the telephone begins to ring. He put the book on the side of the bath, got up and threw a towel around himself. Placing his feet in his traditional slippers he exited the bathroom and shuffled out to the hallway. He picked up the phone.

'Hello?'

'Uncle? It's Lisa.'

'I was in the bath, I couldn't...'

'Uncle, you have to put the TV on.'

'Lisa, you know I hate that thing, I can't hear it very well and...'

'Please, uncle, put it on and turn to channel two.'

The professor sighed and placed the receiver on the hook. He crossed the room to where his small black and white portable stood, dusty, in the corner. He blew some of the dust off the screen and turned it on. He waited for a moment for it to warm up and show the picture. As the image on the screen slowly began to emerge the professor recognised the face of the girl he had seen that day. They were displaying her photograph. Somehow, though, the professor thought her face looked different. She was smiling; there was none of the panic he had seen earlier in the day. It had none of the terror, none of the fear.

The professor turned up the sound.

'Passers-by say the girl ran into the temple to escape

four men who had been seen earlier that day following her. The girl is said to be twenty-six years old and thought to come from one of the small islands around Hong Kong or possibly the New Territories. The police say her body was found near the altar of the temple. She had clearly committed suicide. No one has come forward to help them with their enquiries.'

The professor turned the TV off. The young woman he had seen that day, who had rushed into the classroom, was dead. He sat down, barely able to believe it. No wonder she had seemed in so much trouble, he thought to himself, no wonder she looked frightened for her life. She was. Slowly the professor returned to the bath and again lowered himself in. He thought again about why she had chosen him that day before entering the temple and why she had chosen to take her own life. What does it take, he thought, to make a fully grown girl with everything life has to offer kill herself in such a public way – and what had he to do with it?

He thought of Lisa and of how he would feel if anything were to happen to her. He wondered about the girl's family. What kind of father allows his daughter to run about a big city like a crazy person, giving elderly professors presents of books and then disappearing? What kind of people had she been raised by? Who would let their daughter do such a thing?

Miles away on the small island of Ap Lei Chau they were lowering the body of Matsuo Amichi into the ground just hours after his death. Inside one of the small houses, the photograph of his granddaughter, the one that had been used on the news that evening, lay on the table covered with a white cloth. The villagers said prayers for Amichi, who had never had a day's peace since moving there,

26

who always looked so sad and so uncomfortable, who always slept so badly. They prayed for his soul and wished that he might find more happiness in the next world. They had all heard him at night, after he had been drinking, shouting at the devils he saw before him, screaming at them to leave him. They had all seen him tear at his eyes and his skin, terrified of what the morning might bring. Some said he was in the army once, the Japanese Army but, of course, he never talked of such things; just lived drunkenly but quietly with his grand-daughter, who had inherited his sad eyes and his dark hair.

All the villagers bowed their heads over the grave and wished the curse that had afflicted the dead man while he was alive could be halted now. They wished too that news of his granddaughter would arrive from Hong Kong and that she would return safely to be by her grandfather's grave, as a granddaughter should. They prayed for him even though by his own admission he was dammed to spend eternity in limbo, neither progressing nor retreating. Some of the women threw flowers on his coffin, others just patted it on the way past, hoping that whatever had made him so unhappy would never visit them.

The professor let the water wash over him. He threw the book over to the other side of the room. Later, he thought to himself, he would give it a proper examination. At the moment he was content to just let his thoughts wander.

He woke with a start. The telephone was ringing again. The professor looked round. He realised he had been asleep for an hour or more. Quickly he pulled himself out of the bath, dressed and made his way again to the telephone. Whoever it was, they were persistent.

He picked up the phone. 'Lisa?' There was nothing.

'Lisa? Yes, I saw the programme on TV. Very interesting. Do you think it was her?'

Still no answer.

'Who is this?' he asked. 'Speak or I will put the phone down.'

There was silence. The professor slammed the receiver down and went into his bedroom. The phone rang again. He sighed. Do they never get tired of playing these games, he thought. He picked up the phone in the bedroom.

'I think this is pretty unfunny. I might be waiting for a call, or...'

A voice on the other end sounded, slowly and menacingly. 'The book, professor.'

The professor was startled for a moment. He caught his breath even though his mind was reeling. 'Who is this? What are you talking about? What book?'

'Professor, I know you have the book. The girl did not kill herself today, she had help.'

'Look,' the professor stammered nervously. 'I have no idea who this is but I warn you I am recording this conversation.'

'Really, professor? It doesn't look that way from here.'

The professor turned round quickly. He crossed to his bedroom window and looked out. Across the street was a telephone box but there was no one in it. The apartment opposite was empty and there were no lights on. There was nowhere else where he could be seen from; there was nowhere anyone could be. Just then he noticed a glint from the top of the building opposite. In the dim light of the Hong Kong evening he could just make out a figure on the roof opposite, a figure holding a phone. He quickly pulled the blind and once again put the phone up to his ear. Again he heard the voice.

'You know, professor, you really should close your blinds more often.'

The professor slammed the phone on the hook and darted round his apartment, pulling tight all the blinds and curtains he could find. He turned off the lights and gingerly peeked out of the window. He could see nothing now – the figure was gone. Quickly his eyes darted down into the street. Nothing. All he could see were the usual people milling around, going out, coming back. Tanaka was expert in mind games. The professor felt the sweat moistening his back and then it happened again – the phone.

His heart leaped again. The ring sounded so harsh against the silence of the empty room, it seemed to bounce off the walls and be twice as loud as it should have been. He crossed the room and, like a child, picked up the receiver.

'Uncle?'

It was Lisa. The professor felt the hairs on the back of his neck relax and his whole body lost some of the tenseness.

'Lisa, I'm glad it's you.'

'Why? Who did you think it was?'

'Never mind. Look, how are you?'

'I'm fine. Did you see the news?'

'You haven't had any phone calls?'

'Only from Fraser.'

'Anyone else?'

'No. Uncle, what's wrong?'

The professor suddenly thought, what if the phone was tapped, what if they were listening right now and he had given them Lisa's name? What if they didn't know about her until now? What if they were on their way over to her apartment as they spoke? He felt his muscles tighten again as he looked around.

'Look, Lisa, something has happened. I think we should meet.'

'Uncle? What's happened?'

He could hear the change in her voice.

'Nothing,' he tried to reassure her, unsuccessfully. 'Just something small, something very small, but I want to talk to you about it.'

'OK, do you want to come over here or shall I come to you...?'

'No,' he interrupted. 'It's such a nice night, why don't we meet at that place you wanted to go to, the one your friend owns.'

'But you said you hated the look of it.'

The professor did hate the look of it. It was red and shiny and the seats were plastic. The waitresses there had nametags that declared they were happy to serve you and their uniforms were too clean and too pressed. The professor liked his waitresses to look a little harried, a little unkempt; it made you think that the restaurant was busy and that the food was brought to the tables quickly. The same as you didn't want your furniture to look as if it had just been made, you didn't want your waitress to look as though she had just been washed.

Times, however, were desperate and it was a fool who would suggest he meet his niece at either hers or his.

'Yes, a great mind, however, can always be changed. Remember that.'

'Well, I guess you're right.'

'What I want you to do is call a cab, don't walk. Take a cab to the place and if I am not there waiting outside go straight in and get a table.'

'OK, uncle, but I really think you should tell me what's up.'

'There's no need and there really isn't the time.'

He put the phone down and went to the cupboard where he found his coat. He put it on, and his hat, and walked to the door. He turned and stopped. Quickly he went into the bathroom where he had left the book on the floor. He picked it up and placed it inside his pocket. With one last look over his shoulder he shut the door and ventured out into the hallway.

Outside the air was crisp and clear. The smell from the docks made its way through the streets and seemed to permeate everything with a thick salty odour. The professor decided to get a cab at the stand just around the corner from his apartment building. With his hand in his pocket clutching the book he strode up to the first car. He looked in the window. The driver was asleep with a cigarette dangling between his lips. The professor knocked on the window and made the man inside wake with a start.

'Benji's?' the professor asked.

The cab driver rubbed his eyes, thought for a moment then flicked his head backwards toward the back seat. 'Get in.'

All the way there the professor looked behind him. It was a journey of about ten minutes but it seemed to last hours. About halfway through the driver looked into his rear view mirror.

'You running?'

The professor replied, looking forward, 'Running?'

'Yeah, you keep looking out that window, you got to be running from someone.'

'No, I'm not running.'

'You sure look like you're running. I have seen runners and they always look out the back window. You know a runner, they always want to look out the window.'

The professor replied again, 'I'm not running. I am making sure I am not being followed.'

'They in a blue Nissan?'

The professor started. 'I have no idea.'

The driver nodded to himself wisely. 'Yeah, they're in

a blue Nissan, been following ever since we left. They police?'

The professor felt embarrassed and a little grieved at this. 'Not at all.'

'They gangs? Lot of gangs nowadays, betting, drugs, girls, you name it they deal in it.'

'It's none of those things ... in fact I have no idea who they are.'

'Ah,' the driver said scratching his nose with the corner of his driver's identification card. 'That's the worst kind.'

The cab pulled up outside the restaurant and the professor got out. He gave the driver the fare, and the driver leaned out towards him.

'If you're ever in trouble,' he said, 'Call my cousin, Joey Hutchins.'

He handed over a dirty tattered calling card that looked as if it had been printed in an airport. 'He's little crazy these days, but still good, still reliable ... if you are desperate.'

The professor took the card. He was desperate.

He could see Lisa was already inside.

In the restaurant the professor thought it was too loud and too light. Everywhere he looked, pink and blue waitresses with nametags moved with an energy that was almost superhuman, their eyes twinkling like robots, their legs barely moving as they skipped between tables. The music that played was a mixture of loud banging and heavy guitar; needless to say the professor hated it. He had never particularly understood music at the best of times, even less when it was forced in your ears in a kind of aural enema that left you feeling as though someone had sponged your thoughts. At least here, however, it was light and the music made it hard for anyone to overhear.

He looked behind him at the street as he closed the

door but could see no blue Nissan. Perhaps the cabby had been wrong, he thought to himself, they have been known to be ... on occasion.

Lisa was seated at a table and waved to the professor across the floor. Seated with her was a tall, nervous-looking Englishman, Fraser. He had met Lisa at university when they were both studying and had gone on to work in one of the bigger Hong Kong banks. He stood up as the professor neared the table, and shook his hand.

'Hello professor, nice to meet you again.'

They had only met on a number of occasions. Lisa, next to him, looked worried.

'Uncle, I hope you don't mind me bringing Fraser, only I didn't know what to think. I was worried when you said you wanted to meet up. What is this all about? You look terrified.'

The professor sat down heavily and ordered a glass of water. 'My apartment...' he stumbled. 'Someone was watching me through the window – they phoned and threatened me.'

'Why on earth would they do that?' Lisa asked.

'The book. They wanted the book.'

'The book the girl gave you?'

'Yes.'

The professor looked at Fraser. He didn't know if he could be trusted. Friends, it seemed, were hard to come by at the moment so he pushed on.

'They phoned, and said that the girl today had been killed. Lisa, she didn't kill herself, someone else did.'

Lisa looked shocked. Fraser dabbed at the corners of his mouth with a napkin.

'Whatever do they want with the book?' Lisa asked.

'I have no idea,' the professor said. 'But whatever it is, they will do anything to get it, even kill.'

They were interrupted by the waitress. 'Can I take your

order?' she asked with a friendliness that the professor found off-putting.

After they had ordered, the professor told Lisa and Fraser about the cab ride to the restaurant. They both sat, dumbfounded, through his story, hearing but not hearing, listening but not quite understanding. To them it sounded like the ravings of an old man who had spent too many years inside dusty classrooms. The professor began to see their doubt. He sighed.

'I can see you are not with me,' he said.

Lisa smiled. 'Uncle, of course I am with you. It's just ... well, a little hard to take in. This is a book after all.'

Fraser leaned forward. 'Have you got the book, Professor?'

He reached into his pocket, removed the book and handed it to Fraser, who gave it a cursory glance. Turning it over in his hands he opened the front cover. 'Looks like it's a book about Chinese Buddhist temples.'

Lisa laughed. 'We are aware of that.'

Fraser shrugged this off. 'Looks like some kind of calf skin, nicely done. Would have been a beauty a few years back. We see these in the bank, believe it or not. People leave them in deposit boxes, god knows what for. Suppose they think they're worth something. Only Americans ever bring them.'

'Are they worth something?' Lisa asked. 'That could be why they are after uncle.'

'Oh no, practically worthless, but it's old, no doubt about that.'

The professor pointed to the spine. 'That's why the spine has gone. Look, it doesn't close properly.'

Fraser fiddled with it. 'Well, generally the spine was the best part; it was the part the binder would be most proud of. The calf skin would have been soaked and stretched just right. These particular books very rarely perish in the binding.'

34

Fraser peered into the spine. 'There's something lodged in it, that's the problem. I wonder if it's a love letter. You haven't been receiving any *billets-doux*, have you, professor?'

The professor blushed. 'Not for many years, no.'

Fraser grabbed a chopstick from Lisa's plate and thrust it into the spine. After a few seconds of digging the map fell out onto the table. 'There,' Fraser said in a triumphant tone.

'What is it?' asked the professor. Fraser unfolded the paper.

'Looks like a map of some sort,' Lisa said.

'Where of?' asked the professor.

Fraser turned the map over in his hands. 'Do you know, I have no idea. Could be anywhere. There's jungle, there's a river, there's more jungle...' He thought. 'I'd say it was the jungle, wouldn't you?'

Lisa grabbed it. 'There's writing on it. Look – on the back. It must have been written at a different time. It's not nearly as faded,' she said and held the map up to her eye. 'Ami ... Amichi?'

Everyone looked puzzled. The professor was just about to offer a solution when his thoughts were interrupted by the waitress bringing their food. Fraser folded the piece of paper back into its tight square and replaced it back into the spine of the book. The professor still looked worried. Lisa watched as he ate, barely able to swallow, looking around him, trying his best not to let his feelings show but failing miserably.

'Uncle, why don't we walk you home and we can look at the map there. You look like a fish out of water here.'

The professor smiled. Now that she mentioned it he was feeling a little tired and his head hurt so much from the excitement. He was not used to such action, a man of his age and constitution.

After they had paid for the food, they walked home in the cool evening, chatting, trying to keep their minds off things. Every now and then the professor would stop and look behind him, desperately looking for the blue Nissan, but he could see nothing; either they had given up or he really was a stupid old man with too much imagination.

He put his key in the lock and opened the door. Before him his apartment lay in total disarray. Everything was turned upside down. His bookcase was lying on the floor next to a pile of books that had smashed the glass table in the middle of the room. His TV had been thrown to the floor and lay in pieces with the cord still plugged into the wall. In his bedroom his clothes had been strewn over the floor, paint had been thrown over his bed and his mirror had been obliterated.

The professor couldn't believe his eyes. Everywhere about him lay the debris of his life as if a hurricane had smashed every memory, everything that he held sacred. Every personal item had been either broken or defiled. From the other room, he heard Lisa screaming and he rushed in to see her.

On the kitchen table was a long lock of black hair and the distinctive red shirt of the girl they had seen that day and beside it a piece of paper with word BOOK, written in what looked like blood. The professor sank to his knees. His imagination had just seeped into reality.

2

It was strange how the city seemed alive some nights, the breathing of its people combining to form one great mass that moved in and out with mechanical regularity; the lights in the harbour blinked like its scales. The professor poured another drink into a glass that was already half full and took a gulp. He had always said to himself that at moments of extreme stress one needed to be at one's best, not fall apart or fall into drink. In this case, though, none of that seemed relevant and all he wanted to do was get smashed, absolutely smashed.

Fortunately, Lisa was on hand. She pulled the glass gently away from his lips. He barely noticed, and rested it on the table. Then she straightened his collar and kissed him on the forehead.

'You should go to the police, uncle.'

The professor stared ahead making no sound.

'They have gone too far doing this, whoever they are. Do you know who they are, uncle?'

The professor shook his head absently-mindedly, not wanting to rejoin the world – not yet. Fraser brought Lisa a coffee from the kitchen.

'It's a mess everywhere,' he said. 'Even in there. Were they looking for the book?'

Lisa nodded. 'I think so, don't you, uncle?'

'The book,' the professor answered.

'Uncle, you really must get some sleep. Fraser and I will stay here tonight, if you want.'

The professor stood up. 'No,' he said, kindly, drawing

what little strength he had left back into his heart and mind. 'No, they won't be back tonight; they have done what they came here to do. They have terrified an old man – that was their intent.'

Lisa patted his shoulder, then hugged him. 'Are you sure you don't want us to stay?'

'Yes, yes, you go. Be careful. I'll go to bed. I'll go to bed straight away.'

Lisa and Fraser left, leaving the professor alone in his apartment. Outside, the city hummed and throbbed, its dark shadows closed in around it, its winds encircled anyone walking along its streets. The lights, pink and orange neon, shone brightly against the black background of the night sky and the cars moved eerily along the roads.

Silently, a wisp of blue smoke twirled around the street lamp and spiralled up into the light. Quickly and quietly, it made its way along the horizontal of the lamp and, as if carried by some invisible internal force, flew into the air with languor. It weaved and swirled on the thermals of the night sky until it reached the professor's window where it crept through the crack between the glass pane and the wall. It moved through the apartment until it found the professor, asleep in bed.

All was black and he was unable to breathe. There was no light anywhere. He scrabbled with his hands and felt only cold hard mud. The walls seemed to be closing in and there was a smell of iron in the air. Reaching down, he felt, on the floor, something hard, something brittle – it snapped as he picked it up and fell into shards in his hands.

He guessed it was bone he was touching and he guessed that this was a place where death had happened, where death had been invited. Gradually, his eyes began to become accustomed to the light and he groped about and felt the artefacts of the dead, shoes, clothing, hats, hair. He was glad that he could

38

barely see, as his fingers drifted over partially recognisable objects that had been left by those who had perished here.

Suddenly he felt a wind on his cheek and turned, expecting to see light, but caught only a glimpse of a bright blue smoke that seemed to contain its own luminescence as it flitted through the black air of the cave. He thought to follow where it was going, hoping that it would lead to the outside, assuming that it was the smoke of some cigarette or camp fire that burned in the open air. He found that he was in a tunnel. Feeling with his hands he made out the distinct rounded construction of a military design. Still he followed the blue smoke; he felt by now as though it were leading him somewhere, although where he didn't know. Then he heard a ringing. He turned his head. The ringing was incessant, constant. He placed his hands over his ears to stop it but it carried on. It got louder and louder until he thought he could bear it no longer. He closed his eyes and held them shut for minutes.

When he opened them again he was in bed. The sun was streaming in through the window. The professor looked at the alarm clock with disgust, reached an arm out and flicked the small switch on its side. Mornings were the worst part of the day. He got out of bed and remembered suddenly the events of the night before. Ignoring the chaos in his apartment he pulled on his trousers and shirt, took the book from his jacket and headed out of the front door. He had decided the night before that he would visit the University library and research the name Amichi as it related to cartography or Chinese Buddhist temples. He knew he didn't have much to go on but libraries were his place, they were his territory and he knew he would be safe there, at least.

By the time he got there Lisa was already at one of the tables surrounded by books and opened newspapers. The professor sat down beside her and whispered, 'How are you getting on?'

Lisa shook her head. 'Not very well. Not one mention of Amichi in any of these books on Chinese Buddhist temples.'

She pointed to a stack of books a metre high. The professor laughed. 'Have you left any books for anyone else?'

Lisa continued: 'There is an Amichi mentioned in this volume by someone called Carter, but it's far too early, probably two hundred years off, no way would this Amichi be our one.'

The professor sat back and thought a while. He pressed his hands together in a manner that suggested prayer; Lisa thought perhaps he was praying, but for what she did not know. Slowly, he began to speak.

'What if ... what if he is not connected with Buddhist temples at all, what if the book was merely a way of hiding the map? Wouldn't that make sense, to hide a map inside a book that has little relevance to it? Perhaps the Buddhist temples were just a red herring to take us, and anyone, off the scent.'

'But uncle, that takes us further away from finding an answer. How do we even start to look for someone called Amichi?'

The professor thought. 'The girl,' he said finally. 'The television said that the girl was from a small island off the mainland. We have to find out which island. Perhaps she was related to this Amichi. Perhaps she *is* Amichi.'

'Uncle, how do we even go about finding which of the islands we are looking for? There could be dozens of possibilities.'

The professor smiled. 'The television also said that they were driving her body back tonight.'

Lisa asked, 'How does that help us? We can't follow them. We don't know where she is or when she might be leaving.'

The professor tapped his forehead. 'Listen, Lisa, they are *driving* her back tonight.'

'Yes, but I still do not see how that helps us, they could drive her anywhere.'

'To an island?'

Lisa stopped for a moment. 'If the police are driving her to an island it must have a bridge. Why would they not say, be flying her back, or sailing her back. How many inhabited islands are connected to the mainland via bridge?'

Lisa stood and rushed off to the reference section to see if she could find a detailed map of Hong Kong, while the professor sat back in his chair. The smile on his face gave something of his satisfaction away and the slight tapping of his fingers on the desk suggested the rest.

Lisa came back with an arm full of maps and booklets.

'There are five main bridges to inhabited islands. There are smaller ones but I guess records there would not be up to date anyhow. There is the Tsing Ma Bridge, of course – we can discount that, the Kap Sui Mun between Ma Wan and Lantau, the Ting Kau that connects the airport with Lantau, the Tsing Yi bridge that connects Tsing Yi and Tsing Chau and, lastly, the Ap Lei Chau bridge.'

The professor looked impressed. 'Good work,' he said. 'Out of all those only the last leads to a small island off the mainland, Ap Lei Chau. It would be obvious that the police could use the bridge to take her home. There is a large population there and it is an easy place to hide if you wanted to. I am sure, however, that they would keep records of births, deaths and such like.'

'Shall I get their number?' Lisa asked.

'Yes,' the professor replied.

Lisa returned with the number for the small police station that was housed on the island of Ap Lei Chau.

The professor looked at it quizzically. 'Good job,' he said. 'Very good job indeed.'

Outside the city bustled and the air was thick with smoke and exhaust fumes. In amongst the traders that floated by the docks sat a man, thirty-five, one of those people that you find difficult to place. He looked Caucasian, yet there was something distinctly Oriental about him. His face had the easy grace of someone who had once had money but had had to come to terms with losing most of it in needless ways. On his head was perched an American air force cap that jarred with the dirty white shirt that he wore open to the waist. It was early in the morning and already Joe Hutchins had been drinking.

He was finding it hard to sleep these days. It was too noisy for one thing, this big city; there were too many things going on that he wanted to be a part of. Every time he closed his eyes he would think of something and have to get out of bed, but that wasn't all. There were the visions. He called them visions but they were dreams, really – strange, weird dreams that seemed to come out of nowhere – that had suddenly started to affect him. Dreams of being trapped, of being in the dark, of smoke and flame and of death. He knew the dreams were leading him somewhere but he didn't know where.

So he drank and he drank heavily. It was barely midday and he had already finished a healthy bottle of bourbon, an American drink if ever there was one. Daddy would be proud! He raised the bottle and gave a toast to the brave boys of the American air force of which his father had been part.

'Here's to you, Pops,' he said to no one and swigged another mouthful, gulping it down, trying not to bring it back up again.

He was seated at one of the small stalls that grow like mushrooms about the Hong Kong waterfront. In front of

42

him was a bowl of noodles that he had no intention of eating. Every now and then to appease his stomach he would buy a bowl of noodles and stare at it for a while before taking another sip of bourbon and throwing the whole bowl away. His stomach was fooled for a while and he didn't have to go through the indignity of actually eating anything.

There were some who might argue that Joey Hutchins' life had hit a point of no return. He drank to keep out what was already inside his head but the more he drank the easier it was to sleep and the more he slept the easier life got. His father had been a US airman and his mother a dancer from China, not an unusual combination of nationalities in modern day Hong Kong but it had left him feeling out of place and alien. He was, it seemed, an alien in a land of aliens. He had wanted, of course, to follow in the old man's footsteps, dear old dad, the brave US pilot, but since the ever increasing paranoia of Americans in the 1980s, neither country wanted to claim him for their own and he ended up working a small Cessna out of Hong Kong delivering packages to the more remote of the islands.

That was until his brush with the local law.

It had been a tough time. The increased amount of traffic had slowed the flight paths down to the outer islands and besides he had no idea what was in any of the packages he couriered. He just picked them up and delivered them but, as he also knew, everyone hates the mailman. He should have known, though, he should have seen it coming, he had been in enough bars, enough gambling dens, enough dives to smell the smallest, sweetest smelling rat in the world. Money was tight, though, so he had taken the job.

There were three of them, in big expensive suits, with bulges in their pockets. Each of them wore enough gold to fund a small revolutionary army and had tattoos, in Chinese and English, on their hands, indicating which Chinese gang they were affiliated with. Up until then Joe had made a point of never accepting a job from anyone who smelt of cordite or who had tattoos on a part of their anatomy that couldn't be covered up by a shirt but, as you already know, money was short.

It was the smallest of the three men who spoke: 'How much do you want for taking this over?'

Joe replied, 'The usual rate – five hundred dollars.'

The man slammed a handful of bills on the table. 'There's a thousand, do you want to take it on?'

Joe gulped. OK, he thought, let me weigh up the situation. I have never seen any of these guys before, all of them look as though they have one muscle too many, they are obviously packing guns, they are wearing suits that Trump would die for and they lay double the amount of money on the table. He looked at them again. He felt a trickle of sweat running down his neck. These were the moments his mother had warned him about before she killed herself. These were the type of men she had said his father was – a louse, losers, criminal. But then again so was he. These were the type of men who paid you in dollars and gave you your change in teeth – your own.

'Hell, yes,' Joe said with a smile. 'Why not?'

So, he knew it now. He knew now it had been a ridiculous thing to want to do. Now he had the knowledge, now he had learned because if there was one thing you could say about Joey Hutchins, he learned from his mistakes. Mistakes were like women – it was never a good idea to visit the same one twice. Now it was easy to see he should have said thanks but no thanks and taken a beating. That would have been it, that would have been the end of it and he would still have had his plane. He would never have taken their money; he would never have delivered their parcel. He would never have flown over to some shit-kicking island and he would never have found the Hong Kong police waiting for him as he landed.

They searched his plane, found what they were looking for and impounded the Cessna 'for further investigation'. It was only because he had known the arresting officer through a certain acquaintance of his mother's (who it must be said knew a great many of the arresting officers of the Hong Kong police intimately) that he avoided being slung into jail and forgotten about. It was a bad time to lose the tools of your trade, just as the tourist season meant that the bars were opening. He had a lot of time on his hands and a lot of bars that would help relieve him of the thousand dollars that was burning a hole on his leg. He now also had a couple or three unknown thugs after him, eager to either get their property back or exchange it for one of his arms. He was rather attached to his arms or rather they were rather attached to him. That was when the dreams had started.

He could not remember exactly what day it was but it was definitely shortly after the bust. At first he had put them down to the drink. The type of bourbon they sold in the bars around Hong Kong could blind a normal man at thirty paces. Numerous times he had seen shiny faced tourists wandering through the dock with a sign saying 'Drunk and foreign, please steal from me' written on their backs or so it seemed to every petty thief and criminal that came their way. Hong Kong bourbon was made of the squeezings of old Kentucky liquor, the dregs that were left behind in the barrels. If Jack Daniels ever rose from the grave and wandered abroad he wanted to stay away from Hong Kong bars lest he end up crying in his sweet Southern whine: 'What have they done, ma, what have they done to my wonderful brew?'

Soon, though, the dreams happened whatever state he

45

was in. If he drank harder to forget them, there they were; if he went on the wagon to see if they would stop they would continue right over. It always started the same. The smoke, blue smoke swirling through his head then suddenly he was in blackness, a tunnel, he could barely see his hand in front of his face but he knew he was in a tunnel because of the walls, they bore down on him and threatened to crush him at any moment. He could smell the staleness of air that had been trapped for years and feel the oppressive atmosphere of a place of pain, fear and death. There was only the smoke that seemed to lead him in a direction that he had no choice but to go.

As he stepped he could feel his feet catching on stones and material but he could still see nothing. He stumbled and reached out to the wall of the tunnel – it was damp and cold. Treading carefully he made his way along the tunnel, running his hand along the wall for stability. Suddenly the wall on one side of him gave way to nothing and he realised he was standing in a large space in the tunnel. There was a presence here; the smoke got thicker around him. It smelt now of burning fires, hot and choking; the smoke got worse as he tried not to breathe it in. He put his hand to his mouth and nose and tried not to breathe but he could feel himself getting woozy. His head began to spin, he began to fall, a strange slow motion fall as if inch by inch, centimetre by centimetre.

Before he hit the ground he always woke up. He would jolt up, the sweat running down his forehead and into his eyes. He was more scared and more lonely than he had ever been since these dreams had started. There was something in them, an immense sadness that could not be expressed in any other way. Somehow he knew that something terrible had happened, something that had changed the balance of the world forever, something that was unforgivable – but what? He could not say.

So he drank, he did not mind telling you if you asked. If you bought him a drink and asked: 'Say, Joe, are you a drunk?' he would look right back at you and nod his head.

'You know?' he would say. 'I am drunker today than I been all my life and that's saying something.'

He raised his bottle to the sky and gave a toast to whatever god was looking down on him. 'Whoever you are up there, can you be sure to fill my bottle and empty my head for the night? Thanks.'

He drank heavily from the bottle, drained it of its contents and tossed it into the harbour. He looked up. There was a commotion, somewhere in the docks someone was making themselves known. Without looking round Joey Hutchins knew who it was: the guys in the suits who could crack heads for the Chinese Olympic team. Quickly he pushed his way through the crowd that had gathered outside the small café where he had bought his noodles. These places were on the dockside and very often had a back way to the harbour where the owners would unload essentials like rice, flour and illegal relatives.

He could hear the thugs behind him as he pushed his way to the back. Only this place hadn't got a back way and unlike most of the shanty buildings round here this was built like the Hoover dam. He looked around him – nothing. Nowhere to go and nowhere to hide. This place must have just recently been taken over; there was very little in the way of weaponry about, just some old chopsticks, a pan and a huge bucket of fish heads that was waiting to go out with the trash.

Joe heard the thugs outside. They had seen him come – at least that's what they thought they saw. Without thinking Joe climbed into the bin of fish heads. It stank like nothing he had ever experienced before. As he felt the juice slurping into his shoes, he could feel his stomach turn and he retched slightly as his shoulders hit the wet fish. Their eyes stared at his as he lowered his head under. He was glad he never ate now, he would hate to do this on a full stomach. It was hard to hear in the barrel but he could just make out voices and the scuffing of feet on a damp wooden floor.

Joe held his breath, more through the smell than any anxiety about being heard. There were voices, sharp and angry. The men stamped on the floor and thumped the walls.

'Are you sure you saw him come in here?'

'Yes, I told you, he pushed past everyone and came in here.'

'These waterfront places all look the same from a distance.'

'It was this one I tell you, the guy out front with the one tooth pointed in here.'

'He could've been pointing next door as well.'

Suddenly the voices stopped and Joe guessed they had spotted the barrel. Quietly but easily audible through the wood and the wet fish heads, Joe heard footsteps inch over to where he was hiding.

There was silence for a while. Joe could almost hear the cogs in their heads working. Neither of them was blessed with brains, he thought to himself, neither of them was over-endowed in the head department.

One of them spoke. 'What do you think?'

There was a pause. 'Smells like tuna.'

Then the sound of a head being slapped with an open palm.

'Is he in there?'

Joe could feel one of the figures closing in on him.

'If he is,' the voice said, 'I don't want him. Maybe you're right; maybe he did go next door.'

There was a scuffling of feet and Joe heard the men

barge their way out of the small space. He sighed with relief and breathed deeply again. All of sudden he remembered where he was and coughed as the thick smell of the fish hit the back of his throat. He fought his way out of the barrel and stood, soaking on the floor of the hut. His clothes were covered in fish guts and fish brains but he felt as if he had achieved something, something that he didn't think was possible anymore – he'd outwitted someone. OK, so that someone was two rather dim hoods who were after his blood but he had still done it. He had proved to himself that he could still do it.

'Let's celebrate,' he said aloud to no one and jangled the change in his pocket for effect.

3

Fraser had come along for the ride. The window was open and the Hong Kong highway was fresh and clear. The professor, Lisa and Fraser were travelling to Ap Lei Chau. Lisa had phoned the police but all they could say was there may have been someone by the name of Amichi living on the island, but they could not disclose any information. Lisa had had contact with these small provincial police forces before and knew very well that memories could be freshened up with money, especially if she gave it to them. They loved a pretty girl in distress.

Right now, however, most of that was forgotten as she drove along the road to the Ap Lei Chau bridge which would take them over the bay to the island. Fraser and the professor were in the back and the latter was giving an enlightening speech to the former about rock formations in certain parts of Europe. Fraser gazed out of the window with a glazed look upon his face; he was obviously regretting coming on the trip at all.

The trip to the bridge took about half an hour but all the while Lisa looked in her rear view mirror every second or so. She was taking no chances; any minute she expected to see a car following her or someone by the roadside brandishing a gun. She could not quite believe she was doing these things. One day she was a quiet research student at a reasonable-sized university, the next she was running from god knew who. She was reminded of that old Chinese curse, 'May you have an interesting life'.

The bridge was clear at this time of day and the car

sped across it, the wheels making rattling sounds on the grates at either end. As she crossed it Lisa thought to herself how beautiful it looked; the sea was so blue and calm, just the white tips of the waves betraying any kind of movement at all. She thought to herself that she would rather be nowhere else on earth than this city with its mixture of high-rises and fishing boats, the traditional with the modern.

Ap Lei Chau is a strange island to visit. It was a fishing village before the first opium war and lies to the south west of Hong Kong, next to Aberdeen harbour. It formed part of the Treaty of Nanking when the British took over Hong Kong in 1841 but was always the ugly sister to the larger island. It is a place where someone, anyone, could easily disappear if they wanted to. Its main inhabitants live in two large estates filled with state-built houses that served to house the homeless after the great fire of Aberdeen harbour. It is, however, its own world when it needs to be: surrounded by water, you can drive from one end to the other in less than half an hour.

Lisa stopped off at the police station. She left Fraser and the professor in the car while she went inside. The professor was still talking about the minutiae of European rock striation. His eyes lit up as he talked of the various strata of the rocks he had seen in Italy and France – of course, as he told Fraser, they are so similar and so startlingly different. Fraser lit a cigarette. It was going to be long trip.

He had taken time off from work to help Lisa. He didn't know what it was about her, perhaps it was her stupidly consistent devotion to her obviously crazy uncle, but he liked to be in her company. She had a sort of strength to her character that he had never found in girls back home in England. He nodded politely and opened a window to flick ash onto the road. He had noticed something: there were no other cars about. He thought how, even here in this tiny little island, it was odd not to have any cars about at all. It was almost as if some great sadness had descended over the place, as if some event had taken place that had robbed the island of its life.

Lisa came out of the station and walked around the car to the open window. Fraser thought how good she looked with the morning sunlight glancing off her skin and the sea breeze moving her hair. She stood with her hands on her hips like an angry schoolgirl in mid tantrum.

'No luck,' she said. 'They say they've never heard of Amichi.'

'Did you give them money?' Fraser asked.

'Of course, but someone else is obviously giving them more.'

'You think someone else got here first?'

'Well, when was the last time you heard of a Hong Kong cop not accepting a bribe?'

'When someone else was bribing him more.'

'Exactly.'

Lisa looked out across the island. It had an end of the world quality about it, the end of the line at least. This was a place that existed outside of time and normal society, a place that could swallow you up if you were not careful and never let you go. It was green but lifeless. The growing things on it seemed to do so out of spite. They were challenging the ground not to allow them, the dead dry ground full of salt from the sea.

'We'll have to look around,' she said. 'Do you want me to drive still?'

Fraser looked across at the professor. 'Hmm, perhaps you'd better let me,' he said and opened the door of the car.

After a few minutes' drive they entered a large estate

full of tall tower blocks. Fraser slowed down as they passed row upon row of tenement buildings. In the back the professor was quiet and stared out of the window at the growing number of food stalls and small shops that lined the pavements. Smells of all sorts wafted through the open window reminding him that he hadn't had any breakfast that day. He sniffed at the air and felt his stomach rumbling.

'Perhaps, er...' he began, 'we could stop and take a little air, or perhaps a little food.'

Lisa thought a while. 'You know, it might be a good idea to stop and ask someone about Amichi. We hardly know where to start here.'

Fraser pulled up in a nearby alley and he, Lisa and the professor got out. The professor straightaway headed for a fried crab stall, rubbing his hands together and moving faster than either of the other two had seen him move for years. As he neared the stall he reached into his pocket and pulled out a handful of change. Lisa laughed.

'Where do we start?' she said to Fraser.

Fraser thought a while. 'Well, we know that he liked books. Perhaps we should scout around to see if there's a bookshop nearby?'

'But would they know him?'

'Possible on a small island. It's worth a try anyway.'

Lisa agreed. They decided to split up to look for a bookshop and leave the professor to his crab. An hour passed and they still hadn't found anything. Fraser and Lisa returned to where the car and the professor stood, the latter covered in grease.

'Where have you two been?' he asked.

'Well, Fraser thought there might be a bookshop on the island, or at least someone who would remember Amichi. We went to look but...'

'Nothing,' the professor finished.

'No, nothing.'

'It is to be expected,' the professor said rather pompously. Lisa felt disgruntled. She was, after all doing this for the old man; she would much rather be at home now, studying for her exams that were fast approaching.

The professor licked his fingers. 'Hung Shing,' he said.

Fraser and Lisa looked at each other. 'What?'

'The oldest and largest temple on the island is Hung Shing. It's on Main Street about a mile away. They'll know Amichi there.'

Fraser stood open mouthed. 'How do you know that?'

'The girl. The girl committed suicide in a temple. It was a place of safety for her, a place of refuge, a place where she had gone since she was a child, perhaps. I had a student once from England, highly strung and very sensitive but a brilliant student. Every time she had an exam she would go missing and I always found her in the stationery cupboard. It got so that every time she went missing I would just go to the stationery cupboard knock on the door and say, 'Janet, I am waiting for your presence,' and five minutes later she would come out and get on with her exam. Do you know why she did this? Habit. When she was a small girl she had a panic attack and, not being used to these things, her mother locked her in a cupboard to calm her down. The dark and the warmth worked and ever since at times of stress she would seek out a similar place. The same with our girl – she was under great pressure and wanted to find somewhere she knew.'

'Uncle, that's brilliant, I am sure you're right. Where did you say it was?'

'About a mile away, I think, but before we go, perhaps we could just stop at the soup stall?'

The silence in the temple made it seem a million miles

away from the street as they walked in. Fraser's shoes tapped gently on the floor as they made their way through the main entrance and into the temple's inner rooms. The professor began to examine the many golden artefacts that lined the walls. He neared a statue of the Buddha and gazed lovingly at its curves and its grace. The air was spiced with incense that seemed to waft on some unnoticeable breeze and imbue anyone who entered with its scent.

Lisa noticed a priest bowed in silent prayer in front a large golden idol. She quietly made her way over to him. After a while the priest opened his eyes, bowed at the Buddha and turned to her.

'Yes?'

Lisa was taken aback: he was a young man, no older than her. She had assumed that all of the priests would be at least as old as her uncle and this one's youth surprised her. His eyes were a deep brown and seemed to sparkle with an inner strength that caught her off guard.

'Can I help you?' he asked.

Lisa stammered for her words. 'I ... I ... was wondering if you could help with a small problem I am having.'

The priest stood. 'I will if I can. Tell me, what is it?'

'I am looking for a cousin of mine.'

Lisa swallowed hard. Not only was the priest her age but she was now lying to him. She gave a quick glance to the golden figure on her left. She had never been particularly religious, in fact her father had been an atheist for most of his life, but she had always been drawn to spiritual people and had a respect for the beliefs of all religions, more for their psychological strength than for anything else. 'A cousin of mine called, Amichi? Do you know him?'

The priest thought a moment. 'Amichi? Amichi? No, I do not know him.'

Lisa was crestfallen. She had put her faith in her uncle's ideas; and thought that every idea he had would bear fruit. She turned to go.

'I do know *her* though.'

Lisa stopped. 'Her?'

'Yes, Akina. A beautiful but unfortunate girl. She came into the temple often, sometimes just to look around, sometimes to pray. She was a good soul.'

'Was?'

'Yes, she died very recently. She was not, I assume, your relative, otherwise you would have been aware.'

Lisa caught herself. 'Oh, oh no, I was not related, but I would like to pay my respects. Have you her address? Perhaps I can make some small amends.'

'A kind gesture,' the priest said. 'A kind gesture indeed. Yes, and I know she lived in Lee Tung. That's about ten minutes' drive away.'

Lisa thanked the priest and on the way out dropped a donation into the collection box. She explained to Fraser and the professor about the girl and about the priest never having heard of Amichi, the man.

'Perhaps he wasn't religious?' Fraser ventured.

'Possible,' the professor added. 'Or perhaps he never gave his name away. Perhaps he was too busy hiding from someone or something.'

By the time they reached the Lee Tung estate it was beginning to get dark. Lisa parked some way from the main buildings and they made their way on foot to the tall high-rise apartments. They asked around, had anyone heard of the girl? Did anyone know Amichi? Did anyone remember anything about her? But no one said anything, everyone was tight-lipped. It was Lisa who spoke first.

'If I didn't know any better I would say that they knew but were keeping quiet.'

'I thought the same thing,' Fraser answered. 'Everyone

we ask hesitates as if they mean to answer but think the better of it. Perhaps I'm just being paranoid.'

'Perhaps not,' the professor answered. 'Whoever was following me, whoever broke into my apartment would have a lot of weight in small place like this. Word of mouth soon gets around.'

Fraser and Lisa agreed. There was something odd about the whole place, something strange, like walking into a party and having all the chattering stop or the obligatory scene in a Western where the stranger would walk into a bar and the piano player would stop. They decided to return to the car and plan their next move. As they neared it they noticed a shadow hovering around the bonnet. The falling dusk made it difficult to see but they could all clearly make out the figure of a small boy. They rushed up to him and Fraser caught him by the arm.

'What the hell are you doing?' he yelled and the boy struggled to free himself. Fraser shook the boy. 'What were you doing to the car? Tell me, tell me.'

The boy seemed scared and began to cry a little as Fraser shook the life out of him. 'I was waiting,' he stammered. 'I was waiting for you to come back. I heard you were looking for Amichi.'

Lisa stepped in and pulled the boy from Fraser. 'Leave him alone! Leave him alone, he was trying to help us,' she said and set the boy on the ground.

'Are you OK?' she asked.

'You want to control your dog,' the boy said, and Lisa laughed.

'What's you name?'

'Huen.'

'Do you want ten dollars, Huen?'

The boy thought a moment. 'You got to be kidding me, lady, the information I got for you is worth a hundred at least.'

Lisa struggled to control her laughter. She liked this little street kid, who was dirty and smelled but was wise for his age.

'Well, I'll be the judge of that, shall I? What information have you got?'

'About Amichi. I heard you were looking for him.'

Fraser interrupted. 'Him? You said him?'

Huen recoiled. 'You want to give him a bone or something.'

Lisa turned to Fraser. 'It's OK, Fraser, let me handle this.'

'Yeah, let her handle this,' Huen said.

'Yes, we are looking for Amichi. Do you know anything about him?'

'Do I know anything about him?' Huen laughed. 'He was only my neighbour for most of my life. I only knew the whole family, him, her, the other her and the her that died.'

'Where do you live?'

'Well, I did live there.' He pointed behind him at the huge tenement block. 'Until my dad died. Now I live in lots of places.'

Lisa bought her hand to the boy's face. He flinched a little and then stood still. 'On the streets?' she asked.

'Yeah, the streets, the drains, the back of people's houses, anywhere I can find. So, you want to know about Amichi then?'

'Yes,' said Lisa, and pulled out a roll of dollars from her handbag. The boy's eyes lit up, then faded as he looked around himself with a paranoiac air. 'You don't want to go flashing that around here, lady. There are some tough people around here.'

Lisa laughed a little. 'I think I'll be OK.'

'Well,' said the boy. 'It's your money. Did we say one fifty?'

Fraser leapt forward. 'We said one hundred, you little creep.'

Lisa shot him a glance. 'One fifty it is.'

She handed the boy the money and he counted it before bending over and stuffing the notes in his sock. He straightened himself and looked all about him, his bright eyes shining in the gloom of the evening.

'Amichi's granddaughter committed suicide recently in Hong Kong. They say his family is cursed now. They say that anyone who has their blood is sure to be in great danger. First Amichi dies, suddenly, after years of great misery, then all this business with his granddaughter, it was terrible, horrible. People round here found it hard to believe.' He looked around him again. 'They say that Amichi was a devil.'

There was silence. The professor looked at Fraser, Fraser at the professor.

'Is that it?' Fraser asked. 'Is that what we have paid you a hundred and fifty dollars for? Some mumbo-jumbo about a guy called Amichi, who we knew about anyway, whose granddaughter killed herself, that we could have guessed anyway. Why did she do it?'

'The curse,' the boy replied.

Fraser threw his hands up into the air. 'The curse! Well, that's money well spent.'

The boy lifted a finger to his lips. 'Don't make light of the curse. It's all around you. If it can affect a great soldier it can affect anyone.'

'Even if you don't believe in it?' Fraser retorted,

'Listen, my friend, curse or no curse, I think you should seriously watch your step.'

'Hang on...' Lisa interrupted. 'What was that last bit?'

The boy spoke. 'If it can affect a great soldier it can affect anyone.'

'A great soldier?'

'Yes, Amichi was a famous captain, fought alongside many of the best generals in the war.'

The boy looked at Fraser. 'I thought you would have known that.'

Lisa thought. 'No, no we didn't. But if we looked through the records we could find out how many Amichis there were and how many served under well-known generals. That would give us a start in finding out where the map came from.'

Huen's ears pricked up. 'Map?'

Fraser pushed him to one side. 'Never mind that. Yes, you're right. Perhaps we should be out of here – there doesn't seem like anything else we could hope to find here.' He got into the car and started tapping on the wheel.

Lisa sighed. 'Perhaps we should be getting back, uncle. There are things that need to be checked out.'

'You said a map?' the boy asked.

'It's nothing,' Lisa said. 'Really, it's nothing.'

Lisa and the professor both got into the car and Fraser started it. As Lisa waved to Huen, they sped off into the dim Hong Kong evening, leaving a trail of stone chippings to spray up into the cooling air. They moved away so fast they did not see the shadowy figure make its way from the nearest tower block. It moved quickly but silently, just visible in the bleak light, over to where Huen stood still rubbing the bulge in his sock where the money rested against his leg. The figure reached the boy and bent down to whisper in his ear whereupon the boy talked back. There were few words spoken between the two but what was said was clearly understood. A hand reached out and gave the boy more money than he had ever seen in his life and then they parted, one leaving to the right, back to the bridge, the other back to the storm drain where he spent the nights.

In the car Lisa was excited and she and the professor chatted furiously in Japanese, a trait that annoyed Fraser, who only spoke a smattering of it. He concentrated on the road and the lights that constantly flashed across his face. The bridge was almost full to capacity now and the cars on it crept along with a dull regularity. As he turned off the bridge and down towards the dock he noticed something: lights in his mirror. They looked as though they were following him, every turn he made, every stop, they would turn or stop too. He resolved to test his theory and made a right turn, then another, then another, resulting in him arriving back at the same place he had started from.

He looked in his mirror. They were still there. The left light of the car was slightly duller than the right – the bulb must be old, he thought to himself – so he knew it was the same car. He strained his eyes to see the colour but the rapidly closing darkness made it virtually impossible. He turned into Hong Kong Central and noticed with a sigh of relief that the place was swarming with cars. Soon he was so lost in the crowd that even he did not know where he was any more. He looked in his mirror but could not see the distinctive lopsided lights.

'We lost them,' he said, but neither Lisa nor the professor was listening. They still chatted about maps and books and strange soldiers called Amichi whose family suffered from a curse that followed them about like a blue Nissan.

4

Lisa staggered over to where the professor sat, where he always sat. She dumped the armful of books down on the table and slumped on the seat next to him.

'These are all the army registers since 1930. Every name of every soldier enlisted during the period 1930 to 1945. There must be thousands of names here, uncle.'

'Hundreds of thousands, I'd say.'

'Well, how are we going to get through them all?'

'Well,' the professor said, 'We know he was a soldier during the war, so we can discount every entry after, say, 1943. It is unlikely that a raw recruit would reach the rank of captain in so short a space of time. We can also discount anyone who joined before about 1935 – they would be far too old to be our Amichi. So there's an eight-year space. However, we can also discount anyone joining from the very poor districts. You have seen Amichi's handwriting. It was the script of an educated man, which would cut, say twenty per cent of the names. Also we know that he survived the war, so we could first check the register of war deaths; this would leave only about fifteen per cent of the names to check.'

The professor leaned back with his legs on the table and his arms behind his head. 'Shouldn't take you more than an hour or so, Lisa. If you need me, just ask.'

Lisa gave a laugh of incredulity and opened the first book.

The smoke rose about him but the wind had stopped completely.

He was in the darkness again but this time he could hear movement.

'Who's there?' he asked, but heard no reply. He became agitated. He wanted nothing more than to get out of the darkness – to see the light again, to breathe the fresh air of the outside, to be free of this oppression. He grasped at his throat and gasped for air but the harder he tried the more difficult it became; the walls seemed as if they were closing in. Once again he heard the sound of movement and once again he cried out in the darkness.

'Who's there? Who is it? Speak, please!'

He felt a hand on his shoulder and was suddenly calm and quiet. The hand felt warm and reassuring, like a blanket thrown about him. He fell to his knees and still it caressed his shoulder and made him feel that he was not alone. The professor raised his own hand and placed it on top of the other. He knew he was safe now, he knew this presence would not let harm come to him; he felt as if everything had fallen into place suddenly, as if the world had become still.

He looked up and saw the smiling face of a man he did not recognise. It was a harsh face, a face that had seen things, evil things, but a face that had come through. The skin that was stretched tight over the cheekbones was stained with mud and blood but it radiated a beauty that was easily discernable. The kind eyes looked down on the professor and seemed to absolve him of any sin he had committed, to take away any pain. For the briefest of moments the professor thought that he was witnessing a god.

The man lifted the professor up off of his knees and onto his feet. He took him by the hand and led him down the tunnel. As they walked, a strange eerie glow lit the tunnel and the professor was able to see the marks in the earth that had been left by the diggers. Here and there were finger marks scratched into the tunnel's surface – a testament to the last few desperate hours spent here. He followed his guide deeper and deeper into

63

the tunnel; the air became thicker and thicker but somehow it did not worry the professor any more. He held onto the hand of the man in front who walked with a sure-footed step and was happy to be led wherever he wished. Eventually they came to a door and they both stood for a moment.

Lisa tried to wake the professor to tell him that she had found three Amichis but no matter how hard she tried he would not budge and his snoring, quite frankly, was becoming a little embarrassing in the University library. His face had a kind of calm written upon it that she had never seen before so she decided to leave him and go to the refectory for a coffee instead.

Sitting at a table drinking it, she idly glanced through the copy of the army register. Without quite being aware of what was happening, her attention was drawn to the street below and to the form of a running man. For the second time that week she watched a person weave in and out of the crowds below, desperate to get away; this time, however, they did not enter the University doors but kept on going, towards the docks. Looking along the street, Lisa saw three others chasing him. They were all wearing black suits and were finding it difficult to keep up. To her surprise one of the men pulled out a gun and fired it at the fleeing man, who ducked into a side street, the bullet missing him and hitting the side of a building instead, sending a shower of brick dust into the air. There were screams from the street.

In the alley, Joe breathed heavily. The day had started badly and had got worse. He had met guys like this before but they had always given up by this point. It was a strange sensation to have to watch your back as soon as you woke up; an almost impossibility to everyone but a contortionist.

He peered out of the alley and looked around him. He couldn't see them any more, only the hole in the building that they had left. His glance took his eye up to the window of the university where the eyes of a pretty girl met his; they both looked away in embarrassment.

He quickly looked around him and darted off down the street. Swinging on the awning that stood outside, he ducked into the Club One Hundred, a place where he had spent many an afternoon in recent weeks staring into the bottom of a glass and trying to block out the sound of the awful music they played constantly through large speakers on the wall. Of course, the music was made somewhat more bearable by the presence of the Club One Hundred dancers, who would give you anything you wanted for the price of the name of the club.

Inside it was as dark as it always was. That was why Joe liked it there. It was too dark to see anyone's face clearly so you blended into the background without risking too much. He strode up to the bar and ordered a drink. The barman turned slowly.

'You back again?' he said in a clipped tone. Joe looked sheepish. The last time he had been in the Club One Hundred he had been rather the worse for wear and had started a fight over the price of a book of matches; looking back he could see their point, it was only ten cents but at the time it had seemed extortionate. He gave a wry smile to the waiter.

'Yeah ... erm ... you got that drink?'

'You want a match?'

Joe laughed and the memory of the beating he took from the doormen came back to him in a flash. 'No,' he said. 'I bought a lighter.'

'Very wise,' the barman said. 'Very wise.'

The music suddenly changed and the lights went even dimmer than usual. Joe turned around and propped himself up on the bar. Beside him the barman placed a small grubby glass with thick brown liquid in it. Joe took a swig and felt it hit him like a Hong Kong doorman – fast and low.

On the stage, the curtains opened to reveal a woman in a pair of boots and very little else. As Joe watched she writhed on the stage and turned and shook like a strange exotic play of light. Her body sparkled in the dim glow of the club and shot waves of energy to anyone who had come in out of the afternoon sunshine. Joe stared, his eyes desperate to take in everything they could. He reached into his pocket and felt the last of the grand that he had been paid. It must have been at least five hundred dollars.

He ordered another drink and sat on a bar stool to take in more of the girl on stage. Her eyes were half closed in a languid display of orgasmic tension. She would twirl around the pole in the centre of the stage, glide up it, licking its shiny surface and letting the coldness touch her skin. Joe brushed a bead of sweat from his forehead and let another run down his spine. The girl's set was coming to end. She gave a final twist to the pole and fell, clinging to it, to the ground.

The music stopped and she sat, head bowed, staring at the stage. The club was silent. Slowly, from the back Joe began to applaud. Only his hands could be heard clapping in the silence of the club. He stopped. Their eyes met for a moment, and the girl got up, thanked her audience and left.

Joe turned round to the barman and lit a cigarette. 'Who's she? Haven't seen her before,' he said.

'She's new, straight in from the mainland. She's cute, yeah?'

'Yeah, she's cute.'

'You want me to have a word with her?' the barman asked.

Joe thought for a moment. He felt the money in his pocket again. It's moments like these, he thought, that

66

you need to make the right decision. It's moments like these that need a cool head and a wise brain. I need to weigh up the pros and cons here, take each decision as it comes. I only have this five hundred dollars left, when that's gone there's nothing. I have no plane and no job. I have some guys after me who want my blood and the police aren't too happy to see my face either. He thought hard and long.

'Yeah, sure. Why not?' he said and ordered another drink.

She had the eyes of a cat and the long black hair of a horse's mane. She moved with the fluid grace of someone who knew what she was doing to those around her. Joe watched as she crossed the club, her heels making a slight clicking on the dance floor that was quite audible above the sound of the music. Her dress was open at the front and allowed him to glimpse the pure honeyed tone of her chest. Joe swallowed a mouthful of the cheap bourbon and the two things together – the booze and the girl – made him choke.

She eased her way onto the seat next to him.

'You want a drink?' Joe asked.

'Sure,' she said. 'Whatever you're having.'

Joe hesitated. There was something about a woman who could take strong liquor; perhaps it was his innate sexism but somehow it made him nervous. He shrugged it off and ordered.

'You from China?' he asked and she nodded. 'What's your name?'

'Gem.'

This took Joe by surprise. He had expected a Chinese name, though he did not push. He guessed it was her stage name.

'Nice, like a diamond,' he said feebly and the girl made an attempt at laughter. Joe gave her the drink and she looked at him with those eyes of hers. Quietly she leaned forward to whisper in Joe's ear.

'You want to go somewhere else?' she asked and for the second time that day the situation and the drink got the better of Joe and he coughed in his glass.

'Sure,' he said, composing himself. 'Sure.'

'I'll just get my things.'

Joe paid up and waited for the girl to come out from her dressing room. He knew a small place where they could go for only a few dollars. Hong Kong was full of places where you could go for an hour or so and no one would ask you what you were doing or, more importantly, who you were doing it to.

Outside the day was in full swing. As they came blinking into the sunlight like two moles exiting their burrow they crossed over the road and entered the front door of a small hotel that catered for the patrons of the Club One Hundred on numerous occasions.

The guy behind the counter found them a room and they ascended the stairs. Inside it looked as though the previous occupants had only just left and had had a fine old time. There were beer bottles and cigarette stubs on the bed, condoms in the toilet, the TV had been stolen leaving only a bare wire and an aerial, and the smell of sweat and bodies permeated the air. Joe gingerly stepped over the detritus of someone else's good time and sat on the bed. Gem sat beside him. He held her face and they kissed for what seemed like minutes. Joe felt as though he had found the calm in the eye of the hurricane with this quite beautiful girl he hardly even knew. As he felt her hair and her body his hands rejoiced that, finally, they had something worthy to touch; her breasts were firm and rounded, her thighs were small and smooth. Joe lay back and pulled her beside him, feeling the light breath from her mouth flick over his face.

The breeze gently roughed his hair and everything was quiet. The hands upon his shoulders were gentle but heavy. For some reason he looked up and saw the face of a man staring at him; the eyes were gentle and still and seemed to fill Joe with a calm and an awe that left him breathless. All about him the tunnel was becoming lighter, things were becoming clearer. It was obvious now that whoever this man was he was leading Joe to some other place, some place that was dangerous but that was vital and important. Joe closed his eyes and let the man lead wherever he needed to. His feet scraped and tore at the earth, his legs moved through their own volition.

Joe awoke and saw that the sun was just going down. It took him a while to realise where he was and what had happened. He looked around him. The girl was gone and the mess in the room remained. He stroked his head and wondered what had been in the drink he'd been served. He felt as though he had been sat on by a rhino. Suddenly he thought and checked his pockets. The five hundred was gone.

Meanwhile in the library Lisa looked up from the book with triumph.

'Captain Amichi,' she said. 'Served under a General Takimoto in the Philippines. Had an honourable career until his disappearance just before the war ended.'

The professor opened an eye and stared at the ceiling. He placed his hands behind his head and leaned back in his chair. 'What's that book?'

'A history of the Japanese military. He barely gets a mention and then only because of his disappearance.'

'Does it say why he went missing?'

'No, just that he was in the Philippines and that he went missing before the end of the war.'

'It would explain why he went into hiding.'

Lisa read from the book: '"A certain Captain Amichi, who had served under General Takimoto, disgraced himself in the eyes of the Imperial Army by deserting shortly after a period of serving in the company of General Yamashita. Yamashita will be well known to the reader of this volume." That's it, that's all there is on him. There's still not a lot to go on, is there, uncle? Uncle?'

The professor's eyes had glazed over and he stared ahead of him like a man possessed by some strange spirit. His face shone with an inner light that seemed to illuminate the entire library. Lisa put the book on the desk and leaned further towards her uncle.

'Uncle?' she asked. 'Are you OK?'

'Read that again, Lisa. Read it again.'

Lisa read it again. The professor's mouth lifted slowly at the corners until he broke out into the biggest grin Lisa had ever seen him produce.

'Amichi...' he said to no one in particular. 'Yamashita!!!'

Lisa shook him by the arm. 'Uncle, are you OK? What's the matter? Do you know this Yamashita? Have you heard about him?'

The professor slowly turned his head and looked at Lisa, his eyes barely registering her presence. 'The dreams. They have been leading me here all along. Oh, those spirits of the forest, they know how to get their man.'

'What are you talking about, uncle? What's the matter? Who is Yamashita?'

'It was during the war. People did bad things, people looked out for themselves. I thought it wasn't true, I thought it couldn't be true but here it is, this proves it, this proves it exists.'

'What, uncle? Tell me. This proves what?'

Her uncle sat bolt upright, the light still shining out of his eyes and Lisa thought he looked young again. It was as if the news, whatever was in his head, had taken the lines from his face, blackened the grey in his hair and made him a boy again.

'Yamashita's gold,' he said at last, barely able to contain his excitement. He clasped his hands together and his eyes opened wide. 'Amichi's map – it must be for Yamashita's gold.'

5

Lisa and the professor sat across from each other in the University canteen, staring into their respective cups of steaming beverage: Lisa with hot chocolate, the professor camomile tea. For at least ten minutes neither had said a word to the other and the only sound they heard was the dull roar of a fairly busy restaurant: people coming and going, plates being stacked, the buzz of voices as people made their way to their tables. The professor held his cup in both hands and circled it in his saucer; Lisa occasionally dipped a little finger into the liquid, pulled it out covered in chocolate and licked it – more for something to do than actually wanting to taste it.

The full meaning of their discovery of the morning had not sunk into either of their minds but it kept circling them. Suddenly, breaking the silence, the professor spoke: 'Of course, this could be the making of us.'

Lisa did not answer.

'The mystery of Yamashita's gold has puzzled experts for years, ever since his death in 1944. There were rumours of what he had done but no one has ever authenticated it.'

'Do you think we can? Do you think this does?' she asked.

The professor lowered his eyes. 'The romantic in me says yes. The scholar says no. After all, what have we but a map that purports to be from a captain we are not sure exists from a time and battalion we don't know existed in a place we don't know?'

Lisa stirred her chocolate. 'But the girl, uncle, the girl was murdered for that map. And those men, why would they do that to your apartment if it wasn't important, if they didn't think you were on to something?'

The professor thought, 'Yes, of course you are right.' Then he slapped his head. 'Anderson! Why didn't I think of him first?'

'Who's Anderson?'

'An expert on Japanese military history. He's an Englishman, his family moved over here about twenty years ago. They moved back and he stayed here. I'm sure he'd know if there were any truth in the stories or the map.'

'But where is he, uncle? Is he far away?'

Her uncle chuckled to himself. 'About a hundred yards,' he said, and pointed in the direction of the corridor.

Lisa and her uncle set off down the corridor. Lisa expected them to turn right into the stairwell that led to the history department. She stopped at the top of the stairs and waited for her uncle but to her surprise he wandered straight past her and carried on down the hall. Lisa sighed to herself. She was used to her uncle's little inconsistencies. She was used to him not knowing what day it was or that he had put on the wrong shirt with the wrong tie but, she thought to herself, considering all the time he had been at the university she might have assumed that he knew his way around.

'Uncle!' she called after him. 'The history block is on 2B.'

Her uncle shuffled ahead and turned back to face her. 'Yes,' he said. 'But maintenance is on 3F.'

Lisa was taken aback for a moment but eventually followed her uncle.

The door was barely noticeable among the discarded waste paper baskets and the old vending machines that stood around like open bodies in a graveyard, their bright lights dimmed by time and neglect. On the floor, wires and sockets and tape and all manner of things stuck to their feet at every step. Lisa carefully picked her way through it all.

'Uncle,' she said. 'What the hell are we doing here?'

Her uncle stopped by a tiny blue door that was no bigger than himself. He turned round and put his finger to his lip.

'Quiet, he is often asleep.' Gently, the professor knocked on the door and listened. Nothing. He tapped again and still nothing. Then, slowly, Lisa began to hear a shuffling. It was slight at first and then got louder and louder until, after a series of locks were pulled back, opened and set free, a small face appeared at the door, blinking in the sunlight like a mole.

'Yes?' it said.

The professor answered him. 'Anderson, it's Okada. I am after some information.'

Anderson was about thirty-five years of age, with brown hair that fell about his shoulders, a small goatee beard and eyes of deepest blue that would flash as he talked enthusiastically about this general or that battle. Lisa guessed he was a janitor at the university but was not sure; he could well be a professor, or he could be from the street. They entered his room and the first thing she noticed was the smell: a mixture of patchouli oil and sweat. In the corner was a huge stack of books, some in Japanese, some in English, some in Cantonese. On a table in the middle of the room was a typewriter, a pipe and an ashtray full of ash. Towards the back of the room was a chair that had obviously been recently vacated.

As if asking for an audience with a dignitary, Lisa and her uncle shuffled towards Anderson. He asked if they wanted any tea but they declined.

'What can I do for you?' he asked in a clipped English

74

accent that seemed to belie the state of the room and himself.

The professor was obviously quite nervous, the first time Lisa had seen him so ever since she had been old enough to notice. He fiddled with his hands and stammered his words.

'Well, my niece and ... er ... I are ... – this is my niece by the way, Lisa – are completing a little project on ... er ... Japanese military history...'

Anderson sat down. 'You're a rocks man aren't you? Geology?'

'Yes, yes, er ... usually I'm a geologist but I have come into some er ... information that I thought you might be able to help us with.'

'Information, eh?' Anderson seemed intrigued. 'Carry on. Carry on.'

'Well,' the professor said. 'Well, we'd like some information on Yamashita.'

'The general?'

'Yes, the general.'

'Why? What have you found out, professor?'

The professor looked coy. He obviously was not going to give anything away even though he felt he trusted Anderson. 'Well, just some things, it may be nothing. I just want it validated.'

Anderson looked at Lisa and back at the professor. He stood up and crossed the room to where a large filing cabinet sat. Thoughtfully he pulled out a huge set of keys and began searching through them. Finally he found the one he was after and placed it in the lock of the filing cabinet. Lisa heard the separate locks on all of the drawers spring open. Anderson opened the top drawer and searched inside. Eventually he brought out a smooth white saki bottle which he carried back to the table. He poured himself a cup.

'Professor?' he offered but the professor declined. He did not offer Lisa any.

Anderson sat back and drank. 'At the end of the war,' he said, 'The Japanese were well aware of what fate had in store for them. Like the Nazis in Europe they had counted upon winning in order to cover up their activities. It's not so uncommon really; there are new rules in war, not no rules. People live differently, they live from day to day, they are not answerable to anyone. As early as 1936 Hirohito had begun to plunder the areas around South East Asia. He knew a war was coming and in order to defeat the Americans he would need might – money and might. So they began what was known as Operation Golden Lily that, erm ... acquired all the gold they could in the areas that they had conquered. They must have amassed millions, in fact so much that the only thing they could do was bury it and wait until they needed it.'

'So they began all this before the war?' Lisa asked.

'Sure, they had been doing it for years. You have heard of the Rape of Nanking; well, that was purportedly part of the operation. Whole areas were decimated, art treasures were stolen, religious artefacts, money stored in banks, the wealth of ancient families. Everything was taken. There was even a rumour that many of the Netherlands' national treasures had been moved to the Dutch Indies (which of course is now Indonesia) prior to the war for safe keeping. They thought moving them there would remove them from the path of the Nazis. However, they were, ironically, stolen by the Japanese. The whole area was stripped; there was virtually nothing left.'

'What happened to it?'

'Well, as I said, much of it was buried since there was no chance of selling it.'

'Why?'

'Think about it. You have half the world's gold reserves

sitting in your back garden. If you sell it, not only will your rather nefarious past catch up with you sooner or later but, more to the point, the price of gold goes down the pan; you literally flood the market, making what you have got virtually useless. Hirohito and his advisers knew that if their scheme was to be worth anything in the long run they had to store it somewhere, so that's what they did. They dug huge complex tunnels systems in the Philippines and stored the gold underground.'

'They got the army to dig?'

'At first, but the gold kept on coming and coming. Imagine it, it must have been a nightmare. You desperately need gold, cash, so you steal it from largely defenceless countries. You're happy now, you have all the money you want, but you can't stop once you've started, you have to keep on going. Pretty soon, you have more than you need and, finally, you have more than you can handle. The more holes you dig to put the gold in the more the gold comes flooding in from all over your territory. You need more holes but now you haven't got the manpower – most of your soldiers are fighting in Burma or on the borders of India. So what do you do? You take slaves, you take prisoners of war, civilians though, and make them dig the tunnels.'

'It's chilling,' Lisa said.

'It makes perfect sense when you think about it. You are getting the very people you stole the gold from in the first place to dig the holes. It has the kind of perverse logic that I associate only with military minds. Anyway, as the war progressed this situation carried on. The more they stole, the more tunnels they dug, the more they had to make slaves of the native Filipinos. When they had finished with a tunnel they would simply blow it up leaving whoever was inside to die. No one quite knows how many died like this but it must have run into hundreds, perhaps even thousands.'

'So,' Lisa began. 'Who was Yamashita?'

'Well, to be honest he was just another general whose operation this was. He was no more or less barbaric than any of them; his story happens to be the one that has become famous because of his public execution. Just before the war ended Hirohito ordered a massive surge in operations and a huge percentage of the Japanese army was dedicated to burying gold and artworks. However, this time it was not to store in order to provide money to fight the Americans but to cover up their activities during the last five years. You see, all of this wealth could not only be used for reparations and the like but it also meant evidence of war crime. Put it this way – it was the embarrassing dust that the Empire wanted to brush under the carpet.'

Anderson poured another cup full of saki and gulped it down. 'People have been looking for Yamashita's gold for years, ever since it was buried. Some of it has been found, but no one actually knows how much was actually hidden. There could be troves still out there.'

'Why? Where would you look? I mean there's only jungle there, no one left to talk about it, no maps.' The professor said the last word with hesitation. He studied the look on Anderson's face.

'You haven't any information in that line, have you, professor?'

The professor looked the picture of innocence. 'Of course not, dear Anderson, I am merely interested in your tales.'

Anderson suddenly became as white as the bottle of saki that he held within his thin bony fingers. 'Because it would be bad news, professor, to try and recover any of the gold.'

'Why?'

'The aswang.'

'What is that?' Lisa asked.

'The spirits of the Filipinos – best not tarried with if you ask my opinion. I have seen things that would make you age twenty years in five minutes where the aswang are concerned. They enter the body and can manipulate you from inside. They can appear in any form they choose, and they do not take kindly to their habitat being invaded.'

Suddenly the professor thought about the dreams he had been having – the smoke, the feeling of oppression, the smell, the darkness and the terror. He swallowed hard and tried to pull himself together. 'So Yamashita's gold would be in the Philippines?' he asked, rather overstepping his own mark of secrecy.

'Yes,' Anderson said.

There was silence.

'You have got something, haven't you?'

The professor looked around the room. He crossed over and pressed an ear to the door then returned to his seat at the table.

'We have come into possession of a map, of the location of Yamashita's gold.'

To their surprise, Anderson burst out laughing. He rocked forward in his seat, holding his stomach and showing his brown crooked teeth. For the first time since she had arrived Lisa wondered whether she could trust Anderson, he seemed duplicitous all of a sudden. For a brief moment he looked ugly in the half-light of the room with the darkness making shadows on his face and causing his skin to appear more and more wrinkled. Perhaps it was the way he threw his head back but, to Lisa, he suddenly became the laughing face of a demon.

Anderson stopped finally and allowed himself to calm down. 'Please excuse me, professor, but it was the seriousness with which you said that you had a map. Honestly, I don't think there is a day goes past without someone saying to me that they have a map to Yamashita's gold. I mean, you are an intelligent man, you are a scholar; I am surprised you are fooled by such ridiculousness.'

The professor looked placid and stared at Anderson. 'You know of Amichi?'

Anderson thought. 'Yes, yes, I have heard the story. Wait a minute.'

Again he crossed over to the filing cabinet but this time he opened the drawer second from the top. It was filled with manila files and sheaves of dirty yellowing paper. He flicked through them, eventually stopping on one in particular. He looked at it surreptitiously, then pulled it from the cabinet. He crossed the room and slammed it on the table.

'Amichi, Captain, served under General Yamashita, 1943 to 1945 when he deserted, believed to have been killed.'

Lisa gasped. 'Killed?'

'Yes. It was thought that he was killed by Filipino workers in 1946 after Yamashita himself had been hanged in the prison.'

'Was there any proof of this?' the professor asked.

'Only a body. Is that who you are after, professor? A dead man?'

The professor thought for a moment. 'His death comes as no surprise to me,' he said slowly. 'But the time of it does. You see, we were under the impression that he died only recently. His granddaughter, you see...'

'His granddaughter?'

'Yes, his granddaughter. It was she who gave me the map.'

Anderson looked interested all of a sudden. 'Who is his granddaughter?'

'You heard of the girl in the temple?'

'The one recently who was found dead?'

'Yes, the very same.'

'But it's impossible. Amichi died in 1946 after Yamashita.'

'Did they ever identify the body?'

'No, of course not. He was merely a captain and besides they would not have let his body return home. They would have scattered it in the jungle as punishment.'

'So it's possible it was not him and that our Amichi was alive and well and managed to smuggle a map of the gold tunnels out?'

Anderson thought for a moment. 'Well, of course it's possible,' he said. 'But it's highly unlikely.'

'Well,' the professor said. 'I'll settle for possible.' He got up to leave. 'Good day, Anderson. Thank you for your information.'

'Wait!' Anderson grabbed his arm. 'Have you got the map?'

The professor smiled and tapped his pocket. 'Always,' he said.

'Can I see it?'

The professor hesitated; he looked across at Lisa who nodded slightly. The professor reached a hand into his coat pocket and pulled out the map. He spread it on the table. Anderson looked at it intently.

'Well, it looks as though it's about the right age. Obviously I can't recognise any of these features.'

'What would you suggest?' the professor asked.

'For finding it? Hmm, well, it will be difficult whatever you do. If I were you I'd hire a plane to take you all over the jungle to look for these distinguishing features – look, here there is a ridge and a small hillock, there is a distinctive collection of large trees. They will be still there – it is a remote place, there would be no loggers around there.'

Anderson poured the last of the saki into his cup. 'You know, professor, for my help I might ask for a little ... er ... restitution.'

'Now or later?' the professor asked.

Anderson laughed. 'What with the aswang and the jungle I'd prefer it now if you don't mind. For you there may not be a later.' He laughed again and the sight of his teeth sent shivers down Lisa's spine. The professor opened his wallet and took some notes out. He placed them on the table, picked up the map and put it back into his pocket.

'Don't drink it all at once,' he said and Anderson laughed.

As they turned to go Anderson stopped them. 'Professor,' he said. 'Be careful of the jungle. It bites.'

The professor and Lisa made their way along the corridor again to the canteen. Their talk with Anderson had made them all the more eager to find out all they could about the map and possibly even find the gold for themselves. They chatted casually about what might happen and their feet made short sharp tapping sounds on the floor. They passed the stairwell and headed off back into the refectory. Behind them a pair of deep brown eyes watched them from the level of the floor. As the professor and Lisa opened the door to the busy University restaurant, the eyes revealed themselves to belong to Kono, one of Tanaka's men. He slowly and silently travelled up the stairs and made sure Lisa and the professor were out of sight before making his way along the corridor to the door that he had just seen them exiting from.

Anderson opened the door. 'Have you forgotten it all already?' he said, thinking that it was the professor at the door but his words were cut short by a hand to the throat that nearly lifted him off the ground. Kono barged his way in to the small room, knocking the small saki bottle from the table.

6

Fraser was standing in the professor's office. He flicked through some of the books on the table – they were filled with black and white pictures of rock formations, crystalline diagrams and long-dead geologists. A clock ticked sonorously in the background and seemed to thicken the air with its gentle swaying rhythm. Fraser had been on his way home from the bank and had decided to call in on the professor. It had been a few days since he had heard from him or Lisa and he wondered how the story with the book was going.

Slowly, he walked around the desk. Every now and then he would pick up a scrap of paper, read it, consider its meaning and place it exactly as he had found it on the desk. He hated the word snooping – what he was doing was reconnoitring. Glancing over his shoulder at the door, he opened the drawer and inside found a notebook with the words 'Japanese Military' written, he assumed, in the professor's hand. He opened the book and read. It was just a series of names, but he recognised one of them, Yamashita. He had heard of Yamashita's gold before, the secret network of underground tunnels which housed the spoils of war.

He read on but most of the writing seemed to be in some kind of code created by the professor – either that or his handwriting was so bad Fraser could not decipher it. He knew enough about the workings of the professor's mind to understand that it would be privileged information indeed if he had gone to the extent of inventing a code to keep people from reading it. Fraser assumed that that professor had always known more about the book that he had been given than he was letting on.

He thought to himself: 'So that was the significance of the map, but the old fool doesn't believe that, does he? He doesn't believe in such fairy stories?' He thought that it would be as well to keep the professor as close as possible.

Suddenly, behind him he heard the professor and Lisa walking down the hallway. They talked excitedly about someone called Anderson and what they were going to do next.

As the door burst open Fraser had just enough time to close the notebook and throw it in the drawer before banging it shut. The professor and Lisa walked in.

'Fraser!' the professor started excitedly. 'How good of you to come. We have exciting news concerning our map.'

'Really?' Fraser said, trying not to sound too interested. 'I just dropped by, I was on my way home.'

'It's a good day for just walking,' the professor replied. 'Come, sit by the window and I will tell you everything. Lisa, go and get a coffee for Fraser, would you?'

Lisa looked offended. She was fine with being treated as her uncle's unpaid servant but it was quite another thing to be asked to run around after others. She pursed her lips and stood still.

After about a minute of being ignored she turned and headed out of the door, thinking to herself that she really needed to assert herself in these situations as she made her way to the coffee machine in the canteen.

The professor told Fraser what they had learned that day, about Anderson and his knowledge of the map, about Amichi and Yamashita, about his talk with Lisa and about how they were considering finding the tunnels once and for all.

'It's odd, Fraser,' the professor said. 'But I feel I have a calling. For some weeks now I have been having these dreams – oh, they mean nothing, I know. I am an old man now. In my younger years I would have dismissed them as a glass of saki or a piece of stuck salmon but now, now I'm older, I find I want to believe.'

'In Yamashita's gold?'

'Yes, in that, but more than that, I think I want to believe in the spirits that draw me to it. Anderson called them the aswang and they are very powerful, so he says.'

'But surely that's just myth, professor. You can't believe in it?'

The professor tapped the side of his head with a finger. 'The more I learn,' he said, 'The less I seem to know. I have known a frog to escape from rock strata thousands of years old, just like that...' He snapped his fingers. 'Out of the rock as they drilled, its skin almost translucent, its bones as dry as the dust. Who put it there? Who enabled it to survive? God? Nature? Who knows? These are merely different words for the same thing. I am a man of science, but who owns the science?'

Fraser tipped back in his chair. 'So what next?' he asked.

The professor shrugged. 'Who knows? Hire a plane, perhaps, make a trip to the Philippines?'

There was a knock at the door and the professor turned to look. However, as he did, it stopped. 'Perhaps that's something you could do, Fraser. Do you know anyone in the aviation business?'

Fraser thought. 'I once knew an old pilot from Guam but he would be dead by now. He flew into Vietnam, nearly fried him. Not sure he would make a good choice, anyway.'

The knocking began again. 'Lisa, come in!' the professor said.

'I know very little about planes, professor, I'm afraid.

I flew over here and that's about it. To tell you the truth it rather makes me feel sick just thinking about it. I was never a great flyer. I'll tell you one day about my experience coming over here; it wasn't a good start.'

The knocking at the door continued. It was a slow, insistent sound that seemed to permeate the room and be of just the right pitch to cause the professor the most aggravation. He placed his hands to his ears in a show of frustration that shocked Fraser. 'OK, Lisa, I am coming,' he shouted. 'I am coming. If you could only put the cups down I could...'

He stopped in his tracks. The sight that greeted him as he opened the door would have stopped a lesser man's heart. Suspended from the door jamb by his belt was Anderson, his face blue and his eyes open in a display of fearful death. As he swung, urine seeped out of his bladder, ran down his trouser leg and pooled on the floor below him and his corpse swung this way and that causing his foot to tap gently on the wooden panel of the door.

The professor raised a hand to his mouth as Lisa came along the corridor. As soon as she saw the body she screamed, dropped the cups of hot coffee on the floor and then stood unable to move, the only sound the slight creak of the leather of the belt brushing up against the door frame. Fraser came out to see what was occurring.

'Professor, I just thought...' His words were taken from him as he saw the body.

The professor looked at Fraser. 'Anderson,' he explained.

Fraser grabbed the professor and Lisa and pulled them into the room. He reached for a letter opener that sat on the professor's desk and cut Anderson down, letting him fall onto his shoulders. Struggling to cope under the weight of even this small man, Fraser dumped him down behind a pile of books and noticed that one of them, ironically, concerned the Book of the Dead.

'We have to get out sooner rather than later,' he explained. 'This is more than a treasure map now. Whoever did this did it for a reason and they will probably do it again.'

'But it's no good going back to the flat, uncle, they know where you live,' said Lisa.

The professor thought. 'And they know where I am here now.'

She said: 'We need to get to the Philippines, uncle.'

Fraser interrupted, 'We need to go to the police.'

'The police?' Lisa asked. 'You saw what they were like, they would be twice as bad here. This is a big city. People get lost here easily. The police can make very little difference so they don't try. We need to find the gold, because whoever is after my uncle is really after the gold.'

Fraser sat on the chair. 'Lisa, a man is dead, a girl is dead. How many more have to die before you go to the police and get this sorted out?'

The professor spoke. 'He is right, Lisa. We cannot take matters into our own hands. I am too old for adventure. Besides, we need to arrange things for Anderson.'

'Anderson's dead, uncle, and you could be too.'

Fraser turned round to look at the corpse that was nestled in the corner of the room. 'Talking of Anderson,' he said. 'What do we do with him? We *have* to go to the police.'

The professor thought. 'No one saw us go into Anderson's, right?'

'Right,' Lisa said. 'So technically we weren't there.'

'If we go to the police,' the professor offered. 'They'll ask how he came to be in this state. We were the last ones to see him alive – all except the murderer. At best they would find out about the map.'

'At worst we would be charged with murder,' Lisa offered.

87

'I think you might be right, Lisa, but no one saw us enter Anderson's room. All we need do is get rid of the body.'

'Is that all?' Fraser asked sarcastically.

'Push him in the harbour?' Lisa said. 'Cut him up and flush him down the toilet?'

Fraser stared at Lisa, hardly believing what he was hearing. She smiled at him sweetly and he felt the hairs on the back of his neck stand on end.

The professor walked over to the body of Anderson and looked at it. He saw now the fear in the face, blue and contorted in death, his eyes open to the world, his fingers still stiff from trying to claw at whatever or whoever killed him. The professor put a hand on his friend's head and bowed his own in silent prayer. The sun came in through the window and lit the two figures up in a curious golden glow; the air had a sacred skin to it.

Lisa walked up behind her uncle and placed a hand on his shoulder, causing a chain of concern, from the dead man to the young woman. Suddenly the professor opened his eyes.

'To the basement,' he said, and left the room, leaving Lisa and Fraser staring at each other. When he realised they were not following him, the professor's head reappeared from behind the door jamb.

'Well, come on, to the basement,' he said again. 'Oh, and bring him.' He nodded at Anderson.

Fraser looked around. 'How do we get him down to the basement without anyone seeing him?' he asked Lisa, who shrugged and looked blank for a moment.

Then, as if connecting a circuit in her head, an idea appeared and she snapped her fingers triumphantly. 'Wait here,' she said and disappeared out of the door.

A few moments later she appeared pushing a trolley with a large television on it. 'The film theory department,' she explained. 'Help me get him on the shelf at the bottom.'

Lisa and Fraser picked up Anderson and placed him unceremoniously on the lower shelf of the video trolley. Lisa looked round for something to cover him with. She saw an old Japanese flag that was covered in mould lying in the corner and draped it over the trolley so that the body could not be seen.

'You want me to push?' she asked, but did so herself anyway.

Fraser stood back and watched her from behind. There was something in the way she walked that sent him crazy, just the small, insignificant things she did with her body, unknowing but full of an easy sensuality and imbued with a confidence that he had never experienced in a woman before. She sometimes seemed a tiny girl and sometimes a fully grown woman and it both maddened him and excited him. He loved to watch her move, to listen to her speak, to be near her elegant but easy grace.

As he followed her down the hall he noticed how her hair swayed when she walked, how black it was, how shiny. He saw the whiteness of her neck and how smooth her skin was. He noticed that she walked with her feet slightly splayed and how it made her buttocks sway with a gentle rhythm that was almost hypnotic. He noticed a lot of things as he walked behind her, making sure that the arm of the dead man did not fall out of its covering in an inopportune moment.

When they got to the lift Fraser pressed the button to open the door and stood directly behind Lisa. He could smell her now; he breathed in slightly, trying to grasp as much of her as he could. There was nothing extraordinary about her, nothing spectacular, she was just an ordinary girl from an ordinary suburb of Tokyo who had come to study at a rather ordinary university but that ordinariness, that everyday quality, made her all the more appealing.

He had known many women in this area and each one of them was either beautiful or rich; eventually he had got used to the wide variety of partners on offer to an ex pat with a future. Lisa was different because she had not been spoilt by the big city; she still had that sense of the town about her; the willingness to believe in things that the hard-hearted would not.

As they exited the lift in the basement, they heard a noise like a huge bull elephant sighing, or a train coming to rest. Lisa looked at Fraser, who gazed dreamily into her face.

'Are you OK?' she asked.

'Yes, why?'

'You look as though you are catching flies with your mouth.'

Yes, it was her ordinariness that he liked most of all.

When they found the professor, he was hopping around on one leg clutching the other.

'Are you hurt, professor?' Fraser ventured.

'It's the light down here,' the professor explained. 'I can barely see where I am treading and every now and then I walk into something hard.'

'Why don't you put the light on?' Fraser asked.

'Would you put the light on to kill a man?' the professor said.

'Erm ... no ... probably not. Who are you killing?'

'He's already killed; should I have said disposing of?'

'Uncle! You're leaving him down here?'

The professor looked sheepish. 'In a manner of speaking,' he said and suddenly behind him a jet of steam shot out and filled the basement. 'This is the boiler,' he said. 'Where they strip bones for display. Those animal skeletons you see in classes are not bought like that – they are samples brought in that are stripped and then mounted.'

Lisa's face looked horrified. The whole scenario seemed surreal to her. 'You're going to strip Anderson?'

'Can you think of anything better?'

Lisa looked at Anderson, then at Fraser, who just shrugged.

'I'll have him in my study for always,' the professor said and smiled. 'Help me get him in there.'

Lisa began to see her uncle in a different light.

Carefully, the three of them opened the giant brass lid of the boiler and placed it to one side while they picked up Anderson and gently lowered him into the bubbling water. The professor put the lid back on the large brass drum and tightened the four screwed locks that were placed around its edge.

'What do we do now?' Lisa asked.

'Now, we wait,' the professor said.

It was about three hours later that they returned to the huge boiler that had by now stopped bubbling away like a slow cooker. Cautiously, they undid the locks, opened the lid, shone a light and peered in.

Lisa gasped and placed a hand over her mouth. In the water of the tank, floating like a bleached white buoy was Anderson's skull, its blank eyes staring up at her. She stepped down on to the floor of the basement and started taking deep breaths. Part of her could not believe she was in this position; death had sometimes been close to her but never like this, never in such a way that she felt complicit in it. She felt guilty because she hadn't known about the danger Anderson had been in. She felt guilty because she should have gone to the police. She felt guilty because she should have talked her uncle out of this. Closing her eyes, she felt her head swoon but she composed herself and helped lift parts of the skeleton out of the

91

tank feeling all the while glad that it was dark enough not to be able to see the whole scene.

Carefully, bit by bit, they laid Anderson's bones on the floor, then wrapped him in the flag again and carried him upstairs to the office. The professor sat in his swivel chair and stared out of the window. The sun was just going down over the buildings opposite, which looked almost magical in the early evening dusk. He glanced over at the bundle on a pile of books and silently saluted; Anderson would have wanted it that way.

7

Lisa was tidying up the books in the professor's apartment. She tried to place them in alphabetical order on the shelves but quickly gave up. She had bought some carnations at the supermarket on the way home and was arranging them on the desk, making it seem a little less like a waiting room for the death chamber. Her uncle was with Fraser in the kitchen discussing plans for hiring a plane. She picked up a jacket from the floor and a card fell out of the pocket. She reached for it and noticed it was a cheap business card. There was a plane etched in blue ink on one side and 'Joe Hutchins – Pilot' written on the other with a phone number underneath it.

She took it in to her uncle. 'Uncle? Who's this Joe Hutchins? Is he a pilot?'

The professor looked at her blankly. 'Joe Hutchins? Never heard that name before. Is he a friend of yours?'

'No, I found this in one of your jackets. It fell out as I was picking it up. All it says is Joe Hutchins – Pilot. Then there's a number.'

She handed the card to the professor, who studied it closely. After a while, his furrowed brown turned into smooth recognition.

'The taxi driver gave it to me on the night I met you at the bar. My, it seems like weeks ago now. He told me if ever I was in trouble I was to call his cousin. Then he gave me this.'

'We're in trouble now, aren't we?' asked Fraser.

Lisa swiped the card from her uncle and ran over to

the telephone. She dialled, waited, then spoke. 'Joe? Joe Hutchins?'

There was silence in the room as Lisa listened. She twirled the phone cord in her fingers and nervously fidgeted with the things on the desk.

'Well,' she said after a while. 'Do you know where he might have gone? What about a forwarding address, a telephone number? Anything?'

The professor and Fraser's hearts sank. They knew that card had not delivered on its own meagre promises. Lisa put the phone down and joined them, looking despondent.

'Well, it was worth a try,' she said.

Fraser patted her shoulders. 'Yeah, it's always worth a try,' he said, but the professor was silent. He had his finger up to his forehead and his eyes half closed. Without opening his eyes fully he crossed the room to the desk, opened the drawer and pulled out a stack of dollar bills of small denominations.

'If ever I split a twenty or a fifty and I am given the change, if there are ones in there I put them in this drawer. Every now and then I take it to the market and buy a huge tub of ice cream, which I bring home and eat, all to myself.'

Lisa and Fraser were perplexed.

'It's a bit late for ice cream, professor,' Fraser offered.

'Not ice cream, Fraser, taxi cabs. The driver of my taxi was the cousin of Joe, right? Well, all we have to do is split up, take a handful of bills each, and take short, two dollar journeys in every cab we find.'

'Hmm, there must be thousands of cabs in Hong Kong.'

'Can you think of a better way?' the professor asked.

'Wait,' Lisa interrupted. 'How will we know we aren't testing the same cab? I mean, I get in a cab, ask the driver if he is the cousin of Joe, he says no, I get out. Five minutes later Fraser gets in the same cab and asks the same thing, by which time I have forgotten what the back of his head looks like and I get in his cab again. We could be paying three cab drivers all the money and none of them will be Joe's cousin – no matter how many times we ask them.'

'Hmmm, yes, that's a point,' the professor acquiesced. His shoulders dropped and his hands, with the bills inside, fell to his sides.

'What if we each take...' Lisa looked around her. 'Some flowers...' She picked a handful from the vase that she had placed on the desk. 'We put one on the parcel shelf at the back of the cab when we have checked it. It would be easy to see from the outside. If there's a flower, it's been checked. Who's going to notice a flower on the parcel shelf other than someone who is looking for it?'

Fraser spoke. 'But there still must be thousands of taxi cabs in Hong Kong.'

'There are,' the professor said. 'But only maybe fifty or so in the area that I took. It would take a couple of hours at the most for all three of us to check them out. In fact we could start at the restaurant and work backwards. We know he works that area.'

So, it was set and the plan was in place. On the way to the restaurant they picked up more flowers, which made all three of them resemble mobile florists and, one by one, they hired cabs. Inside each one the conversation was the same.

'Busy tonight?'

'No, not really.'

'Say, you wouldn't know a Joe Hutchins would you?'

'Joe Hutchins? No, don't think so, he a friend of yours?'

'Yeah, anyway, look I think here is far enough actually, I'll walk the rest of the way.'

'But it's only been about a hundred yards.'

'Yeah, that's fine, I can walk the rest of the way.'

95

They would leave a flower on the parcel shelf of each cab they visited, pay their money and exit, leaving a trail of petals behind them.

As the night wore on it became harder and harder to find a cab that did not have a flower on the parcel shelf. The professor was right, it only took about two hours for there to be no cab driver they hadn't asked. Every time they saw a taxi, one of the three would hail and find, to their disappointment, that there was a flower on the parcel shelf. By one o'clock in the morning, the professor had given up hope. He sat on the pavement, placed his bunch of carnations next to him and studied his face in the rain water that was by now collecting in the gutter.

A few miles down the road, Lisa was doing the same. She sat on the curb dandling her one last carnation between her fingers, sniffing its tender white petals and letting her hair fall about her face in the drizzle. Suddenly her face was lit up with a harsh white light and a spray of water covered her from head to foot.

'You been stood up?' a voice said and she looked up. It was a cab. She sighed. 'Maybe.'

'Well, he's nuts. Do you wanna go somewhere?'

'Away,' she said, only half joking.

'Get in the back,' the voice said. Lisa stood up and as she stepped into the road noticed that there was no flower on the parcel shelf. She quickly got in and started the routine that had by now become second nature.

'Busy night?'

The taxi driver sighed. 'Don't know really. I have been ill. I've only just come on. I hope it's quiet. I prefer the quiet ones.'

'Say, you wouldn't know Joe Hutchins would you?'

Suddenly the car pulled over and the driver stared at Lisa through the rear view mirror.

'Who wants to know?'

Lisa gulped. 'Me.'

'Look, I don't want any trouble. Like I just said, I have been ill and I could do without shit tonight. I don't care what he's said to you or how he has promised to marry you, or whose daughter you are. As far as I am concerned Joey's sex life is his own business and that's that.'

Lisa felt her heart leap out of her chest. 'So you know him then?'

The driver turned round to face her for the first time in the conversation. 'Know him? Sure, he's my cousin.'

'Look,' said Lisa. 'Will you come with me to my uncle's flat? We really need to speak to Joey.'

'Look, I told you I don't want any trouble.'

Lisa laughed. 'There's no trouble. We want to hire him and his plane. We'll give you something for your help too.'

The cab driver looked Lisa over. His eyes rested on her breasts and made their way up to her slender neck and large brown eyes.

'OK,' he said finally. 'Where to?'

By the time Lisa and the taxi driver had got to the apartment, Fraser and the professor were already there. As soon as they burst through the door Lisa started explaining excitedly what had happened. She told the professor how she had given up hope and had been sitting on the curb by the side of the road when he had just driven past, soaking her dress, but how that did not matter because they were here now and that Joe could not be far away.

The taxi driver remained silent until he caught sight of the professor.

'Hey, you're the guy who was running. I heard you want my cousin Joe. Yeah, he's a damn good pilot.'

Fraser whispered underneath his breath. 'He needs to be.'

They fixed the cab driver a drink and sat round the table.

'So?' Lisa asked, but the taxi driver remained blank-looking.

'So what?'

'So where's Joe?'

'Hong Kong,' he said.

'Yes, we guessed Hong Kong, where exactly?'

The cab driver shrugged his shoulders. 'Don't know, did you phone that number I gave you?'

'Yes, but they said he moved out about three months ago.'

The driver sat back in his chair and rubbed his stomach. 'Yep, that sounds like Joe. He could never keep in one place very long. It's not so much he wants to move as other people want him to; they either drive him out or try to kill him.'

Lisa felt exasperated but was determined to see this thing through. 'Well, do you know where we could find him?'

'You could try the docks, he sometimes drinks down there. Oh, and the Club Hundred, he goes there a lot.' He stared at Lisa. 'You'd fit in down there.'

Lisa shifted nervously in her seat. 'Right, and you say he's a pilot?'

'Yep.'

'And he'll be able to fly us?'

'Nope.'

Lisa felt like giving up. 'Why?'

'Got no plane any more. Last time I heard it had been impounded by the police. This is grapevine stuff, you understand, it's been a good while since I seen his face.'

'But, if we got a plane, he could fly it?'

'Oh yeah, you pay him, he'll fly anywhere. That's why he's got no plane.' The taxi driver laughed a raspy, smoky laugh which segued into a raspy, smoky cough.

'Well, that sounds like just the sort of person we need,' Lisa said. 'The Club Hundred, you say?'

'Yep.'

Lisa stood up. 'Thank you Mr ... er...'

'Just call me Lee,' the taxi driver said.

Lisa smiled. 'Lee.'

'Now you said there might be something for me, if I could ... er ... help you with your business?'

Lisa looked at him and her skin crawled. 'Er, yes,' she said, and looked round.

'Here,' Fraser said and offered Lee a handful of the one dollar bills, which he took with a scowl.

'Thanks,' he said with heavy sarcasm and left, slamming the door behind him.

The Club One Hundred was its usual precipitous self. The smoke hung low below the ceiling and the music bounced off the walls in a lugubrious display of rhythmic suggestion. Lisa, Fraser and the professor walked straight in after paying their cover charge and started to weave in and out of the other customers who all jostled to see the stage. They found a table in a corner and sat down.

Fraser said that he would order some drinks and ask about Joe at the bar, so he left the professor and Lisa alone at the table. Lisa tapped nervously to the rhythm of the music and noticed that pair of eyes was staring at her. They were small and blue and piercing, easily noticeable through the smoke of the club. They belonged to a small man in a white coat who was standing over by the door. He could have only been five feet one and was as skinny as a rake but wore the most outlandishly wide white hat. With consternation, Lisa realised that the man was walking towards her. His gait bobbed to the beat of the music as his feet slid across the polished floor of the club. As he got nearer she could smell his cologne. It smelt of incense and roses, a little too sweet and cloying to be pleasant. He stood at the table, in front of her and the professor.

'You want to trade?' he said to the professor, who in turn looked blankly back. 'You wanna trade? I got a whole room full of women here you can have, black ones, white ones, Japanese, Korean, European, you wanna European? Yeah, course you do.'

Lisa suddenly realised that he was making her uncle an offer for her. She put on her most indignant face and said, 'I'm not for trade.'

But the man ignored her. 'You want a couple for this one, eh? How about these two?'

He snapped his fingers and two scantily-clad women ran up and draped themselves over his shoulders.

'They look good, yes? You can have them both for this one, she's got something.'

'Yes, I have,' said Lisa. 'A degree in chemistry.'

'A brainy one. I like it. Maybe you want three?'

The professor leaned forward. 'You know, I am thinking seriously about your offer, but perhaps another day.'

The man in white shrugged his shoulders. 'Whatever you say, you know where I am if you need a little something.'

He clicked his tongue and winked as he turned you go. Fraser passed him on the way. 'Who was that?' he asked.

'My future pimp,' Lisa said.

Fraser looked puzzled. He set down the drinks. 'I asked at the bar and they said they know Joe and he was in last night, got absolutely smashed by all accounts, so will probably be in today for the hair of the dog.'

'How will we know him?'

'The woman at the bar said she'd send him over. I said we wanted to offer him a job and she seemed to think he would go for that, if only to pay his bar tab here.'

Suddenly there was a deafening noise. The main show

had started and a deep bass was coming crashing out of the speakers. The stage began to revolve, uneasily, and lights were flicked on. The professor and Fraser stared as a tall half-Asian, half-European girl with long black hair sauntered out to the middle of the stage and started to dance erotically by the pole.

'I think perhaps we might go easy on him when we see him,' she said, but got no response. 'I thought perhaps I'd better try it with him first, he might respond better to a woman, he might not feel so ... hello, is either of you two listening to me any more?'

The professor and Fraser stared open mouthed at the girl on the stage, who could contort her small frame in ways that they hardly thought were possible. Every now and then the professor would blot his forehead with his tie and his eyes opened wide as they tried to gain every last piece of information they could about this beautiful thing. His face was contorted into an idiotic smile that seemed to make him seem about four years old again. She sighed to herself and took a sip of her drink. Then, noticing that the man in white was still watching her, she lowered her head and studied the enormously interesting marks that had been left by a thousand cocktail glasses in the varnish of the table.

After the show, the girl glided from the stage and mingled with the audience, displaying all the sexual allure of a cat. Her eyes darted around the club for someone but no matter how far they searched they always came up blank. She lazily brushed a hand over a businessman's shoulder and made him sit bolt upright in his chair as if electricity had passed through him; she dangled a lock of hair in the face of a foreign sailor who seemed to smell in it a thousand lusty nights in port. She wiggled her hips at a group of young Japanese youths at the bar and they nudged each other and nodded in her direction but they were all just boys to her and they were sent spinning into the distance by her lackadaisical smile.

The air was thick with cigarette smoke and sweat and the floor was sticky with spilt booze. Lisa got up out of her seat and made to go to the bar before Fraser tugged at her arm.

'Where are you going?' he asked.

'To get a drink.'

He pushed her back in her seat. 'I think I'd better go, don't you?' he said, and stood up himself.

Lisa crossed her legs in a manner that suggested she was not happy. She liked to be taken care of as much as anyone but she was up to ordering a drink, even here. Fraser's gallant actions were welcome at certain times, in certain situations, but when they became *de rigueur* she felt awkward and uncomfortable, as if she were expected to reciprocate in some way.

The professor had been watching her and as she turned to face him he smiled.

'You could do worse,' he said, sensing the moment. Lisa wrinkled her nose and then looked across the bar at Fraser, shoving his way through the crowd in a manly way. She could do worse, she said to herself … but she could also do better.

Suddenly her thoughts were broken by a commotion at the bar. A man, small but muscular, was being manhandled by three men in black suits. The small man struggled for all he was worth. He looked quite comical pitting his might against the three hulking brutes who flanked him. He flailed his arms about and kicked in the air, all to very little avail, until Lisa noticed the barman lean over and whisper into his ear. The little man stopped and shrugged off his guards. He dusted himself down, straightened his white cap and ordered a drink from the bar.

To her horror, the small man strolled over to her table. She could see now he was in his thirties. His hair was jet black and hung down beneath his white cap, which had some sort of insignia on it. It was dark so she could not see but she assumed it was a military badge, even though it did not look like a uniform cap. He wore a pair of baggy white trousers and blue deck shoes, with a striped blue and white T-shirt that even in the half light of the club looked as though it been slept in for weeks and never washed.

The man stood for a moment, saying nothing. Lisa thought she could smell fish as he stood there but put it down to the smoky air of the club and the fact that she had been drinking strong liquor. He placed his glass down on the table.

'You the one looking for me?' he said.

Lisa had dealt with these situations before; she knew how to handle them.

'Perhaps, depends on who you are.'

The man was cagey. He did it as if he had something to hide, perhaps lots of things. 'Well, that would depend on who you are.'

Lisa smiled. 'I'm no one special.'

The man looked her over. 'Oh, I wouldn't say that,' he said. 'You look pretty special from where I'm standing.'

Lisa felt herself blush and cursed herself for it. The man held out his hand. 'Joe Hutchins. They said at the bar that you might want to see me.'

'Lisa Okada,' Lisa said. 'And this is my uncle, Professor Okada.'

Joe lifted Lisa's hand and kissed it gently. 'Pleased to meet you, Lisa,' he said, and looked deeply into her eyes. 'Professor,' he added, without looking.

There was a cough behind. Joe spun round and sent the tray of drinks that Fraser was holding flying into the

103

air. Joe and Fraser squared up to each although it was obvious that this was a new experience for both of them. Lisa sighed, introduced Fraser and the two men warily relaxed.

'So,' Lisa added. 'Sit here and I'll tell you what my plan is. Fraser, go and get another round, would you?'

This time she relished being able to order him about. Fraser disconcertedly turned and headed towards the bar again.

'We have a proposition,' Lisa began. 'It's totally legal, it's totally above board, there's nothing to it. It's just a flight, that's all.'

Joe looked wary. He had been in these situations before and they never led to anywhere nice, although this pretty girl who looked as though she might be more at home in a classroom than a strip joint was an authentic touch. He tapped his arm absentmindedly. 'Where to?' he asked.

'The Philippines.'

'OK, so what's the deal?'

'Well, we'll tell you that when you agree.'

'Who says I will?'

'Well, when you know what you will be paid.'

'OK, what's the money?'

Lisa stopped for a minute and looked around her. 'A tenth of what we find,' she said.

Joe laughed. 'Right! A tenth of what?'

'A tenth of everything we're going to get.'

'And what's that?'

Lisa realised the paradox she had landed herself in. 'Er... I can't tell you unless you agree.'

Joe sat back in his seat and sipped his drink. 'So, you want me to agree to something before I know what it is, for a tenth share of whatever it is I'm agreeing to.'

Lisa thought. 'Yes,' she said.

'Well, have a good night,' Joe said and stood up.

'Wait...' Lisa implored. 'You can trust us.'

Joe smiled. 'Look ... Lisa? It's not that I don't trust you, but I have things here, things keeping me around. Women, deals, commitments, that sort of thing. I can't just up sticks and leave when I want. Otherwise, believe me, I would have gone by now.'

Joe looked up and winked at an attractive blonde by the bar. Lisa noticed and felt a tinge of jealousy.

'You see,' Joe said, 'There are things keeping me here, things I can't let go of. Good luck though, finding a pilot. You'll need it around here.'

He pushed the peak of his cap up high on his head with a finger and sauntered off, leaving Lisa feeling dejected and rejected. The professor patted her arm.

'There'll be others,' he said. 'There are others.'

At the bar, Joe walked up to the blonde. He ordered another drink and started small talk. 'You didn't think I'd be back, did you?'

The blonde looked at him. 'You been here before then?'

'Nice, it's always good to be flattered.'

'Sorry but there's a lot of faces in this business.'

'Yeah, I guess. Say, you haven't seen a girl called Gem around?'

'Gem? No, can't say I remember. Like I said, I'm no good with faces.'

'You sure you haven't seen her? She worked in here.'

'What do you want her for?'

'Oh, you know, just want to talk.'

'How much she steal?'

'Five hundred.'

'That's small fry, you got off lightly.'

'Well, I'd still like to talk.'

The blonde girl sucked air in through her teeth. 'There's a few like you about.'

As if the world had stopped moving for a second, as

if it had spun off of its axis and fallen into space, as if the moon had crashed into the earth, as if the oceans had suddenly decided to rise up and challenge the land, Joe felt his head being knocked from his shoulders. The first thing he knew was the sound – it was the sound of someone very near to him being punched, then the pain in the side of his face told him that it was him. Suddenly his teeth moved independently of each other – each one desperately trying to cling on to his gums like thirty-two white and shiny sailors hanging onto a raft. The second thing he felt was his brain hit the side of skull. It knocked all thoughts out of his ears; minor reminiscences, childhood memories, worries, bits of conversation half remembered and half forgotten squirmed about on the carpet eager to get back to where they belonged.

When his eyes had stopped spinning like a roulette wheel Joe turned and saw the faces of the two thugs who had been following him for the past week.

'Don't you guys ever give up?' he said rubbing his jaw and feeling about for his nose.

'We need a talk,' the smaller man said.

Joe thought quickly. 'Well, I'd love to but, I am really busy with this lovely lady for a moment, perhaps we could...'

There was a bang and Joe saw that the girl had fallen from the stool and lay on the floor in agony, a bullet in her arm. Her tears were low and visceral like the dying voice of a beast as it waits to be put out of its misery.

'You seem to be free now,' the man said, holding the still smoking pistol.

Joe swallowed hard, then threw his whiskey squarely into the eyes of the man with the gun, who recoiled in pain, letting fly a volley of bullets into the club. There was a commotion as girls and punters ran and ducked for cover. Joe grabbed one of the bar stools and lifted it above his head before bringing it down smartly on the back of the other thug who merely stood stock still. Joe jumped up on the bar and ran its entire length being shot at all the time. As he ducked the bullets missed him and hit bottles and glasses and customers about him.

He jumped down to where Lisa sat and screamed, 'You know that flight to the Philippines? Well, perhaps I would be interested after all. Do you wanna meet by the docks at twelve tomorrow night? You mind if I go now, I'm er, rather busy.'

Lisa nodded and jumped as a bullet flew near to her face and entered the wall behind her. Joe jumped over the table and ran along the outskirts of the dance floor. He spun around the pole in the middle of the stage and exited out of the back, making his way through the crowds of half-naked girls getting ready to dance.

By the time the hoods had followed him he was out of the door and away into the Hong Kong night.

8

The street vendors and food sellers had packed up now and the only sound that could be heard was the lapping of the waves on the sides of the boats that gently bobbed up and down in the water. Lisa wandered along the dock. She had persuaded Fraser and her uncle not to come – not because she had something to hide or that she didn't want their company but because she wanted to do this on her own. She wanted to contribute to this whole plan without having to answer to either of the two men.

She casually picked up a stone from the ground and tossed it into the harbour. It made no sound.

Around her, occasionally, people chatted and walked. The docks were a strange place for a girl to be on her own at night but she knew them well and was not afraid, even when drunkards would push their way up to her and breathe nasty boozy propositions in her face. She just leaned back, waved them on and did not look back.

It was amazing how quiet the city seemed at this time of night. Of course, all of the noise was underground now, in clubs, in bars, in massage joints, in the many places where she was never allowed to go when she was growing up. She had not really wanted to but, somehow, the places we are kept from are always the places we want to go most of all. She thought about Joe. Was he in one of those places? Was that why she was here on her own when really she should be with someone else? Even a man would probably not have come on his own, or perhaps that was it, perhaps only a woman could come on her own to the dock and not expect to be attacked by a knife or gun.

She realised she barely remembered what Joe looked like. She remembered his hat and strange way of tapping his arm with his fingers but that was about it. She tried to visualise him but always failed. She wondered whether he would turn up. She wondered what type of life he must have, what type of man he must be, what type of lover he would make; rough and quick or slow and considerate. No, she corrected herself, this is a business deal and it must stay that way.

She looked around and saw nothing. Only a cat moved between the barrels of fish heads, sniffing at the ground eager to find a meal or a bed for the night. Somehow the cat again reminded her of Joe.

The light skimmed across Hong Kong bay, making the water look like an expanse of glimmering ink. The moon was high but crescent, giving everywhere a half light that was comforting and yet eerie at the same time. She heard a noise behind her and turned quickly. Joe stood, smiling. One of his eyes was clearly bruised and there was a faint trickle of blood oozing out of his mouth.

'Ah, you made it then?' he said with a smile.

Lisa was shocked. 'What happened to you?' she asked.

'Well, let's say I ran into a spot of trouble today.'

'The same lot as last night?'

Joe laughed. 'If it had been I would be talking to you from the bottom of the harbour. No, this was a new one, a boyfriend.' He rubbed his cheek. 'Never mess with the girl of a soldier. Jesus, those guys can hit.'

Lisa tugged at the bottom of her skirt and licked at the cloth. She raised it to Joe's mouth and dabbed it, taking some of the blood away.

'You'll kill yourself before you take us to the Philippines.'

Joe backed off. 'Ah, yes, I was meaning to talk to you about that.'

For a moment Lisa was taken aback. She had assumed that the deal was settled between them, that Joe was signed up to fly her, Fraser and her uncle to the Philippines. She could not bear to see her hopes dashed at this stage.

'What is it?' she asked with half-closed eyes, waiting for the worst.

'Well,' Joe looked sheepish. 'Well, I am, as they say, grounded at the moment. My wings are currently sitting in a field at the pleasure of the Hong Kong police.'

Lisa dabbed his face a little more. 'I know,' she said.

'You know?'

'Yes, your cousin Lee told me.'

'How the hell did you meet him?'

'In a cab.'

Joe shrugged. 'Yeah, well, I suppose you would. Well, it does complicate things.'

'Not really. We just rent you another plane.'

Joe whistled through his teeth, grabbed Lisa by the shoulders and pushed her away. 'Look,' he said. 'You might have guessed that I'm not exactly law-abiding. I mean, I'm not going to get awarded the fair play award or anything. The mayor is not likely to offer me the contract of chief of police, but I know when I am in trouble and I smell trouble on you, honey. I think you reek of it.'

Lisa's eyes fell.

'I mean, you got money to rent a plane, but you got no money to rent a pilot. What is this?'

Lisa started. 'Well, I need someone who can look after themselves, who wouldn't be in a position to ask too many questions, who would do the job properly.'

'In other words you need someone desperate.'

'Yes, yes, perhaps. We need someone who is desperate enough to take on this job.'

'What is it?'

'I can't tell you yet, not until you're in.'

'I'm not in until I know what it is.'

'I can't. Please, Joe, I can't tell you.'

He turned to go. 'Then there's no deal.'

Lisa stood and watched him walk along the dock. His shoulders were hunched in the half moonlight and his hat was perched comically on his head. She couldn't go through all this with someone else and besides in the little time she had known him she had come to like him, even though he was dirty and abrupt and maddeningly stubborn.

'OK!' she shouted after him. 'OK, I'll tell you what the plan is. I'll tell you everything.'

Joe stopped, turned and inched his way back towards Lisa.

'OK,' he said. 'I'm listening.'

Lisa began. She told him about the girl and about her death, how they had traced the map to Amichi, how they had talked to Anderson and what had happened to Anderson in the basement of the university. She told him about Yamashita's gold and the legend of the aswang and about her uncle's visions and about all the strange things that had happened to him. Then she told him about how they had found his cousin and about how they had looked in virtually every cab in Hong Kong to find him, then how they had sat in the club until he had come in the night before.

When she had finished Joe sat, staring into the water. His face was a blank slate; his eyes stared straight ahead of him seeming to see something move in the water. In his head he was revisiting the cramped darkness of his dreams. While Lisa had been telling him about Yamashita's gold, about the tunnels where it was buried, about the aswang and the strange visions of her uncle, Joe recalled his own dreams and the visions that they produced in his mind. He realised that they were calling to him; they were trying to tell him something, to make him go somewhere.

He shook his head. It wasn't possible that he was having the same dreams as her uncle. It wasn't possible that whoever was beckoning to him was also beckoning someone else. Joe could not believe it, he would not let himself believe it, it could not be happening. He took off his hat and ran his fingers through his hair. This cannot be happening, he told himself again, this is not real.

'Have you spoken to your uncle about his dreams?' Joe asked.

Lisa was taken by surprise. 'Well, only in passing. He very rarely wants to speak about them. They scare him, I think.'

Joe gulped. He knew them too and he knew how frightening they could be. 'Where is your uncle?' he asked.

'Back at his apartment, with Fraser. Ever since it was broken into I don't like to leave him alone there.'

'Can we go to him? I need to speak with him.'

'Why, what's wrong? You look as white as a sheet.'

'I just need to speak to him.'

The night was folding around them like a blanket and the water lapped at the edges of the island. In the harbour something moved. Its eyes darted this way and that and its sinuous body changed shape again. In the dim light of the crescent moon the aswang strained each muscle of its form until it became something else, something more human, and it began to follow the two figures, the man in the cap and the pretty young woman, along the dockside. Each turn they made it turned too, each step they took it made too, but its feet made no sound on the damp concrete of the Hong Kong night.

112

Joe and Lisa walked to the professor's apartment oblivious to the half shadow half man that followed them.

The light was on in the apartment and Lisa found the professor and Fraser playing cards in the bedroom. Fraser sat with a look of absolute horror on his face and the professor sat with a pile of what Lisa assumed was Fraser's money in front of him and a smile on his face. Both of them jumped up as Joe entered the room.

The professor crossed immediately and shook Joe by the hand.

'I am so glad we caught up with you, Joe,' he said and shook his hand a little more.

Fraser was less enthusiastic and stood by the window with his hands in his pockets.

Joe said, 'Professor, I need to talk to you about something, something that I think we might have in common.'

'Sit,' the professor said. 'Sit down.'

'Well, but I feel a little foolish talking to you about it in front of er ... strangers.'

He nodded at Fraser and the professor answered, 'Of course, of course. Fraser, will you go and make us some tea? Do you drink tea, Joe?'

'Only when there is no whiskey.'

'Well, I may have a little scotch left over from...'

'Tea will be fine, thanks. Lisa, would you help him?'

Lisa screwed her nose up. Now she was being ordered around by Joe as well as Fraser and her uncle, but she desperately wanted this trip to go ahead and she was not going to spoil it due to a little thing like an ego. She groaned slightly and stormed out of the bedroom. Joe shut the door and sat down on the bed.

'I have heard you have dreams, professor.'

The professor laughed. 'We all dream, Joe.'

'But I have heard you have specific dreams, special ones, particular ones.'

113

The professor looked concerned. 'Well, yes,' he said. 'There have been certain dreams lately that have, how shall we say, disturbed me.'

'Describe them to me.'

'Well, I am in a tunnel of some sort, yes, a tunnel. It's black but I know it's a tunnel because when I reach up I can feel the roof and it's arched and cold and damp like earth. There is a musty smell and the smell of bad air. I know there is death there. I know there has been suffering and great pain but, no matter how badly I want to leave something pulls me along. I feel my feet moving even though I don't want them to. It's like something pulling me onwards, something that I cannot control.'

'What then, professor, what happens then?'

'Well, I see faces, faces of dead men, skulls some of them and they look at me as if to ask where have I been, why didn't I come earlier. Oh, it's so horrible there – the air is so thick it chokes me, I want to die, to expire, but I never do. No matter how much I want to I never lose consciousness. It's like something is keeping me awake to do whatever it wants me to do.'

'And what does it want you to do professor? What is it leading you on to do?'

'It wants me to open the door, open the door in the wall. It's an old wooden slatted door that looks as though it has not been opened for decades. I reach out my hand and I can see that it's shaking. My fingers touch the door knob and I turn it ... but then I usually wake up. I feel, though, I just feel as though I'm being called somewhere, that something is asking me to follow it, that something is pulling me somewhere.'

Joe was silent for a while. He sat with his hands in his lap looking at the professor.

'What would you say,' he said finally, 'If I told you that

I had exactly the same dream and exactly the same feelings?'

The professor stared at him. 'I'd say you were lying, Joe. Either that or we are both mad.'

'Well, we must both be crazy, professor, because I'm not lying and I have exactly the same dream virtually every night, right down to the feel of the tunnel roof above my head.'

The professor got up and crossed over to the window. He looked down into the street below and thought he saw, just for a brief second, the figure of a man disappear before his eyes. One moment he was there, the next he was gone. He checked himself and reasoned that the night and the light play tricks on the eye when one is tired and afraid and he put the thought out of his head.

'What does it mean, professor?'

'I wish I could tell you, Joe, but I have no idea myself.'

'You don't think it has anything to do with this treasure, do you?'

The professor laughed. 'Joe, I am a man of science, I can't believe in such nonsense stories.'

Joe looked at him hard. 'What are your real feelings?'

'My real feelings are that we are both being told something by someone or something and all we need to do is listen and they will make sure we come out of it alive. Are you going to fly us?'

Joe thought. His mind was a whirl of different emotions and images, there were so many practical reasons why he should not do this stupid trip, why he should just pack up now and go: walk out of the door and never look back. However, there was the matter of the two guys who wanted to dance the fandango on his face and the police who were investigating him. There was also the opportunity of making some real money if this thing were to come off. He had heard about Yamashita's gold, had also heard that it was a myth put about by the Philippine government to ensure that a steady stream of suckers would come knocking at their door looking for treasure. They survived on kickbacks and shady licences from your average workaday American now that the drug trade was gradually losing favour.

He thought of his plane. If nothing else this would get him flying again. He hadn't flown for a number of months now and he missed it. He never thought he would say it but he actually missed being up in the air out of the way of everyone on the street who wanted him dead. He was never a romantic but, in the air, you were free, not quite as a bird perhaps, but freer than anything that walked on two legs on the ground. If this whole stupid trip came to nothing in the Philippines then he could always get his wings back and, as his father used to say to him, a man's wings are his best friend.

Joe stared hard at the professor and held out his hand. 'OK, professor, you got yourself a pilot.'

The two men shook hands. The door burst open and Lisa fell through it, rushing over to hug her uncle and then Joe. The professor stared intently at her. 'I do hope you weren't listening,' he said to Lisa.

'Do you want sugar in your tea, uncle?' she replied.

Later that evening they sat around the table discussing the plan.

'Of course,' said Joe, 'The main problem is how do we get a plane to take us over there?'

'I told you. We hire one,' Lisa replied.

Joe shook his head. 'To be brutally honest with you it might not be that easy. You see in order for us to be able to hire a plane I need to be insured and, well, since, I have had problems with the aviation authorities over here – well, they haven't exactly been my best friends.'

'Have you actually got a licence?'

116

Joe rubbed the back of his head. 'Well, that all depends on what you call a licence.'

'Usually it means a bit of paper that says you can fly a plane.'

'Oh, yeah, well, I have one of those.'

'Good, so what's the problem?'

'Well, it was kind of...' Joe paused for a moment, 'Taken momentarily, due to an unfortunate incident with a few kilograms of heroin. I mean, I'm still legal, technically, I just don't have the bit of paper to prove it. The police do.'

'Great!' Fraser said, and slammed his hands on the table. 'Where the hell did we get this guy?'

Joe looked at him angrily. 'Look, do you want to fly the plane yourself, buddy? I know what this looks like but I didn't know what I was carrying and I have suffered since, right? Now, when we're out of Hong Kong air space, none of this matters any more. All I need to do is take off and we are virtually there.'

'So how do we get a plane?' Lisa asked.

'Well, I've been thinking about that,' Joe answered. 'I say we just take my one.'

The group were stunned.

'Yeah, we try to bribe the guard they have at the airfield. You know what Hong Kong cops are, right? We just waltz in, flash some money and take my plane right out of there.'

'Just like that?' asked Fraser.

'Yes, just like that. Have you any better ideas?'

Fraser was quiet. He didn't have any better ideas, just a gut feeling that this was one of the worst ones he had heard in a long time.

'So when do we go?' Joe asked.

Lisa shrugged. 'Uncle?'

'We have all we need,' the professor said. 'Next week?'

There was silence for a while as each of them contemplated what they were about to do.

'We need things, uncle,' said Lisa. 'Provisions, permits maybe, and we need to organise food and tools.'

Her uncle waved her concerns away. 'Yes, yes, I am sure you and Fraser can sort all of that out. You are excellent at logistics. Me, I need to decide what we need in terms of texts, books, maps, and so on. It would be best, I think, to be in and out as quickly as possible.'

Fraser started to speak. 'How do we know what part of the Philippines to start looking in? I mean it's a vast area and the map only shows local landmarks. We could theoretically be flying over Philippine airspace for months before we even saw anything that was remotely like the features on the map.'

'He's right, uncle,' said Lisa. 'Anderson was sure we would recognise the features once we flew over them but how do we even know we're in the right area?'

The professor thought for a moment. 'I'm thinking,' he said, with his lips pursed. 'I'm thinking.'

The other three looked at him. They watched as his skin became a little damper and his temples became a little redder. He closed his eyes and sat down squarely on the bed for what seemed like hours. Then, suddenly, as if waking from a dream, his face lit up with a smile, he got up from the bed and shuffled, quickly out of the door. A moment later he came back with a book in his hand.

'I found this in the library last week, when you were researching the Japanese military, Lisa. It is a history of the army, written at the end of the war by a Dutchman of all things, Van Broek. It details that there was heavy fighting with the US army in the last months of war, especially on the island of Mindanao. Here, here is the part: 'The US army dedicated hundreds of men to pursuing

118

the Japanese army through the jungle of Mindanao. After three weeks of continuous attrition, many of those left alive were taken prisoner, relieved that they might be given rations and a dry bed again.' There it is on page 67.'

The room was silent. Finally Fraser piped up, 'Professor, this is very interesting but I do not see how it helps our cause.'

The professor looked stunned. 'You do not see? You do not see?'

'I don't see it either, professor,' Joe said. 'What's it got to do with us?'

The professor sighed. 'The island. The small island. What interest had it for the Americans? Why did they pick this tiny island among all the others to conduct a three-week war of attrition? They must have suspected, no, they must have *known* that this was where the gold was buried. They were flying all over the Philippines at this point. I have no doubt in my mind that they would have sent a reconnaissance plane over Mindanao and seen what was going on.'

'Yes, but they wouldn't have found much out in the jungle ... without a map. That's it, uncle, that must be it.'

Fraser was unsure. 'Well, yes, I can see it's a lead anyway.'

'You're a genius professor, do you know that? A damned genius. You're right, I know it. Right, when do we go? I wanna get my plane back in the air as quick as possible.'

'Well, as Lisa said, Joe, there are still provisions to be got and things to be finalised.'

The four of them moved to the living room and stood round the table. They looked at each other in awed silence, not knowing what to say or to do next. Outside, down the corridor someone waited for them to come out,

119

someone who was all too human. He had a dark suit on that was splattered with blood – Anderson's. He tapped his fingers on the wall and kicked at the ground while all the time keeping his eyes on the door and his mind on the job.

Suddenly he felt a tap on his shoulder and when he turned his mouth was covered by a perfumed hand that was covered in gold rings. There was a whisper.

'Shhhhhh! Kono, you fool, it's me, Tanaka.'

Kono relaxed and the hand was taken away from his mouth.

'When did they go in there?'

'About an hour ago.'

'Have you listened at the door?'

'No, I thought it best to stay here and wait for them.'

Tanaka patted the other man on the cheek. 'Good, good. I want them followed, you hear me, wherever they go. I want you to stick with them.'

'You can count on me, boss.'

'Good, good.' Tanaka turned to leave.

'Er ... boss?' Kono said.

Tanaka sighed deeply and stopped. 'Yes, what is it?'

'You don't believe in this, do you?'

'In what?'

'The gold? The buried gold?'

Tanaka inched closer to Kono, who was twice his size. 'Would I have got you to kill the girl if I didn't believe in it?' he said with menace, the corners of his mouth forming a snarl and his eyes closing in tiny snake-like slits.

'No, boss, no, you wouldn't have.'

Tanaka slapped Kono's face. 'You just keep your eyes open, yes? Leave the thinking and the believing to me. Don't worry your ugly little head over it.'

He turned and headed down the corridor. When he

was sure he couldn't see him any more Kono poked his tongue out at the back of his boss before turning around again to fix his eyes solidly on the door.

9

A match was struck in the darkness and lit up a cold, sinuous face. Slowly it was brought nearer to the cigarette that dangled from a pair of thin, white lips – it lit the cigarette, which glowed with a red warmth and fizzled as it was sucked upon, then it was shaken and thrown to the ground.

A voice whispered: 'Do you know that for every one of those you have, you lose five minutes of your life?'

The man smoking just shrugged. 'This life, I could do with losing a few minutes from it.'

They had been waiting for over two hours already and they could feel their fingers growing numb and their legs starting to give way.

'You sure he's coming?'

'No.'

'How did you hear he was here?'

'He's been coming here for a week now. He's hooked himself up with some girl and her uncle. Every day he comes here, spends a few hours in the apartment and then leaves. I've had someone follow him but he just spends the night mooching around, going from place to place, bars, clubs – the usual thing with him.'

'He not sleeping anywhere now?'

'No, just going to that apartment every day, leaving every night.'

They stood in an alley facing the professor's apartment, their expensive suits looking out of place in their tawdry surroundings. They had been tailing Joe for almost a week now and were ready to strike any minute.

'You know the funny thing?' the smoking man said to the other.

'What?'

'I think he's being followed.'

'Yes, by our guy.'

'No, by someone else ... look.'

The other man looked and, sure enough, outside the apartment block stood Kono, reading a newspaper, trying not to look conspicuous but, doing so, looking as conspicuous as hell.

'Who's he?'

'Don't know, haven't seen him before.'

'Is he part of Yuen's mob?'

'No, I would have recognised him.'

'Lee's?'

'No, I think he's from out of town.'

'You think it means anything?'

'Yeah, I think it means our friend Joe is about to go somewhere.'

'Where?'

'I have no idea. What's that?'

The two men were suddenly quiet and still as they saw four figures exiting the door at the bottom of the apartment block.

'What are they carrying?' the one said to the other.

'Bags. They look heavy. Go and get the car. We'll keep close, see where they go.'

Over by the apartment block, Lisa was struggling with the bags. 'Fraser, do you want to help me with this one?'

Fraser screwed his forehead up. 'Lisa, that's your bag. If you really want to take all that rubbish, well, I think you should be responsible enough to carry it yourself.'

Joe offered to help but was cut short by Fraser's arm. 'However, I can never bear to see a woman in distress,' he said gallantly and picked up the bag, struggling under its weight.

As they neared the pavement a cab pulled up with Joe's cousin at the wheel. Quickly, they put the bags in the boot and clambered in.

'To the airport,' Lisa said, and they sped off.

'The international airport?'

'No, the old airport at Kai Tak.' Joe smiled at the thought of being re-united with his wings.

The city streets were packed, even at this late hour. The neon signs buzzed and blinked in the darkness and the jaywalkers and street walkers cluttered the pavements like ants around honey. Lisa put her face up to the window of the car and watched the world go speeding by. Everything had happened so fast but she had butterflies in her stomach when she thought about what was about to happen. Her eyes moved slowly around the car and rested on Joe, who was busy in conversation with his cousin; they both talked in a frenetic manner, pointing at things, becoming excited, acting crazy. It was his craziness that she liked most. She had spent most of her life with academics, writers and thinkers. Now here she was face to face with a doer, someone who took life and experienced all of it – the joys and the pains.

She liked the way Joe dived head first into everything he did: whatever it was he wrung the most out of it – danger, excitement, action, adventure. She hadn't known him long but already she found herself being attracted by him – his easy manner and his sense of the unknown.

Joe's cousin suddenly addressed the car: 'That blue Nissan's back,' he said, looking in his rear view mirror. 'The one that was tailing you before, professor.'

Joe's cousin craned his neck as he drove. 'And you can call me crazy but ... I think there's someone following that!'

Joe looked round. 'Ah!' he said, guiltily. 'I think the black Merc might be my fault.'

'Your fault? What do you mean your fault?' Fraser asked.

'Well, you know those guys in the club?'

'Yes.'

'They have been tailing me for a week now. I thought I might shake them off but it looks like they stuck.'

Lisa looked out of the rear window just in time to feel her head bang against the door jamb as Joe's cousin sped off into the night. The screech of tyre on tarmac was almost deafening as the cab was thrown this way and that in order to lose the two cars that followed it. It headed down a side street and along by the docks, knocking baskets off into the harbour and causing people to sprawl on the ground; everywhere it went, the blue Nissan and the black Mercedes stuck to it like glue and followed its every move.

Inside the cab, Fraser, the professor and Lisa were being thrown about and were tangled up in each other's arms.

'Slow down, slow down!' Fraser cried, feeling as if his teeth were being rattled out of his head.

The cab swerved out of the harbour district and into Hong Kong city centre. From his vantage point in the front seat, Joe could see the fear on the faces of the crowds as they found themselves face to face with a crazy cab driver and a cab full of scared passengers. His cousin turned into an alleyway which led to a back street and there were sparks as the sides of the car brushed up against the brickwork. Looking back, Joe saw that the two cars were not following them any more.

'They've gone,' he said. 'We've lost them. They must have been too wide to fit through here. You've done it, you done it!'

Suddenly he felt the car come to a grinding halt. There was silence. The only noise that could be heard was the slight creak of metal as it cooled. They were stuck in the alleyway, which narrowed imperceptibly towards the middle. Joe cursed the builders of Hong Kong's streets.

'What do we do now?' Lisa asked.

'All out the roof,' Joe's cousin exclaimed as if this sort of thing happened all the time (which it did). He opened the sunroof and climbed out onto the car, then casually stepped onto the bonnet and hopped down to the ground. When he was safe, he looked back through the windscreen and beckoned to the others.

'Come on,' he said. 'Hurry up.'

Joe placed a foot on the headrest of the driver's seat and climbed out of the car. As the cold air hit him he felt a strange sinking feeling. Turning, he saw that one end of the alleyway had been blocked off by a blue Nissan. Turning back, he saw the face of his cousin, apologetic but smiling.

'I'm sorry, Joey boy, the taxi game is not what it used to be and these people have money.'

Joe sighed. 'You could have given us a chance. You could have done at least that.'

His cousin shrugged. Joe noticed that Kono, Tanaka and about three others had exited their car and were walking towards them. From inside the cab Lisa pushed him.

'What's going on?' she demanded. 'Why are we getting out?'

Joe called down to her. 'We've been double-crossed,' he said. 'By a skunk.' And he looked at his cousin.

Suddenly, he felt a breeze blow past his ear, followed by a loud bang. He turned to see that at the other end of the alleyway the black Mercedes had stopped and the two goons inside were firing at him.

'Great,' Joe said and jumped back in the driver's seat.

'What the hell's going on?' Lisa asked.

'We have company that we really didn't need at this moment,' Joe said and his words were followed by a bullet smashing the back windscreen and almost parting the professor's hair.

'Well,' said Joe. 'Wish me luck.' And he started the engine. It fired into life. He put it into reverse and pressed the accelerator for all it was worth. There was an infernal blast of smoke and sparks as the car desperately tried to free itself from the alleyway. The more he floored the pedal, the more the car churned and screamed, trying to get free. Through the windscreen he saw that Kono and Tanaka were running towards him; through the rear window, he saw the goons aiming to fire again. He closed his eyes and pushed down with his foot and almost immediately the car sped into life and zoomed backwards, causing sparks and smoke to be sent into the night sky.

The cab got faster and faster towards the end of the alleyway, until it hit the black Mercedes and sent it spinning into the road. Joe spun the wheel round, changed gear and sped off, leaving the black Mercedes spinning and reeling on the damp road and Kono and Tanaka running back towards their Nissan.

Joe wrestled with the wheel of the cab, which was by now looking battered and bruised. He looked in the rear view mirror.

'They'll still be after us,' he said. 'We'd better get to the airport and in the air.'

He drove at high speed to the small airport just outside of the city, conscious that all the way they were still being followed by the blue Nissan and the black Mercedes. As they neared the airport, they noticed that the gates were closed, but they were flimsy, only chain and aluminium.

'We're going straight through,' Joe said. 'Hold on.'

The cab crashed through the gates and sent them flying on their hinges. They hung limply for a moment and then

127

fell to the ground like a prize fighter after a hard tenth round. Joe once again pressed on the pedal and sent the cab screaming round the empty spaces of the airfield. Behind him, the two cars that had been following kept on his tail, their tyres screaming on the tarmac, leaving a trail of sticky black rubber and smoke.

'Where is it?' asked Fraser.

'Hangar 26b,' Joe said.

Lisa pointed. 'There's 15, and there's 16. We must be going in the right direction.'

Joe heard the sound of gunfire and ducked. 'Don't those guys ever give up?' he said, and swerved the car so as not to make it an easy target. 'I could get seriously fed up with this.'

Lisa screamed, '21! Come on, just a few more!'

Joe heard the engine of the cab splutter and looked down. 'Damn, we're overheating,' he said, and watched as billows of white steam shot up from the bonnet. 'Come on, come on, just get us there!'

'25!' Lisa shouted. '26a ... 26b!!'

Joe drove the cab straight into the doors of the hangar. Inside it was dark and the air was musty. The cab screeched to a halt and the noise was sent shuddering round the walls. 'Come on,' he said, jumping out of the doors of the cab, which were bare metal now, into the plane.

'We need the bags,' Lisa shouted.

'Forget the bags,' Joe said. 'Forget everything, we have to go.'

'But we need the documents,' the professor said – but as he felt a bullet pass nearby his left earlobe he corrected himself smartly. 'You're right Joe, as long as we have the map, we can leave the rest.'

He quickly made his way to the plane, opened the door and jumped in, followed by Fraser.

Joe pulled Lisa by the waist and forcefully carried her towards the plane.

'We at least need food and bedding,' she screamed.

'Will you get in the crate,' Joe said. 'Or you'll get us both killed. Why don't you just do as you're told for once?'

'How dare you!' Lisa retorted. 'I always have to do everything you or uncle or Fraser says, anything...'

A bullet whipped past her and she felt the first, warm drops of blood on her arm. She realised that these were not her drops of blood but Joe's – he had been hit in the arm and was bleeding slowly.

'You're hit,' she said.

He grinned. 'I'm fine, it's just a scratch, although you might have to carry yourself.'

Together they ran to the plane, opened the doors and climbed in. By this time, both the blue Nissan and the black Mercedes had braked to a halt and their occupants had climbed out. They ran towards the plane, where inside Joe struggled for the key.

'OK, OK, I know I had it,' he said, and furiously fumbled in his pockets.

'Come on, come on,' Fraser shouted.

The two thugs who had been tailing Joe for a week began firing at the plane, ripping holes in the edge of its wings. They tangled with each other as they tried to get near. Kono and Tanaka also struggled to reach it. As if some great beast were awaking inside its belly, the plane leapt into life, the engine spluttered and then caught with a roar that made the propeller turn with furious speed. Joe eased it forward through the hail of bullets. He turned the plane to face the hangar door and started it on its forward run.

Kono ducked this way and that trying to stop the plane and get out of its way at the same time; the men in suits ducked as the wings moved perilously close to their heads. Joe eased the plane forward and felt it go faster and faster along the gravel lined runway. Behind him he saw Kono running and puffing to keep up.

'He's tiring,' Lisa said. 'He can't catch up.'

Kono made a final desperate leap for the plane and managed to grab hold of the landing gear just as they left the ground. Joe pulled back on the joystick and sent the plane skywards. What he didn't see was that while underneath them, Kono had attached a small device to the undercarriage. Then he had fallen to the ground, where he lay bruised and breathless watching the tail lights of the small plane disappear into the night.

Joe smiled. 'There,' he said, and patted the control board of the plane. 'Knew we'd do it.' He turned and saw the terrified faces of his three passengers all staring, white as sheets, out of the cockpit widow. 'Come on, now, it wasn't that bad, was it? I mean, I have had better take-offs, but at least we are still alive.'

The professor had caused ten indentations on the back of the pilot's seat. Lisa was clutching on to her seat belt and Fraser was wiping a tear away from his cheek.

'I think it went rather well, actually. We are in the air, that's all that counts. Look at that down there, that's Hong Kong, right? Look at it. Isn't it beautiful? It looks like a million diamonds shining. We are on our way. When we come back, we are going to be rich.'

He banked the plane, a move which caused Fraser to groan from the back seat.

'All we really need is to keep to our course and we're home free.' He reached in to the map compartment of the plane, pulled out an old aviation map and threw it at Lisa. 'You're navigator,' he said. 'Just keep us on course.'

The sea below was black and inky as they skimmed above its surface. There was very little to navigate by, only the map and the compass, but Lisa found that navigating was a skill she took to quite easily. Before long, Fraser and the professor were snoring in the back seats, lulled to sleep by the sound of the engine and the vast expanse of nothing outside the window. In the dim light of the cockpit, Joe and Lisa chatted.

'So, how did you get to be a pilot?'

'Ah, you know, family.'

'Family?'

'Yeah, my dad was a pilot in the US air force. He met my mom when he was over here and bingo, a few months later she had me. They say I was born with a pair of wings on my shoulder.'

'You like it, then?'

'Look around you. There isn't anyone who will bother you up here. There ain't no one going to shoot at you or tell you what to do. You're free.'

'Sometimes, it's good not to be free.'

'Yeah? You say! That's all I ever wanted – to be free, to just be able to go wherever I choose.'

'Have you ever been married?'

'Nah, I been close once or twice, I am a sucker for a hard luck story, especially if it's told by a girl but fate always steps in – don't know if that's a good thing or a bad thing, probably good. I wouldn't want to marry. What about you? You ever want to marry? Settle down?'

Lisa thought. 'Maybe, but I want to do a lot first. Everyone I went to school with, every girl, is married and settled down now. They all have their homes or their children or their small jobs, they all go out at the weekend to the theatre or to see family in the country, they all drive new cars that are never more than three years old and all have grey hairs and big asses.'

Joe laughed. 'Not for you, eh?'

'Well, I'm here, aren't I?'

'Yep, you are here all right, but why are you here? That's what I want to know.'

'Well, I guess for the same reason you are.'

'The money?'

'You're not only here for that, are you?'

Joe looked at her, her big eyes shining under the dim bulb of the cockpit lamp. 'No,' he said finally. 'No, I guess not.'

'All of that gold is stolen from somewhere. We can't forget that, none of it is ours or the Japanese army's or Yamashita's – it's the people of Manila's, the Buddhists of Japan's, the Chinese merchants', who knows? It could have come from anywhere in Asia. The things in the tunnels have real importance to real people's lives; it can't be just left there forever. Once, people worshipped the Buddha there, kissed the statues, drank wine from the cups and wore the jewellery; once they revered the icons and handed down the artefacts to their children. It can't be left in a tunnel, never to be seen again, never to be freed.'

Joe was quiet. He thought for a moment. 'You make it sound like a calling you have.'

'Haven't you got a calling?' she replied. 'Is that not what part of this is about?'

Joe didn't reply, he just looked out of the cockpit window at the stars shining overhead. In the dim distance he saw the sun begin to rise; its slow orange beauty was just beginning to infiltrate the sanctity of the purple and black sky.

'Look,' he said to Lisa. 'The sunrise.'

10

Lisa awoke to the sound of Joe banging his fist on the control board.

'Come on!' he was shouting. 'Come on!'

She rubbed her eyes.

'I think we're in trouble,' he said.

'What?'

'Fuel, we're running low.'

Quickly, Lisa grabbed the aviation map that lay on the floor of cockpit. By this time Fraser and the professor had also woken and were straining to hear from the back seats.

'What's wrong?' the professor asked.

'Nothing,' Lisa lied. 'Just a little problem with fuel.'

Fraser screamed, 'Didn't you check when we left?'

'Well, I had a quick look, yeah.'

'A quick look!' Fraser exclaimed. 'We're hundreds of feet above the South China Sea and you say you had a quick look!'

Joe turned. 'Do you want to fly this thing?'

Fraser sat back in his seat and looked out of the window, wishing he were somewhere else.

Joe fiddled with the controls on the panel, while Lisa studied the map.

'Look,' she said. 'I think we should be near land by now. If we could just glide for a bit we might make it.'

Joe was sweating as he flicked the fuel gauge. 'This ain't no glider,' he said in a panic. 'If we go down we go down ... fast.'

Lisa pointed to a lush green island in the near distance. 'There it is, there it is, surely we can make it.'

Beside them the engines spluttered their last as they were starved of the fuel they needed to keep functioning.

'I think they're going,' Joe said.

Suddenly there was silence. The steady hum that they had got used over the last few hours stopped and all they heard was the wind rushing past the windows as the plane fell steadily.

'I'll try to bring her in near the island,' Joe said. 'But you might have to get wet.'

Lisa leaned over and held Joe's hand. She squeezed it a little and he looked at her. For the first time since he had known her she looked scared. He reciprocated and tightened his grip on her fingers.

'You'll be OK,' he said. 'Professor, can you swim?'

The professor was busy getting himself ready. He had taken his shoes off and stuffed them into the pockets of his jacket.

'Oh, yes, Joe, don't worry about me, I manage ten lengths a day. I'll be on the island before you.'

Joe laughed. 'Fraser?'

Fraser didn't say anything.

'Fraser.'

'Er ... yes?'

'You ready?'

'Course, er, course. I can't actually, er, swim.'

'Well, this would be a damn good time to start,' the professor said. 'If you can stick by me as we hit the water, I'll try to carry you.'

Fraser noticed Lisa looking at Joe and suddenly found his voice again. 'I'll be fine,' he said. 'I'll learn.'

Joe turned to Lisa. 'See you on the beach.'

The first thing each of them noticed was the force of the landing. It threw them forward in their seats and

134

then the whole world seemed to turn upside down. Suddenly it got dark as the plane's wings snapped off with the force and the fuselage rolled underwater. The professor had managed to open the door just as they hit the water but its coldness and the sudden lack of light stunned him for a moment. With all his strength he kicked his way out of the plane, pulling Fraser behind him. Quickly he headed for the surface where the water was a lighter blue. Behind him, Joe and Lisa were pulling themselves free. He saw them exiting the plane and, kicking elegantly, make their way to the surface.

The professor realised that Fraser was weighing him down – something was not right. He tugged at his shoulder but he didn't move. The professor swam down to look at his face but it was too dark. He placed a hand over his mouth and felt bubbles coming out, a sure sign that he was breathing but that he was unconscious, unable to hold his breath. The professor assumed that the force of the landing had knocked him out cold, so he grabbed hold of his shoulders and kicked for all he was worth towards the surface. The more he kicked and struggled the heavier Fraser became, and the heavier Fraser became the harder it was to drag him to the air.

The professor flailed his legs and arms but to no avail. He felt himself being dragged under by the dead weight of the man he was clinging on to. Above him Joe and Lisa had realised something was up when the professor and Fraser hadn't surfaced. They ducked under the water but again could see nothing. Lisa dived under the water frantically searching with her arms in the darkness. It was so cold she could no longer feel her fingers. She knew that none of them could last long in the water; they had to get out on to dry land and warm themselves.

Eventually, her hands caught hold of her uncle's jacket collar and she kicked for all she was worth. Gradually, with Joe's help, she managed to pull both the professor and the unconscious Fraser to the surface, where they trod water for a while, breathless and scared. Joe held Fraser's chin above the surface.

Lisa looked concerned. 'How is he?' she asked, nodding towards Fraser.

The professor swam over. 'He's still breathing. Better take him to the shore where we can have a look. It might only be concussion.'

Lisa, the professor and Joe, carrying Fraser, swam to the shore where they lay for a while in the early morning sun. Joe looked at the ocean just in time to see the wings of his plane disappearing below the surface.

'There she goes,' he said.

'This island looks too small to be Mindanao. What if we're miles away?' Lisa asked but no one answered; they just watched the bubbles breaking the surface of the ocean that, every now and then, brought forth a fresh piece of debris and deposited it on the beach. The sun was only just above the horizon but it spread a warm glow on to the faces of Joe, Lisa, Fraser and the professor and seemed to give life to their bodies which were wet and cold.

Lisa held Fraser's head in her arms and, as if coming back from the dead, he opened his eyes and stared at her thinking that she was, perhaps, an angel. Suddenly he started fighting for his life. The last image he had in his mind was of the plane under water, he struggled with the waves, gasping for breath, not wanting to let them win, to drown him. Lisa held his head and whispered in his ear, 'Easy, easy, you're safe now. We are on the beach.'

Fraser became calm. Lisa felt his body relax under her grip as his eyes and his mind became adjusted to the situation.

'You nearly pulled us all under there,' Joe said. 'I thought we had all had it for a moment.'

Fraser sat up. 'Is she gone?' he said, nodding to the ocean.

'Yes, just now,' Lisa explained.

Fraser's head fell back onto her arm and he gave a sign that seemed to speak for them all. Slowly, the professor adjusted the collar of his shirt.

'The sun will be fully up soon; we should be getting along.'

'Where would we go to?' Lisa asked.

'To find the gold,' he said.

'But where? We needed the plane. The plan was to spot the area by plane. Now that's gone.'

'We can walk. This island's not so big. We'll find it, I am sure.'

Joe laughed. 'You are mighty optimistic all of a sudden.'

The professor smiled at him. 'We are here, aren't we? I think that is reason to be optimistic enough.'

About a hundred yards away from the beach, in the shadow of the trees something moved. It was barely noticeable against the dark background of the dense undergrowth of the jungle but, in the early morning sun, the glint of metal shone. It was raised to the horizontal and aimed at those on the beach with a military precision, but no sooner had it locked on to its target than it was lowered again. Now was not the time, it seemed to think, later would be better.

'We need food and provisions, uncle, and how the hell are we going to get off this island? Who knows we're here? No one.'

The professor tried to calm her but the words were hard to find. Tears formed in Lisa's eyes as the shock of the crash and the thought of the island brought home how isolated they were. Joe shifted on the sand and sat next her. He placed a hand on her shoulder. 'We'll make it,' he said tenderly. 'We'll make it.'

And Lisa dried her eyes. 'Now you're sounding optimistic,' she said with a sob. Joe leaned over and kissed Lisa on the cheek, drying one of her tears with his lips. 'Have I ever let you down yet?' Joe asked, and Lisa laughed.

'Once or twice.'

The professor got to his feet. The sun had partly dried his clothes and they hung off his body in a sandy misshapen lump, making him look more comical than usual. He brushed himself down and fumbled in his pocket. He pulled out the map, enclosed in a bag.

'Good, good,' he said. 'Still intact. This, after all, is why we came here. Now, where do you think we should start?'

Fraser raised his head from Lisa's lap. 'We should try to find a base. Are there people on this island?'

The professor scratched his head. 'Yes, yes, there may be inhabitants here, small villages, I don't doubt they have a radio. I'm afraid the modern world stretches everywhere these days. I guess the problem is finding them.'

'So you think we could radio for a plane?' Joe asked.

'Possibly, possibly, if they have one, if we find them … if it works and if there's anyone on the other end.'

'Hmm, that's a lot of possibilities, prof.'

'Yes, but a lot of possibilities is better than one "not at all".'

'Did you get that out of a cracker?' Joe asked.

The professor looked at him. 'Possibly,' he said, and started to walk along the shoreline.

'Wait, uncle,' Lisa shouted after him.

'Well, come on, come on.'

In the undergrowth someone observed them stand and leave. They watched the younger ones go towards the sea and retrieve anything they thought might be useful from the wreckage of the plane that had washed up, then hurry after the older one. They noticed the skin and the eyes and the hair of the two who looked Japanese and they thought that one spoke with an American accent; even this far away it was noticeable and made the hatred and bile rise up in the throat and cause it to burn and sting. A bead of sweat ran down a forehead and was brushed off with an alert arm which was thin but strong. It was hot in the jungle, humid, but they were used to it, they had made it their home, ever since the great general had conferred upon them the sanctity of its boundaries, ever since the Imperial Emperor himself had decreed that it must be protected from whoever tried to take it from them.

They had cooked and eaten and slept and lived and been wounded and cured in the jungle. They had treated it with respect and it had reciprocated with kindness; for almost sixty years it had fed and clothed them, given them water and a place to sleep. They had been given the mandate to protect the jungle and that is what they had done and would do until word came from the Emperor himself. As Lisa and the others disappeared behind the bend in the bay, the figure stepped out from the shadows and stood, in the full glare of the early morning sun, in the uniform of the Imperial Japanese army. Over his shoulder a rifle was slung and in his breast pocket orders from the great General Yamashita who would one day come back and relieve him.

11

The professor was having a hard time navigating the rocks; every other one he slipped on or caught his foot so that he lurched forward; he cursed and puffed his way through the rock pools that led to the open clearing of the jungle, the place that would begin their journey. Fraser had shaken most of the salt water from his ears and walked along in the sunlight studying the horizon for any sign of a plane or a boat. Joe lagged behind, puffing and wheezing, resting on the rocks as he took a few faltering steps forward.

'Look,' he said, sweating profusely. 'Can we stop a moment, I mean, I'm not meant for walking this far.'

'We've only gone a few hundred yards,' Lisa said with a laugh.

'Boy, I could do with a drink,' Joe said.

'There must be a stream around here somewhere we can drink from,' the professor answered.

'Unless it's a whiskey stream I'm not interested,' Joe said, and bent down to scoop up some of the water from a rock pool and splashed it on his face.

Lisa was beginning to like this island and the thought that there might be a radio on it somewhere that could get them off it pleased her even more. She craned her neck and heard all kinds of different sounds she had not heard before, sounds that she assumed were animals rather than spirits.

'What did Anderson say about the aswang again, uncle?'

'He said they were best left alone.'

'What do you know of them, professor?' Fraser asked.

'The locals of these islands believe in them fiercely. It's rumoured they live in the villages and can change shape to look just like you or me. Some are good, some are – well, most Filipinos think of them as a type of vampire that will stop at nothing to get you, if they so desire. They could be watching us right now.'

Fraser suddenly felt cold. He drew his damp coat about his shoulders and gazed into the jungle. It looked dark and mysterious. He didn't know quite what he was doing here anyway and the last thing he wanted was to hear about the spirits that were after him. Ever since they had started on this walk he had had the strange feeling that he was being stared at. Every time he looked around to see who it was he saw nothing but, somehow, he knew that in the jungle eyes were on him.

He whistled a little but his lips were so dry he could make no noise. Behind him the professor had stopped. 'Ah,' he said. 'I see fascinating strata here, untouched, undisturbed for millions of years. I'm sure I could dig up some seashells to prove that these islands were born from the sea. To a geologist it is a blank book waiting to be written.'

'Can we keep moving, uncle? We want to find a camp before we go any further really.'

'How come you know all this stuff about open air living, you a girl guide or something?' Joe asked.

Lisa turned. 'Yes, actually I was, but really it's just common sense, something that may pass you by,' she said with a giggle.

Joe knelt down in a pool and felt the cool water seep into the legs of his trousers.

Miles away, in the capital, Manila, Kono and Tanaka were

making the last arrangements for their flight. They checked their luggage and made sure that the tracking device was still working. The red light flashed a constant pulse and a tiny beep was emitted from a speaker.

Tanaka handed over a wad of dollars to the guard at the airport and whispered in his ear; this was going to be an easy trip, he had decided. Once they were on the island, the usual rules did not apply. There were no police who would come sniffing round, no university authorities getting in the way, and all he had to do was follow the professor to the gold and pluck it out of his hands. In a way this was almost better than stealing the map. If he had done that he would have had to find the tunnels, dig them out, pay for local workers to carry the gold to the plane and fly it home. Now all he had to do was find them, follow them and steal from them.

The airport guard waved him through the terminus where he climbed aboard a pontoon plane. Beside him, Kono squeezed his bulky frame into the spare seat.

'Do you have to sit so close?' Tanaka said.

'I'll shove over a bit,' Kono replied, moving his sizeable buttocks a fraction of an inch to the left.

Tanaka pushed him so that he was flush up against the window. 'Just stay there, will you, you fool.'

'Sorry, boss.'

'Just keep to your own side. Ah, why couldn't I have got a decent right hand man?'

'Sorry, boss.'

'Just stay there.'

Tanaka did up his seat belt and tapped the pilot on the shoulder.

'There it is!' Lisa said. 'There's the exact spot where we should build our temporary camp.'

She raced through the last few pools of water to the clearing by the edge of the jungle and threw herself on the ground.

'It's got overhanging trees, not too shady though. It's big enough, clear enough. There are no ants. This is feeling like home already.'

Joe wearily made his way to where she lay. 'You sure have an imagination,' he said, and slumped down on the ground.

The professor and Fraser joined them.

'Yes, yes, I think you are right, Lisa. I think this will make a perfect camp site, if only for tonight,' the professor said.

'Shall I make a start finding materials?' Lisa said, and made her way into the undergrowth.

'I'll help,' said Fraser and ran behind her, kicking at her heels. Joe and the professor stared out over the ocean.

'You really think we'll find anything, professor?'

'Sure,' the professor answered. 'What, though, I don't know.'

'What d'you mean?'

'Well, these are mysterious islands, Joe. I have been reading about nothing else lately, thinking about nothing else. They have overtaken my thoughts. There are physical things in the tunnels, actual dangers: gas, cave-ins, disease, rats – and then there are the things we don't know about or can't explain.'

'Aswang?'

'Yes, aswang, but also others. Has it not occurred to you that none of this was an accident?'

'What you mean?'

'Getting the map, finding you, finding the way here, the plane crashing. Has it not occurred to you that it could all be part of their plan?'

'Who are they, professor?'

143

The professor looked about nervously. 'Them,' he said, and nodded into the jungle. 'The spirits in there. The things in our dreams, Joe, the things that brought us here.'

Joe was silent for a while. The waves lapped slowly up on the beach and caused a ripple of sound to pass through the air.

'Perhaps you're right, professor. We're here for the same reasons, you and me.'

Joe put his hands behind his head and lay back in the sand, staring up at the sky. There were wisps of white cloud floating over him which seemed to take forever to pass. He closed his eyes and felt the sun on his face and for the first time in years felt free and at peace. Here, on this island, there was no one who wanted him dead, no one who wanted to skin him alive and, more importantly, no bars that would take his money and leave him feeling like death. He crossed his legs.

'You know,' he said. 'I could get used to this.' He stared along the line of the shore and sighed. Suddenly his eye was caught by something glinting. 'What was that?'

The professor snapped out of his doze and looked around. 'What? What's happening?'

'I saw something,' Joe said. 'Glinting, over there.' He pointed to a dense patch of foliage that lay on the outskirts of the jungle. 'I swear it was metal.'

'Probably a rockpool, Joe, they take on quite a metallic sheen if the sun hits them in the right spot.'

'It was no rockpool. I swear it was metal or glass – real shiny, you know?'

Joe got to his feet. He strained his eyes towards the thicket but could see nothing. He sat back down again. 'Jeez, just as I was getting a little relaxed I make myself all jumpy again.'

'You want to forget about things for a while, Joe, take it easy.'

Joe sighed. 'I have been running ever since I was born, professor. It's a little hard to stop now.'

Behind them, Lisa and Fraser returned with armfuls of green vegetation. 'How's this?' Lisa said smiling. 'I think we could make a whole apartment block out of this.' She dumped the leaves on the sand. 'And these huge leaves to wrap ourselves in to sleep.'

Ordering everyone else about, Lisa set to making the shelter; she and Fraser cleared a space where the sand met the damp earth of the jungle floor and the professor and Joe began to make the frame of the shelter out of branches and fronds that had fallen or could be easily pulled free.

By the time they had finished it was nearing evening. The sat in their shelter examining the inside for leaks.

'There are a million holes in this thing,' Fraser said as he pushed his finger through the leaves.

'It will do for tonight,' Lisa said. 'Tomorrow we'll be off.'

'I've heard it gets freezing cold, here,' Fraser said. 'I hope we don't freeze to death, after all this.'

'We won't if we huddle,' replied Lisa and comically cuddled into Fraser's side. Fraser gulped and placed his arm around her.

'I think, if we leave early tomorrow,' the professor said, 'We might be able to traverse the jungle, looking for these landmarks. This might not be a bad situation after all.'

He placed the map on the floor of the shelter. 'These high hills, you see, and this river, should be easily located.'

'If we find the river,' Joe said, 'We only have to follow it. It will lead us right into the heart of the tunnels.'

'But where is the river?'

'That is for tomorrow,' the professor said.

That night, the stars were brighter than Joe had ever thought possible. He lay on his back outside the shelter looking up at them, trying to count each one. Lisa came to join him.

'You keep staring,' she said.

'Have you ever seen them looking so beautiful?' Joe asked. 'As if each one were made from cut glass.'

Lisa laughed. 'I have seen the stars before.'

'I've only ever seen them through the haze of the city fog or against the lights of Hong Kong. I have never seen them like this, not even when I've been flying.'

'You've lived in Hong Kong all your life?'

'Yes, most of it.'

'You've never been to the country at all?'

'Well, my grandmother lived about a hundred miles out of the city but we hardly ever saw her. She was sick a lot and died when I was five. Wow, look at that one there, it's so beautiful.'

Lisa looked. 'There's a shooting star,' she said excitedly. 'Look, two of them.'

Joe looked into the black sky. 'That isn't a shooting star,' he said. 'That's the lights of a damn plane.'

He stood up to get a better view and, sure enough, against the black of the sky two small white lights made their way to the other side of the island and disappeared.

'Who do you suppose that was?' Lisa asked.

Joe scratched his head. 'I don't know. A doctor, perhaps. It's possible they were going to another island, they are so close round here it's difficult to tell which one is being visited. It looked like a pontoon plane.'

'A pontoon plane?'

'Yeah, you know, one that can land on water. Perhaps they were treasure hunters too.'

Lisa laughed. 'Well, they won't have a map, will they?'

Joe thought for a moment. 'Who were those guys in Hong Kong, the ones we saw at the hangar? I mean the ones who weren't after me.'

'They were the ones who broke into my uncle's apartment ... Joe, you don't think...?'

'We'd better be careful is all I am saying, just ... we'd better keep our eyes open.'

Lisa yawned. 'That's easier said than done, although I think I might have nightmares now.'

Joe touched her tenderly on the shoulder. 'I'm here now,' he said. 'Don't worry about a thing.'

The door was closed as usual but somehow he knew he had to get behind it. He put a shoulder to it and pushed with every muscle and sinew in his body; the more he pushed the harder it got until, like a giant wave of release, it fell open and he stumbled inside. It was a dark room, smelling of damp and vegetation. He felt about with his hands but found nothing. Suddenly a match was struck and the face of a young boy was illuminated. 'I have been waiting for you,' he said, in a soft gentle tone.

The boy took his hand and led him to a corner where, covered by a fallen mound of earth, a Golden Buddha sat. The boy leaned forward and pulled at its head. Slowly, he removed it to reveal its hollow body full of emeralds and rubies, diamonds and sapphires, gold coins and all manner of riches, trinkets and chains. 'This is the temple's,' the boy said. 'The temple's.'

Kono woke in a sweat and reached across to his water jug. He splashed some water on his face and poured the rest down his throat. He had been having these dreams for some time now and could make nothing of them. At first he had assumed that they were nothing, just like every other dream he had had in his lifetime but these were different; these demanded more attention – like the niggling pain that never goes away and means something serious.

* * *

The next morning, the professor was the first up. As the others awoke he marched into the clearing.

'I have found the river,' he said. 'Well, its mouth. All we need do is follow it. Breakfast?'

He placed a heap of firewood on the ground and began lighting a fire with a box of matches that he had secreted in his jacket. 'They must be dry by now,' he said and struck one. After a few tries it burst into flame and he lit the dry wood on the ground.

'You know,' he said to no one. 'I think the ocean may be teeming with fish.'

Joe rubbed his eyes. 'It's a bit early for the boy scout stuff, isn't it?' He rolled over and closed his eyes again.

The professor stood and crossed over to the shelter. He kicked the main vine that held it to the tree and the whole thing fell, in a flurry of branches, leaves and vines on top of Joe, Lisa and Fraser.

'Now,' he said. 'Fishing?'

At the water's edge, Joe, Lisa and Fraser were still blurry-eyed and sleepy.

'How the hell do we catch fish with no line?'

Fraser thought for a moment. 'I heard that if you tickle fish they go into a trance. We just need to find their sweet spot.'

'Their sweet spot?' Joe said. 'Do you know where a fish's sweet spot is? Do you know, Lisa? You don't! There's a surprise. I say we go into the jungle, find a big stick and hit them over the head.'

Lisa baulked at this idea. 'That sounds a bit cruel.'

'A bit cruel? You're about to kill them, gut them, cook them and then eat them. You think hitting them is cruel?'

Lisa grabbed her stomach. 'I need something to eat soon, though, I'm starving.'

Joe pointed at her legs. 'Are those tights you have on?'

148

Lisa looked down. 'American tan,' she said. 'I know but, hey, I left my others in the suitcase.'

'Take them off,' Joe said. 'We can use them as a net.'

Lisa was not convinced.

'Why not?' Joe said. 'Look.' He looked around. 'We make a net out of ... this stick here ... and we just scoop them into it. Take them off, take them off.'

'This is the least romantic proposition I have ever had,' Lisa said.

As she took her tights off, Joe fashioned a loop out of the wet branch and strung the tights over it. He held it out in front of him and smiled.

'There, this has to work.'

An hour later it hadn't worked.

'Perhaps it's the colour?' Fraser offered, with a grin.

'Every time we get near and I try to scoop, they get away,' Joe said. 'I can't understand it, I was sure it would work. I was sure it would.'

'I'm so hungry,' Lisa began, 'that I'm hallucinating smelling chicken.' She held her stomach. 'Does that mean I'm going mad?'

Fraser looked around him and pointed at the professor. 'It's coming from the fire,' he said.

They ran up to the fire and the professor, who was busily roasting what looked like a chicken over its roaring flame.

'Where did you get that?' Lisa asked.

'It's a manok,' the professor replied.

'What?'

'Chicken, or cockerel really. There must be a village somewhere near here. They raise them for sport, fighting, then when they get too old, like this poor chap, they are just left to roam.'

Joe sat by the fire. 'What an end. Makes you feel kind of sorry for him.'

149

'Yeah, I will feel sorry for him as I am biting on his leg,' Lisa said and plopped down on the floor.

They ate hungrily, throwing the bones over their shoulders and wiping their mouths with the backs of their hands.

'So, where's the river, uncle?' Lisa asked.

'It's about a mile away. When you get nearer to it you can hear it – very faintly, but you can hear it. I suggest we follow it until we come to the hills on the map.'

'I must say, professor,' Fraser said, with his mouth full. 'This is the best chicken I think I've ever tasted. We should save some for later really.'

The professor pointed. 'The jungle will provide,' he said, and threw another bone into it.

After they had eaten, the group stamped out their fire, broke up their shelter and scattered it. They gathered up what few possessions they had and made their way into the jungle, following the professor. They tramped for what seemed like hours, although in reality it was merely minutes, through dense undergrowth which was spotted and freckled with sunlight and damp. The professor walked at a quick pace that meant the others found it difficult to keep up, especially Joe, who was beginning to feel as though he would trade all of the beauty and the magnificence for a single shot of dry bourbon whiskey. As his feet tramped on the ground, they seemed to get heavier and heavier; his breath also laboured under the weight of his rapidly increasing detox.

He stopped by a tree. 'Wait, wait!' he shouted. 'Do me a favour, would you? Just kill me here.'

'Come on,' the professor said. 'Come on, no time to stop. Must get to the river.'

The others forged ahead while Joe lagged behind. Feeling he could not go on, he slumped to the ground. As he sat, out of the corner of his eye he saw something move; it was black and quick as lightening. It darted from his view into a thicket of dense foliage. Joe followed it on his hands and knees.

'Here chicky chicky,' he said. 'Come to Joey, come on, come on.' He crawled under the hanging branches and the low dangling vines. 'I know you don't want to be eaten but we all do what we have to. We've all got our place in the world, we all...' He stopped as his hand hit something hard. He felt around and recognised the shape of an army boot. Slowly, his eyes followed the boot upwards until it turned into the grey-green colours of the Japanese Imperial army. His eyes continued until they hit the gaze of a gun barrel and then the staring face of the man who held it. It was pointed at the insignia on Joe's US air force cap.

For a moment neither said anything. There was silence in the jungle. Even the screaming birds had stopped for a second in anticipation of what was about to come. Joe smiled and gave a faint laugh and the soldier cocked his rifle. Swiftly, Joe brought his hand squarely between the legs of the soldier, who doubled up in pain; Joe got to his knees and then up and ran for all he was worth. He crashed through the jungle with his arms flailing, shouting at the top of his voice. All around him creatures darted this way and that trying to get out of his way. He tripped over the root of a tree but automatically got up and began running again until he caught up with the group. Without stopping he crashed past them and along the trail made by the professor that morning.

Suddenly his feet gave way and he found himself in a trench, waving wildly in the mud and foliage. Lisa was close behind him.

'What the hell's got into you? What kind of racket are you making?' Joe could barely speak. 'S-s-s-s-someone back there, with a gun,' he said. 'Aiming it ... at ... me ... my ... head.'

151

'What the hell are you talking about?'

'I saw someone with a gun, aiming it at me back there. Jeez, he looked mad. Right at my head.'

Fraser and the professor caught up. 'What's up?' Fraser asked.

'Joe said he saw someone with a gun,' Lisa said. 'We'd better have a look. Uncle, stay here and make sure he's all right. Fraser, come with me, and Joe, keep quiet.'

Lisa and Fraser stepped quietly through the trail they had just made and made their way back to the spot where Joe had met the soldier, but there was no sign of him. As they searched in the bush a bird flew out and roosted in the branches above them.

'What do you think?' Lisa asked Fraser

'I think perhaps he needs a drink.'

'You think he made it up?'

'I think he needs booze and it's affecting his eyesight, or his mind. Whichever, there's no one here.'

'But we saw a plane last night. It could be them.'

'Well, they're not here now and never were if you ask me. Come on, we need to crack on.'

They turned to make their way back to the group. As they walked off, Corporal Yashida checked the bullets in his rifle. He had been waiting for this moment for sixty years and was not going to give up easily. He had been put in charge of this island and that is what he was going to do but he must wait, wait and see if there were others as they said, wait and see who owned the plane that he had seen the night before. For so long he had waited for this moment, he could wait a few more days. He smiled at the thought of the praise of his beloved General Yamashita and at the thought of his Emperor when they learned of his bravery and tenacity. These Americans and their cohorts would regret landing on his island.

12

The jungle was sighing as the professor and the others pushed their way through it. Time was getting on and the sun was getting hotter. Fraser and Joe tried their best to forge a path through the dense growth but it sapped their strength and made them perspire with the effort. With every step they felt themselves getting weaker, until Fraser slumped down onto the jungle floor, his eyes rolling in his head, his hair matted underneath his cap. The professor looked at him closely.

'What do you think?' he said to Lisa. 'He looks bad.'

Lisa bent over Fraser and felt his forehead.

'I think we'd better rest a while here,' she said, and sat down beside Fraser while Joe rested against a tree and began to suck at a twig that he had found digging into his shoe.

Suddenly there was movement all around them. There were no shapes, no tangible sights, just the sense of bodies flying through the canopy. Lisa covered her ears as the noises got louder and louder. All around them they heard the flapping of wings and the sound of the air being torn apart. The professor tried to stand but was knocked to the ground, his face flushed and scarred by tiny invisible talons. He put his hand to his face and felt warm wet blood on his fingertips; something that he could not see, something that was beyond his comprehension had struck him.

Up against the tree, Joe stood transfixed, his eyes flickering from place to place, following as if in a trance. Lisa called to him but he made no reply. She crawled over and tugged on his legs, but Joe was somewhere else. His eyes darted this way and that, searching for something, tracking something that Lisa was not a part of. She screamed at him, pulled at his trouser leg, anything to shake him out of the trance he had fallen into. 'Joe! Joe! Wake up, we need you.'

But Joe didn't hear her. He merely stood, transfixed, looking at the sky and following the demons that were playing in front of his eyes. Lisa knelt on the ground, put her head on her knees, closed her eyes and felt her hair being played with by whatever it was that was surrounding them.

As quickly as it had started it stopped. There was silence. Lisa lifted her head and looked around her. Fraser was seated on the ground, exhausted, barely able to move. The professor was flat on his back with pinpricks of blood on his cheek and Joe – Joe was smiling a huge smile as his head slowly lowered to the vertical again.

'What was that?' Lisa asked.

The professor wiped his cheeks. 'I don't know for certain,' he said. 'But I would guess that that was our first meeting with the aswang.'

They looked at Joe, who had by now recovered.

'The aswang?' he said. 'I see.' And he moved off, through the jungle.

On the other side of the island, Kono and Tanaka were setting up camp. They had spent their first night in the open air of the Filipino jungle and they were little used to roughing it. Kono heaved his bulking frame over the guy ropes that held their canopy up and tripped over it, sending its canvas roof to the ground.

'Idiot!' Tanaka admonished. 'Watch where you are going, can't you?'

Kono apologised for the fifth time already that day and began to tie the roof back up.

Tanaka made his way down to the beach, where the pilot was moored, bobbing up and down on the soft waves. 'You stay here,' he motioned, 'Until we return. We will give you the money when we come back.'

The pilot began to get suspicious and he mimed that he would fly away if they had not returned in two days, then showed Tanaka a bag with what looked like rations in it.

'You'll be able to buy plenty of that when we return,' Tanaka said. 'Just be sure to be here when we come back.'

He turned and walked off up the beach again, making his way through the slight undergrowth to the camp where Kono was fixing the stove. 'I have a bad feeling about that pilot. We should have got a decent one, I think.'

Kono sighed. 'But where do you get a decent pilot that would come on a trip like this?'

Tanaka began to argue, then thought for a moment. 'Yes, you might be right there,' he said. 'Don't bother making yourself too much at home, we are moving soon.'

Kono looked a little disappointed. He had liked camping in the hills with his father when he was young and this reminded him of it. He looked down at his stove, and the bed he had made nicely, with its blanket to keep the cold from coming up from underneath and the sleeping bag that would make sure he would get a good night's sleep. He had owned these things since he had been a boy and had treasured them. With his life, it was hard to partake in things like camping these days. It was difficult to remember the child he had once been, in the life he had now.

'Why are we moving?' he asked.

Tanaka flicked his ear. 'To find the professor and the girl. That's why we are here; they will lead us to the tunnels and the gold. We are not here for you to play at boy scouts.'

Kono sat on his bed. The jungle was noisier than he had imagined. He didn't mind that but he liked the peace and quiet of the hills where he used to go with his father. He liked how they made him feel and he missed them. Tanaka crossed the small patch of ground between their two beds and put a hand on Kono's shoulder.

'I know what you're thinking,' he said, and Kono looked downward. 'Your father loved the outdoors, right? He liked to sleep under the stars and be out in the open air?'

Kono nodded.

'He was a good man,' Tanaka said.

Kono nodded again.

'We can make him proud of you again with this gold. We can make him think of you again as his son. You know you want that, don't you?'

Kono nodded. He thought of his father's face, he thought of his disappointed look.

Tanaka spoke again. 'You know that when you are rich everyone respects you, don't you? You know that your father would have no choice but to see you as his son again.'

There were painful things in Kono and Tanaka knew how to access them, with a simple word or a sentimental reminiscence of their shared childhood. Tanaka knew how to get what he wanted out of Kono, which was usually a violence that didn't come easily to the other.

'Remember that time we camped out and it rained all night?' Tanaka said. 'Remember you came into my tent because yours had split right along the seam and you were shaking and moaning all night because there was thunder and lightening and you couldn't sleep?'

Kono nodded.

156

'Who was it that told you jokes until you eventually fell off to sleep?'

'You.'

'Yeah, and who was it that fixed it so you didn't get scolded when you got back, who exchanged tents with you?'

'You.'

'Yeah, me, so when I say we are going to do something, when I say we've got to move soon, you know I'm doing it for you, aren't I?'

'Yeah, I suppose.'

'I'm doing it because I love you like a brother.'

'You do?'

Tanaka punched Kono's arm playfully, 'Course. Now, get the camp ready, I'm going to talk to that pilot again.'

The plane pitched and rode on the waves as Tanaka waded out to it. He noticed that the pilot was asleep in the cockpit. How dare he question me, he thought to himself as he carefully checked over his shoulder. Climbing aboard and with the speed of the consummate professional, Tanaka pulled a blade from his sleeve, held it under the throat of the pilot and pulled. From the outside of the cockpit all that could be seen was a single spurt of blood on the window. It stayed for a moment as if suspended by the shock of its release and then fell in small rivulets onto the dashboard.

A moment later Tanaka dropped down into the water, washed his hands and the knife in it and strode over to the beach again. As he got to the camp, he placed the knife into the backpack that was suspended from the bed and lay down on it breathing slightly but audibly in the hot air. Kono busied himself unpacking and packing his possessions.

* * *

157

Joe moved through the jungle like a cat through treacle. This wasn't his terrain; he knew about it, he had read a few books about jungle warfare but, when it came down to it, he was a fish out of water and he desperately wanted a drink. The only thing that kept him going was the thoughts and images in his head of the boy he had seen in his dreams. With each step, with each difficult breath, he cursed the journey but somehow he knew it would be worth his while in the end.

He placed his hand on his head and felt that it was damp with sweat. Try as he might he could not shake the sight of the aswang from his head. Until he had spoken to Lisa about it he was unaware that none of the others could see what he had seen. However, they had all sworn that when they looked to where the sound was coming from they saw nothing. Joe though, Joe saw it as clear as the light that shone through the trees. At first he thought it had been a ghost, the type that might appear to children and the superstitious; it was an old woman floating before his eyes, but only part of her body was visible. She had a strange face, old and tired, but eyes that could melt steel – red and violent. He had tried to scream but nothing came out of his mouth, all he could do was stare at her, stare and submit to whatever it was that she wanted. She floated right up to his face and he could smell her breath as it shot out of her mouth in thick, foul clouds. She smiled at him and he felt her lick his skin with her hard, scratchy tongue. Joe had tried to close his eyes but, again, he could do nothing.

Then there was a laugh, a flash and the aswang disappeared, flying off into the canopy of the trees. The first thing Joe remembered was Lisa calling to him. He felt as if he had been out cold; there was sweat running down his face into his eyes and he could still smell the breath of the aswang.

158

The professor was moving more quickly than any of the others in the party. Every now and then he would rush off into the forest, dig around in the undergrowth and return with a prized sample or a handful of earth. They seemed to trek for hours when suddenly Lisa stopped them.

'Shh,' she said. 'What's that noise?'

They all craned their necks to hear.

'I can't hear anything,' Fraser said, but Lisa placed a finger to her lips.

'Yes,' she said. 'Yes, it's there. I can hear it.'

'Hear what, Lisa?' the professor asked.

'The river,' Lisa answered. 'The river.' And she marched off into the jungle.

Joe and Fraser looked at each other, shrugged and followed her. As they parted the last of the branches, Fraser and Joe heard splashing and caught sight of Lisa diving head first into the river. The sun was high above and beat down into golden rivulets, hitting the surface of the water and sending warm rays of light throughout the area. Fraser kicked off his shoes, put his bag down and nervously joined Lisa in the stream. Joe sat by the bank, took his canister from its belt hook and filled it up. The professor stood behind him.

'What's it like?' the professor asked.

'Cold,' Joe answered.

'Not the water. The aswang,' the professor replied.

Joe stopped filling his flask and turned slowly. 'How did you know?'

'Just a hunch,' the professor said.

Joe continued filling his flask. 'Nothing to say, really. Nothing to say at all.'

The professor knelt down beside Joe. 'I guess we'll all find out soon enough, won't we?'

Joe turned and began to speak but thought better of it.

The day was almost over but the sun was still warm. The group decided to camp by the river for the night and began to cut down vines and large leaves to make the shelter. Fraser set to finding dry wood for the fire; in an hour they had the camp as they wanted it and Lisa sat by the fire slowly drying out after her second swim of the day. Fraser looked at her, her skin looking a bright luminescence in the glow of the fire. He loved to watch her in moments like this – moments when he knew she wasn't aware of him. He noticed how she dug her toes into the soft earth to cool them down after the fire had made them too hot; he noticed how she moved her shoulders to and fro so that they did not get burnt and he noticed how she looked at Joe every time he moved and that she laughed every time he spoke.

Fraser wondered why he was here. He was too old for adventure and not nearly old enough for one last fling. He guessed he was here for her, but she was here for someone else. Perhaps that's the way it always goes, he thought. Perhaps, the ones we really want are destined to be with someone else; perhaps that's why we want them. He looked into the flames. They flickered and made his eyes hurt. Of course, he thought to himself, there was always the money; there is always the money.

That night the jungle was quiet; it breathed softly as the moon came out and folded its arms around itself. The night sky looked beneficently down upon the group. The river moved silently on, deep into the jungle's heart.

The jungle gives up her noises easily at night and Lisa lay awake listening to it move and sigh, scream and wail. Every time she closed her eyes, the noises got louder as if the volume were being turned up to full. She tried to block her ears but nothing seemed to work. She could hear Joe breathing heavily over the sounds the jungle made and it reassured her. She reached a hand out and touched his skin; it was warm and damp. Slowly she rose up on her elbows and looked into his face. She could tell he was dreaming. His face flickered, his eyelids moved with rapid intensity, his arms twisted this way and that. She wondered what he was dreaming about; whatever it was, she was glad not to be a part of it.

Eventually she lay back down and tried to concentrate on the sound of the river as it gently flowed.

The morning came quickly and suddenly. As soon as the light came streaming through the canopy, Lisa awoke with a start. She blinked her eyes, barely able to believe how light it was. Beside her, the professor snored so loudly she wondered how she had ever got to sleep. She shook him.

'Uncle, uncle, wake up.'

The professor turned over and the snoring stopped. Glancing over to the other two she saw that they too were fast asleep so she lay back, with her hands behind her head, and closed her eyes. Five minutes later she opened them again, failing to fool herself that she was sleepy. She decided she might as well get up and go for a swim in the river. Whenever she had been camping before she had loved to go swimming just as the sun was coming up, before it could warm the water.

She wriggled out of her covers and quietly set them in a pile to one side, then placed her feet neatly in her shoes and stepped gingerly over the professor, who snored again and rolled over the other way. Feeling free, she skipped through the branches that surrounded their temporary campsite and made her way down to the river.

The sight of the river in the early morning sun was so beautiful it made her sigh as she set eyes on it; the water was so clear and so blue and the light spread itself out on its surface and made it shine. She knelt down by its edge, took her shoes and shorts off, reached down into

161

the water and took a deep drink. She felt the coolness of the water flowing through her body, literally taking the sleep away with it. Suddenly she felt more alive than she had felt for all of her life. Around her the jungle was quieter than it had been during the night. The animals that came out after dark had calmed down now and there was only the slight sound of insects buzzing and the occasional bird somewhere far off.

She took another drink and realised that she had never tasted water so clear or so clean. She had no idea where it had come from or where it was going but this beat mineral water any day. Without looking about her she dived into the water and felt her muscles tense as her body reacted to its coolness. Under the surface, she kicked with her feet and legs, held her breath and swam as far as she could manage. When she had run out of breath she surfaced and felt the sun hit her face in a glorious bath of warmth and light. She smoothed her hair down and dived under again.

Under the water, she could open her eyes and see the bottom of the river that was made of almost pure sand. Tiny rocks and minerals were littered here and there making the whole thing look as if it had been covered in glitter and gold. She dived down and pushed a hand through the silt. It ran through her fingers and disappeared into the ebb and flow of the current. Lisa kicked with her legs and swam further down the river, letting it take her along.

She surfaced again and once more felt the sun on her skin. All about her the sunlight warmed the jungle and made it seem alive and fresh. Lisa kicked and swam against the current, her strong limbs cutting through the water with ease and confidence. She dived and kicked, sending a spray of clear water up in to the air. The current felt strong about her and she swam for all she was worth

162

against it. The harder she kicked the stronger it seemed to get. Suddenly, it was the river that seemed to be in control; suddenly it was the water that moved her rather than the other way round.

She felt herself being taken along on the strong current that ran deep beneath the surface. Every time she tried to put a foot on the river bed the current would take her and she would find herself fighting again. The more she fought the harder it became as she felt the energy being sapped from her. She flayed wildly with her arms trying to get some purchase in the water but nothing she did seemed to help; it was the river who was in control now, the river who showed her where to go.

As if being helped by some malevolent force, Lisa felt her body being carried along. She looked up and could just glimpse the sun through the canopy but it seemed less beautiful, less magical. In a desperate effort she twisted her body and swam with every ounce of energy she had; her arms cut through the water and her legs pushed against the current. Eventually she managed to work her way over to the bank where she clutched at a root that had been exposed by years of erosion. For a moment she hung on, letting the water wash over her body, closing her eyes with the effort.

As the sun warmed her and the feeling began to come back into her legs, she tried to clamber out onto the bank. It was harder than she thought. She hadn't eaten properly for days, she was tired and the swim upstream had taken its toll, but she managed it. Bit by bit, muscle by muscle, she climbed on to the green foliage of the jungle floor and lay down, feeling her body being drained of all life.

Her head began to spin and she felt herself fall into half unconsciousness. Suddenly the jungle became cold, dark and alien. Her eyes felt dim and heavy and her mind wandered. She thought she heard noises about her but was too tired to look. She thought she felt hands upon her and breath upon her skin, but she was too exhausted to see who or what they were. And she thought she smelt blood, but could not be sure whether it was real or imaginary.

When she awoke she felt eyes upon her. With a start she sat up and there in front of her sat a little girl, staring with big brown eyes. Lisa, startled a little, smiled. The child did nothing. Lisa held out her hand but the child remained still.

'Hello,' Lisa said. 'Hello. I guess you can't speak English?'

The child remained still, just looked at Lisa and sat, with her arms round her legs. Lisa got into a kneeling position. She was dry now so she figured she must have been lying on the ground for some time. She thought about the others. They would be worried about her by now; they would be looking for her.

'I ... I tried to take a swim but was caught by the current,' she explained to the girl, who seemed to listen but could obviously not understand. 'I guess I'm not the swimmer I once was, eh?' She laughed and the child, briefly, smiled. Lisa breathed a sigh of relief. 'Do you live round here?' she asked. 'Only I could probably do with knowing someone like you.' She held out her hand. 'I'm Lisa.'

The child leaned over and looked at Lisa's upturned palm as if expecting to see something there.

Lisa withdrew it. 'I guess you don't shake hands, eh?'

The two smiled at each other. Lisa got up and arranged herself. She still had her bikini bottoms on from swimming but they were fine in this heat.

'Well, I really must get back up the river. God knows how far I've come.'

164

Lisa put a hand up to her eyes to shield them from the sun and the little girl quickly got up, crossed over to her and placed her arms around her waist. Lisa was a little disturbed by this.

'Guess you're lost too, then. Great, you're not the only one around here. Guess we are in this together.'

Lisa patted the girl on the head in the most motherly way she could muster and pulled the little girl close to her. She could feel her tremble in her arms and shake softly. Lisa tore a piece of her shirt and gave it to the girl to wipe her eyes, but the girl was brave. She took the cloth and threw it to the ground, making Lisa laugh.

The sun was invisible now; it had hidden itself behind the tall trees that seemed to stretch to the sky anyway. Lisa cuddled the girl, more for her own sake than the girl's and thought about how she would get back up the river.

At the camp, the professor, Joe and Fraser had woken about two hours before and were pacing back and forth trying to work out what had happened to Lisa.

'You know I told you I saw someone yesterday? It was a Japanese soldier, I tell you. I saw him as clear as I am seeing you now,' Joe said. 'He looked angry. Suppose he's got her?'

'We would have heard,' Fraser said. 'Besides, did he snatch her from her bed, then tidy it up before he went?' he said, pointing at the neat sleeping space on the floor.

'Perhaps she's gone to get breakfast?' the professor ventured.

'Nah, she would have been back by now. I mean, how far do you need to go to get breakfast around here?'

Joe looked around him. 'Pretty far, I would imagine,' he said and peered into the jungle.

The professor sat down on his bed. 'I think we wait,' he said. 'I think the most likely scenario is that she is lost and will find her back to us eventually.'

'But if she's lost,' said Joe, 'She might never come back. I mean, do you know how big this damn place is? I say we take a look, find the trail, see if we can track her.'

Fraser looked doubtful but Joe was insistent.

'I know,' Joe said, 'We could split up. Professor, you and Fraser stay here and I'll see if I can track Lisa.'

Fraser was incredulous. 'Won't you get lost?'

Joe tapped the badge on his cap. 'US air force. I won't get lost.'

An hour later Joe was lost deep in the heart of the Filipino jungle. He had left camp with an idea in mind. It was an old trick his uncle had taught him many years before: look for a path and if it looks like someone else has been there you can't go far wrong. Unfortunately, he had never experienced terrain like this before; each clearing looked like a path, each new turning in the jungle looked like it had been created by a host of trekkers walking through but he knew it was just the trick of Nature, encouraging trees to grow their branch width apart, the light causing gaps in the undergrowth.

When there were not deceptive looking 'paths' there was thick jungle that could barely be hacked through. He pushed at it but it seemed as if it just closed around him again, touching him, pulling at his clothes, scratching his skin and making him feel as though he were being torn apart.

All the time he felt, deep in the jungle, as though eyes were upon him, as though the trees were watching him. Occasionally he stopped and looked around, convinced he was being followed but when he looked there was no one there; the jungle, he thought to himself, plays strange tricks on the mind.

166

Joe trekked for what seemed like hours. It was no good, he said to himself, he was most certainly lost. He thought what a good idea it would have been to leave a trail behind, to carve signposts into the trees to remind himself of where he had been or even to make a mental map of the terrain as he passed through it; that would have been what his father would have done. That would have been the first thing on his father's mind, but Joe, Joe was too busy thinking about Lisa, the same as he was always too busy thinking about the girl in the bar, or the woman in the club or some other minor distraction from the real business of trying not to get himself killed.

He pushed through some thick undergrowth and fell on to the jungle floor. It was warm here; the sun beat down on to this area and as he lay down he could hear the river a little distance away gently ripple. Suddenly his eye was caught by something. Usually you would not see such a thing, it would melt into the background, become just another one of the many insignificant finds of the world but here, here in the jungle, it was like a beacon. He turned himself over and stared at it – a small piece of dark blue cloth. He picked it up. It looked like the same material that Lisa's shirt was made out of – same colour, same feel, same weave. He had gazed upon it for long enough – he would know it anywhere.

Quickly he picked himself up and followed what looked like a trail made in the undergrowth. He guessed that Lisa, if she had been here, would have left some time ago but he forged ahead. Somehow, the connection he already felt to her made him sure that he was heading in the right direction and he knew that he would find her if he just followed his instincts, so he pushed through the dense foliage and made his way deep into the heart of the jungle.

13

The day was getting on and the jungle was becoming denser as Joe pushed his way through. Occasionally he would stop and examine the path, more out of a sense of procedure than anything else. The jungle floor was thick with moss, dead and decaying vegetation and insects. Ever since he had been a little kid he had had no time for small things that moved of their own accord; he hated their legs, the way they scuttled, how they felt on his skin and, most of all, he hated the way that they died, crushed under a foot, helpless and unmindful.

Here, though, he was in the insects' kingdom, he knew that and that given time they could crush him just as easily as he crushed them, so he moved onward as best he could, trying to not kill too many as he walked lest they return to haunt him one day.

He stopped to listen to the jungle. He had no idea what he was listening for, just that something seemed out of place here. Something on the wind made him suspicious and wary. He craned his neck and stood on a fallen tree. He heard voices somewhere; they were far off but they were human. He couldn't be sure but he thought there were two voices, one was high and harsh, the other low and soft, but they were too far away for him to make out what they were saying. Joe climbed down from the tree and tried to follow the voices that were so distinctive amongst the animal noises that surrounded them.

In a clearing Kono and Tanaka had stopped. Sweat poured from their bodies and stained their clothes a musty brown. On his back Kono carried a pack that contained everything they would need for a two-day trek on their search to find Joe, Lisa and the others. He dropped it on the ground with relief. Tanaka sat on it.

'You hear something?' he said.

Kono craned his ear. 'Birds, the wind, nothing else.'

'I thought I heard footsteps.'

Kono looked around, surveying the area. 'You think they're here somewhere?'

Tanaka pulled a handkerchief out of his pocket and began to mop his brow with it. 'I think we would have heard them. Besides, they should be miles away over the other side of the island. I'm sure I heard footsteps though.'

It was Tanaka's turn to begin to look around him. He peered into the dense foliage but it was too thick, too dark to see anything.

'Do you think we'll find them?' Kono asked, rummaging in the bag for a rice cake.

'Of course,' Tanaka snapped back. 'You have the tracking device?'

Kono pulled a black box out of the backpack and held it up to his face as it flashed out its message.

'Right,' Tanaka said. 'All we have to do is find their plane and that will lead us directly to them, and the gold.'

Kono smiled and reached for the bag. 'We'd better get on then,' he said, and left Tanaka desperately trying to keep up.

A brief moment after they had left Joe pushed through the trees. He examined the ground and observed that someone had been there. Some of the vegetation had been disturbed, a sure sign – he remembered that from his two weeks' basic training. He assumed he must be on the trail of Lisa and guessed that he was pretty close; he looked around the clearing for an exit point. A gap in the branches assured him of the way to go and he headed for it.

'Soon,' he thought to himself, 'Soon I will be with her.'

Lisa held onto the little girl's hand tightly as the two made their way through the jungle. To Lisa's relief, the girl was not as lost as she had first thought but walked, with sure and steady feet, through the thick trees and over the small rivers that seemed constantly to block their path. Suddenly Lisa felt afraid; she was being led but she had no idea where or for what reason. The girl pushed ahead of her and their two hands strained at times; the one eager to make ground, the other reticent and wanting to slow down. Every now and then, a branch would flick back into Lisa's face, scratching her or catching her eye. The little girl strode ahead with a determination that grew stronger by the minute. Occasionally she would glance backwards to make sure Lisa was still following her but mostly she strode onward and onward with purpose.

This carried on for about half an hour and Lisa felt her head swimming with the running and the lack of water. She stopped and the little girl pulled on her arm.

'I can't go on,' she said. 'I have to rest.'

The little girl looked at her and pointed through the trees, then motioned to Lisa to move forward. Lisa shook her head as she breathed harder than she had ever breathed before. She thought her heart was bursting from her chest and she could feel the sweat running down her forehead and into her eyes. She had to make this girl understand; she had to make her understand that she could not go on any further – there was nothing left. The jungle had won and all she wanted to do was sit and rest. The girl, however, had other ideas; she grabbed Lisa's arm and pulled for all she was worth but Lisa slumped

170

to the ground and would not budge. The girl then spoke in a language that Lisa had never heard before, sounding excited and enthusiastic. Her voice was lighter and higher than Lisa could ever have imaged. It seemed strange to hear it in this jungle, a little girl's voice, when it seemed that they were so far away from anyone.

Lisa shook her head again. 'Please,' she implored. 'No more.'

She felt tears welling up in her eyes as she laid her head on her knees, forlorn, afraid, tired and wanting to see home. The little girl walked up to her and placed an arm around her shoulder. She flicked a strand of hair out of Lisa's eyes and gently wiped a tear from her cheek. Then she sat down next to Lisa and rested her head on her knee. The older girl placed an arm round the younger and they sat for a while just listening to the sound of the jungle.

Suddenly Lisa heard a voice; it sounded like a call. It was obviously an older woman's voice and by the reaction of the little girl she guessed it was her mother. She was surprised as for some reason she had believed the little girl was on her own. The voice sounded high and shrill against the background of the jungle and the little girl shot up and made to go. Remembering, she stopped and turned towards Lisa. She held out her hand and Lisa took it. The two walked through the trees and the sight that greeted Lisa as she did so took her breath away.

Behind the trees, in a large clearing, Lisa was confronted by a village. All around her she saw huts and people milling about and children playing. There were women carrying water and women making bread; there were fires dotted here and there outside some of the huts, and cockerels scratching in the dry earth. Lisa thought she had stepped into another world.

The little girl was spotted by her mother, who ran

171

towards her. Without thinking Lisa held out her hand but the mother was suspicious; she just held onto her daughter and stared with half closed eyes. Lisa realised that this was the place the little girl had been heading to all along; she had known exactly where she was. She had run away from home. Like so many other children in the world, she had been chastised by her mother and to teach her a lesson had run away. The mother held on to her daughter as if she might float away – again, the same as any other mother in her position.

Lisa smiled at this thought. For some reason, in the middle of the jungle she had assumed people's lives might be unimaginably different but here she was confronted by a scene of such everyday tenderness that she could barely believe it. She inched forward to the woman and the girl who, again, merely stood and stared back at her. Lisa held out her hand and the mother looked into it as the girl had done an hour or so before. Lisa smiled and laughed a little. The mother smiled too and Lisa felt that a barrier had been crossed.

The little girl was the first to break the silence. She said something to her mother; Lisa didn't understand her language but she understood its meaning as the mother first looked at Lisa, then the girl, then smiled at Lisa, walked forward and took her hand. She led her into the village.

The first thing Lisa noticed was the amount of activity. It was a busy place, obviously getting ready for the main evening meal. Everywhere she looked there was bread being prepared or placed into large dishes ready to be cooked and the smell of roasting meat from open fires permeated the air. Every step she took she tripped over a child or a cockerel or chicken until she gave up trying to avoid them and instead kicked them out of the way with as little fuss as possible.

The mother took her to what Lisa assumed was her own hut. It was smaller than the rest and was no taller than Lisa herself. Bending down almost to the ground Lisa followed the woman in and the little girl followed them both. Once inside, Lisa saw that it was as small as it had seemed outside but had the kind of cosy closeness that she associated with tents. It was obvious that this was a place for sleeping in and very little more. There was a small fire to the left of the door and the smoke blew in from outside, filling the small space with an acrid smell when the wind changed.

The woman sat down and Lisa did the same. Suddenly there was a noise outside and an old woman walked in. She stared at Lisa, then crossed the floor of the hut and sat next to the mother of the little girl. The two talked briefly for a moment and then stared again at Lisa. Lisa smiled, trying hard not to look too scared or too perturbed. There was a shaft of light as the flap to the hut was opened again and two more women walked in. They too stared at Lisa for a while, then crossed and squeezed themselves next to the women who were already seated. As soon as they had sat down another woman walked in and so it continued until the tiny hut was filled with at least fifteen women, all squashed in together and all staring intently at Lisa, who was by now beginning to feel a little nervous despite trying her best not to.

The voices of the women built into a dull hum as they obviously began discussing what they would do with Lisa. There was clearly an argument breaking out between two of the women over what they should do. Every now and then the mother of the little girl would intervene and say something that would cause everyone else to strongly disagree. One of the women started to shout above the others and pushed her back against the wall of the hut that bowed and strained with her weight. Lisa thought

173

that it was all getting a little too overheated for her and she wondered how she might be able to make a bolt for the door.

Suddenly the old woman raised her hand and said something that made the other women stop. They all looked at the old woman who, as far as Lisa was concerned, had said only three syllables but they must have been the most important, most profound three syllables in the world because all of the women agreed. They started nodding their heads and congratulating the old woman, who looked as pleased as punch with her idea.

The little girl extricated herself from the mêlée and crossed over to where Lisa sat. She took Lisa by the hand and squeezed it. Lisa found it disturbing rather than comforting. It was the kind of squeeze one might give a condemned man just before he was hanged; the kind of squeeze that said 'Be brave, you know this has to be done'.

The old woman shuffled forward and started examining Lisa. She looked in her hair – perhaps for lice, Lisa thought – then in her mouth. She felt Lisa's arms then cupped her breasts as if she were weighing fruit. Lisa felt a little aggrieved at this but she thought it was perhaps best to go along with whatever it was they were thinking, at least until she knew what that was. The old woman continued to examine her, pushing her fingers into Lisa's sides, peering into her eyes. Eventually she slapped Lisa's side and went back to the group, evidently pleased with what she had seen.

The mother of the little girl then got up and stepped forward. She handed Lisa a bowl that was full of water. Lisa drank thirstily. It tasted bitter but it was cold as it ran down her chin and it had been hours since her last drink. She handed the cup back and asked for more but the woman only smiled and returned to the group.

174

The room began to spin and there was a curious ringing in her ears, and it began to feel as though she were standing on the bow of a ship. Lisa realised that she had been drugged. Suddenly her head felt as if it was going to explode and her eyes began to itch. She squeezed her eyelids together and rubbed them. The cup fell to the ground. Lisa could barely make out the women in the hut now, it was spinning so much. She could just hear them chattering and chanting. Suddenly it all become too much to bear. Lisa stumbled out of the door, pushing her way past some of the women who were blocking it.

Out in the sunlight her head felt a little clearer but it still stung and her eyes were still blurred and useless. She veered this way and that, not knowing where she was going or where she had come from. She tripped over something and fell to ground, where slowly she lost consciousness and dreamed about strange shapes and weird faces that loomed at her out of the darkness.

The first thing she saw when she awoke was the fire. It was night and it sent sparks of bright orange up into the black sky. Someone was flicking water on her face; someone was trying to wake her up. Lisa moved to rub her eyes but found that her hands had been tied behind her back. She was lying on the ground in a cage made of thick branches lashed together with vines and there was a bowl of water on the floor in front of her; she craned her neck and licked a few drops from it.

She had no idea where she was; the drugs had hit her pretty hard and she was not sure if this was even the same day. Slowly she became aware of breathing next to her. It was slow and sonorous, it wheezed in and out, occasionally there would be a small insignificant cough that sounded as though given time and enough damp weather it would build into something more serious. The breathing became quicker and more excited as Lisa began to wake up and open her eyes. Without making a sound, Lisa moved her head and came face to face with a pair of the bluest eyes she had ever seen.

'Headache?' a voice said.

Lisa started. It was an English accent, here of all places. She shuffled over to the other side of her cage and stared in wonder at the face that had produced the voice. It was a middle-aged man with a shock of white hair that seemed to take on a holy glow in the light from the flames. He was smoking a pipe that sent billows of fumes up into the air.

'Yes, you'll have a headache for a while. Sorry about that but we never know what you might do. We've had a number of your type coming through here.'

Lisa gulped some of the water. 'My type?' she asked.

'Yes, foreigners.'

Lisa found it strange that this Englishman would refer to her as a foreigner. 'Who are you anyway?' she asked. 'And did you put me in here?'

The man thought for a moment. 'Yes,' he said. 'You'll have to wait in there for a while, at least until we get a little more idea of who you are. I take it you're here for the treasure.'

Lisa wriggled a little at this. She was not sure whether to admit she was there for the treasure or not; was she supposed to be there for the treasure? She decided to change the subject. 'You still haven't told me who you are.'

The man leaned forward and his nose touched the bars of the cage. 'Winthrope,' he said. 'W.G. And you are?'

'Lisa. I doubt we will know each other long enough to get better acquainted.' She wriggled in her bonds but was unable to get herself free.

'Hmmm,' Winthrope said. 'You might have a little trouble there; they are pretty tight, I think.'

176

He laughed a little and sucked on his pipe. As he did so a shy teenage girl appeared from out of the darkness and set down a bowl in front of him. Winthrope looked at her and stroked her naked thigh. He said something to her and the girl giggled a coy laugh. Winthrope leaned forward and kissed her lightly on the cheek; Lisa thought he looked old enough to be the girl's grandfather. Then another girl appeared with some fruit and meat in vine leaves and set it down in front of him. He looked at her lasciviously and stroked her hair. Lisa felt disgusted.

'Are they your daughters?' she asked and Winthrope laughed, nearly choking on the leg of chicken that he was gnawing on.

'Oh no, my dear, they are my wives.'

'Both of them?'

'No, not both of them...' Winthrope smiled. 'All of them, well very nearly all of them, I am working on the others.'

'Don't the other men mind?'

Again Winthrope laughed, throwing his head back and exposing his dark pink gums. 'There aren't any men, my dear.'

Lisa slowly began to remember. It was true: all the people in the village, all those running about, preparing meals, sitting with her in the hut, all had been either women or children. There was not one man among them. There had been women of all ages and certainly boys but no men.

'Where are they? Where are all the men?' Lisa asked.

'Gone. Taken by the aswang. Killed.'

Lisa looked incredulous. 'You believe that?'

Winthrope looked pensive and closed his eyes. 'There are more things than you would care to guess at in this jungle, Lisa. I have seen things that would make you scream.'

'But you don't believe the aswang killed every man in the village? You can't believe in such things.'

Winthrope shooed his two wives away and leaned closer towards Lisa.

'Belief is everything!' he said. 'Lisa, these are simple people with simple minds. They have no understanding of cause and effect, of science. You and I ... well, you and I have been brought up in more sophisticated surroundings. We are people of technology, of reason; we have no need for gods or devils. We do not need spirits to make us see things clearly. We have our minds, our mathematics and our intelligence.'

He stopped and swigged a mouthful of steaming tea from the bowl. As he did so, streams of liquid ran down his chin. His tongue flicked at them and sucked them back into his mouth. 'It's not me that tells them the aswang killed the men folk. It's not me that puts it into their pretty heads; it's their culture to believe – to believe is to relinquish worry and responsibility.'

Lisa felt uncomfortable at this conversation but she was still confused. She had no idea who this man was or what he wanted with her. She thought it best to try and extract as much information as possible, if only to keep him talking so that she could think of a way out of the cage.

'But what did happen to the men?'

Winthrope sighed. 'Something much simpler I'm afraid – economics and microbiology. Most of the men were hired to accompany an expedition by a group of American treasure hunters. They were paid well, as well as could be expected, anyway. They all headed out into the jungle, a party of about fifty men and about five or six hunters from what I can remember. They trekked for a few days, but it travels fast out here. If you are not used to it you can succumb very easily indeed. Once moment, you are fine, walking along; next moment, you're down with it, coughing, spluttering, sneezing, eyes watering, chills, everything.'

Lisa was confused; she strained her ears to hear as Winthrope's voice got quieter and quieter.

'What travels fast here? The aswang?'

Winthrope smiled and leaned in. Lisa could smell the fumes from the tea that he held in his hand, she could see his pulse beat through the veins in his forehead, and smell the musky aroma of sweat on his skin.

'Flu,' he said. 'Simple common or garden flu. The treasure hunters brought it in with them, in their lungs, in their bloodstream, and it was as effective and as deadly as any poison. They could not have known when they hired all the men from the village that they were really condemning them to death and also the womenfolk to a lifetime of celibacy. That was, of course, until I came along.'

'And what did you have to do with this expedition?'

'I was medical officer, wouldn't you know? I had inoculated myself before I came out.'

Winthrope crossed his chest. 'Not guilty,' he said, and smiled.

'But you're leading these women to believe that they're the victims of the jungle when all they time they're victims of your germs.'

Winthrope looked hurt. 'My dear, I am providing a vital natural resource: my genes for the preservation of an entire culture.'

Lisa was unconvinced. 'In the meantime, you have as many wives as you like and are treated like a king by women who are too scared of the stories you've put into their heads.'

Winthrope grew angry. 'What am I? An ogre? A despot? What is the aswang, do you know, Lisa, have you seen one? What really are these spirits of the jungle? What form do they take? What is the difference, Lisa, between the aswang and the germ? Tell me that.'

'Flu germs exist, can you see that? Flu, colds, diseases can be treated, people need not die of them.'

'Gods can be treated too, Lisa, with time and science.'

Lisa fell silent. She stared at the dry ground beneath her knees. 'So what do you want with me?' she asked, hardly wanting to hear the answer.

'The others,' Winthrope replied.

'What others?'

'The others you came with. I'm assuming you did not come here on your own, and I am also assuming that you did not come here with an all-female group of sisterly treasure hunters.'

'What makes you assume I came here to hunt for the treasure?'

Winthrope laughed. 'Why does anyone come here, Lisa?'

She looked about her. 'Well, yes,' she said. 'There are others. I don't know where they are though. I got lost. I was swimming in the river and the current took me. I ended up here.'

She could feel herself begin to cry. It was all getting too much. She had never felt more alone or more afraid than she did now. The flames from the fire glinted in her tears and turned everything a hazy orange.

Winthrope's voice softened slightly. 'We need to find the others, Lisa. I am an old man and I am only one man. We need to expand the programme.'

Lisa could not believe her ears. 'The programme? Are you mad? These women are people, not cattle to be bred and made to produce.'

Winthrope was getting excited. 'Think of it Lisa. A community, right here in the middle of the jungle, a whole new start for mankind and civilisation. We have both seen the big cities, the mess we have made of them, the mess we have made of each other. I have been planning it all out. I know exactly what to do. This could be the start of a whole new world, Lisa. Just imagine, an interdependent community right here in the middle of the jungle.'

Winthrope's eyes flashed wildly as his arms flayed in the air drawing imaginary diagrams of plans and aspirations. 'A community with shared genes, but genes from all over the world: Chinese, Japanese, Filipino, American, English; everyone equal, everyone pulling together for the common good.'

Lisa started to worry – suddenly Winthrope's face had changed. It took on the sheen of madness. She did not know how long he had been alone in the jungle but guessed it had been some time since he had seen the outside world. She moved further into her cage, for once glad that there were bars separating her from him. Winthrope continued to gesticulate wildly.

'This is the ultimate dream of mankind, the only thing worth fighting for, worth dreaming about. Marx proposed it in *Capital*, Thomas More in *Utopia*, William Morris in *News from Nowhere* but we – we have the chance to do it, right here, to start again. To create an Eden here of our very own. But, Lisa, I can't do it on my own, I need help. I am but one man. We need diversification, we need varied stock, varied genes. We need your party.'

Lisa was shocked; suddenly what he was proposing dawned on her. She giggled a bit at the thought of a whole village of Frasers and her uncles running around, examining rock formations and not being able to swim. Winthrope noticed this.

'You find it funny, Lisa? You find the idea of a perfect society amusing?'

Lisa stopped. 'No,' she said. 'I just had a thought, that was all. So what do you want me for?'

'I want you to find your companions and bring them to me. I want you to bring me stock, Lisa, bring me varied stock.'

Lisa realised the position she was in. If she found Joe and the others she would be leading them to this madman; if she didn't, she would be stuck with him herself. Her head spun with the thoughts of what she should do. She felt torn in two, not knowing which way to turn or what to do.

Winthrope snapped his fingers and a middle-aged woman ran up to his side. He said something in her ear and the woman nodded and ran off.

'Something to eat?' he asked Lisa, who nodded doubtfully.

'It's OK,' he said. 'You're quite safe now. Nothing can harm you.'

In their clearing, the professor and Fraser had worn a strip of vegetation away with their pacing up and down. They had been waiting for news from Joe for hours now and had all but given him up for dead.

'I still say we stay here,' the professor said suddenly, breaking the silence for no apparent reason. He and Fraser had been debating the relative merits of going and staying for most of the day. On the one hand, they thought, going would allow them to feel as though they were contributing to things. On the other, it would mean that they relinquished their post and Lisa or Joe might come back to find them gone.

'I think we should go,' Fraser replied. 'We can't stay here forever and perhaps Joe or Lisa needs our help. Anyway, what can we do here? Nothing. All we can do is pace up and down, it's utterly useless.'

The professor slumped down onto the floor. 'I say we stay.'

Fraser turned suddenly. 'What was that?' he said.

The professor looked up.

Fraser continued. 'I heard a noise, nearby.'

The professor waved his arm. 'The jungle is full of noise,' he said. 'Noise and trees.'

Fraser moved over to where it was coming from. 'Hello?' he called. 'Anyone there? Anyone?'

There was a crashing of branches and a rending of foliage. Without knowing what was happening Fraser was confronted with a mass of tangled vines and flailing arms. He put his hands up to cover his face but it made no difference. Whatever it was was coming straight for him. Fraser staggered backwards and fell on to the floor and whatever it was fell on top of him. The professor darted up and pulled the figure off Fraser and rolled it on the ground; it was only when they had done this that they realised the figure was Joe.

The professor dusted the dirt from the jungle off of Joe and steadied him on his feet. The three stood and watched each other for a moment, not knowing what to do or say.

Slowly, Joe spoke: 'I've been walking for these last few hours. I got nowhere. I tried to find her. I walked and walked but couldn't see her anywhere. I know she's out there somewhere. We have to go and find her. She might be in serious trouble.'

Fraser tried to calm him down; he poured Joe a drink from the canteen and made him sit on a pile of leaves they had fashioned to one side of the clearing. The professor sat down in front of it.

'You may be right, Joe, it's been some time now. We need to go and find her, but we need to be careful – we don't want to be getting lost ourselves.'

Fraser butted in. 'We could leave a trail of stones behind us, like they did in the fairy tale.'

The professor nodded. 'Yes, I think that might be a good idea. We need to find our way back here at least, if things should go wrong. But Joe, you need to rest first. You are tired. We shall make you something to eat.'

Joe shook his head. 'No, we need to go now. We need to find her as soon as we can, otherwise I have no idea what might happen. Professor, I'm worried about her. Someone could walk for days and days in that jungle and not know where they are, not come to a clearing, or anything. You can go crazy in there.'

He looked at the thick, dense foliage and shuddered. 'Sometimes, I thought I was going crazy.'

He felt the eyes on him, the eyes of the jungle that always seemed to be trained his way. He pulled his coat a little further round his neck and, for a moment, closed his eyes. The professor picked up the kettle.

'I insist, Joe. First you must rest, stay here overnight and tomorrow we will look for her. The night is drawing in and soon it will be dark. Lisa is a bright girl. She'll know to keep out of trouble and to try to find her way back.'

Joe felt his head bob and his eyes closing slowly. Somewhere in his mind, a light was being turned off and his body began to shut down; he let himself fall into unconsciousness.

He was surrounded by the tunnel again, everywhere he looked there were bodies, skin and bone, teeth, hair. The first thing he was aware of was the smell of blood and the awful oppressive heat. Joe tried to scramble his way backwards but it was no good – something, someone was pushing him forward. He heard the moans and the cries of those around him and he knew they were dying. Even in his dream he knew that something was not right, that the calming, uplifting dreams of the last few weeks were fading and the spirits of the jungle were trying to tell him something. They were trying to tell him that he must hurry, hurry or all would be lost.

He tried to push his way through the mass of bodies that surrounded him. Everywhere he placed his hand it would touch a soft, hot surface of flesh. Those around him were dying. He lit a match and held it up to one of the faces and nearly dropped it as he recognised the face of his mother. Her eyes were bloodshot and staring and the nails of her hands were ripped from their roots in the attempt to claw herself free. He moved the match and saw Lisa, with her hair torn from her head and blood dripping from her face. He lit another match and saw the professor, face pale and bloodless as a death mask, propped up against the wall of the tunnel.

He couldn't stand any more of this. He just wanted to wake up. He knew it was a dream and he knew why they were goading him to continue into the jungle. They did not want him sidetracked by Lisa. They – whoever they were – were jealous of his relationship with her. He knew he was here for a reason, he knew that something was spurring him on but now, now they were punishing him for ignoring them.

Suddenly everything was silent; the moaning and the crying stopped. All that could be heard was a breeze, blowing like those he remembered from when he had been a child on the streets of Hong Kong. A hard breeze, but one that blew old memories and fears away, a breeze that was somewhere forever blowing, that could lift your spirits and send you soaring if only you believed you were light enough. A breeze that carried you away.

He could feel his skin become raw from the wind that blew in the tunnel. Even in his dream he knew such things could never happen, knew that it was absurd – but he just stood, feeling it hit, feeling it washing away his worries and take away his fear. There was a shadow moving in the darkness, a slowly-moving black shadow that seemed to creak as it moved and could barely be distinguished from the darkness that surrounded it. Joe reached out a hand and it touched something cold. The shadow revealed itself as an old woman with deep *brown eyes and white hair. She moved closer to Joe and placed her hand upon his chest. Joe felt as though he had been hit by a lightning bolt, the shock almost sending him backwards onto the pile of bodies behind him.*

'Look for me,' the old woman said. 'Look for me and I will be there.'

14

It was almost dark but the moon ahead was throwing enough light to walk by as Kono and Tanaka trekked through the jungle. Their heavy footsteps crashed through the undergrowth and could be heard for miles in both directions. Every now and then they would stop and examine the tracking device that Tanaka held in his hands.

'I think I need to sleep,' Kono moaned, but Tanaka was having none of it. He pulled on the other's shoulder strap and urged him onward.

'Look,' he said. 'According to this we are almost upon them. We've been walking through this Godforsaken place for days now and we have almost got them.'

Tanaka examined the tracking device which sent a shaft of red light into the black jungle sky and pulsed with an ever-growing regularity. His eyes were fixed firmly on the light as he followed its path through the jungle, tripping over fallen trees as he went; nothing seemed to matter to him but the tracking device and the course it suggested: through the dense foliage, over the thick jungle floor, onward, always following where it led. Kono followed behind like a faithful puppy dog snapping at his master's heels.

Suddenly, Tanaka saw the light flash faster than it had ever done before. His face was lit by its soft red glow and his eyes widened as he surveyed the landscape that the tracking device led him through. He pulled Kono nearer.

'Over this ridge,' he said. 'They must be over this ridge.

This is it. We must keep quiet. They must be near. They must be over this ridge.'

Tanaka inched forward, placing one foot on the steep angle of the ridge in front of him. He kept his eyes fixed firmly on the tracking device as his other foot followed the first and he gingerly made his way up. Kono pushed at his behind in order to stop him from falling backwards. Tanaka could hardly control his breathing. Since Hong Kong he had been following Joe and the others and now he had finally caught up with them. His mind raced as he thought about the gold and the riches he would take from them. He laughed quietly to himself as he neared the top of the ridge. He steeled himself and peered over.

The first thing he noticed was the ocean as it breathed softly in the night air. The second thing was the cool breeze that seemed to wash over his face like the water itself. And the third thing was a white shard of fibreglass with a flashing red light upon it that was caught, eddying on the tide. In his hand the tracking device gave off a furious pulsing light that seemed to taunt him as he stretched his arm out to where the remnants of the plane that had brought Joe and the others to the island had been dumped on the shore by the ocean.

Kono rounded the top of the ridge and looked with wide eyes at the scene. After a moment's silence he spoke. 'Where are they then?' he said. 'Is it safe to talk yet?'

Beside him Tanaka threw the tracking device into the waves. 'Fool,' he shouted. 'They aren't here.'

Kono was confused. He had been tracking them for days with the device that he himself had planted on the plane in Hong Kong.

'But the device?' he asked.

Tanaka calmed himself down. 'They crashed the damn plane. Look, out there on the beach – that's the tracking beacon.'

He grabbed Kono's chin and roughly turned his head to where the tracking device lay.

'They crashed the damn plane and we've been following a piece of it for days.'

The two were silent for a moment then Kono began to feel the information sink in, although he hadn't quite yet made up his mind what it meant. His eyebrows knitted together in thought as he tried desperately to make sense of what he had just been told. 'So,' he said, slowly, 'What does that mean for the treasure?'

'There might not be any treasure,' Tanaka replied. 'If they've gone down with the plane, who knows, the map might have gone down with them. This could be it, the whole plan finished, right here and now. I'll have to think this thing through.'

Kono sat down on the ridge, his feet pointing in opposite directions. In a way he was glad; he really wanted to go back home and forget all about this trip. Tanaka had made him come and, really, all he wanted to do was fire up the plane and get out. He picked up a stone from the ridge and threw it into the jungle, hearing the undergrowth ripple and tear. All he had ever wanted out of life was to be comfortable but, like his father had always said, he was dumb – he was big and dumb, there was nothing more to it. He picked up another stone and threw it into the undergrowth after the first one.

His father's face came into his mind; those eyes, those disappointed eyes. He had tried his best at school but when you were as big as he was people challenged you, they wanted to fight you until all you knew was fighting. He picked up the biggest rock that was within reach and threw it hard against a tree.

'Ouch!'

The tree had cried in pain. Kono stood up. Tanaka beside him continued thinking in silence.

'What was that?' Kono said to no one.

'Quiet!' Tanaka said. 'I'm thinking.'

Kono screwed up his eyes in order to see. He was positive he had heard a voice in the jungle; he was sure that something had cried out in pain as he had thrown the stone. He knew he was stupid but he had never hallucinated before.

'Hello?' he shouted into the jungle but it offered back only silence and the odd sound of an insect buzzing. 'Anyone there?'

'Quiet!' Tanaka shouted. 'I'm trying to think. There's no one there.'

In the jungle, Yamashita's corporal watched his two countrymen on the ridge and rubbed his shin where the rock had hit. He wondered if they could be trusted. He had heard that they paid spies these days to try to flush the faithful like him out. They were wearing the clothes of the enemy, western trousers and western jackets, and they certainly didn't look like any member of the Imperial Army he had seen. As long as there was a war on, he thought to himself, he would trust no one.

The corporal sniffed at the air and pulled his coat tighter around his neck. He had known times like these. He could recognise the scent on the breeze of something about to happen. He had lived on the island now for over sixty years and knew every inch of it. He also knew what it was like when a storm was coming. The corporal looked up to the sky. He could see no stars now. They were covered by the clouds that were full of rain, thunder and lightning. He gave one last look at the two men standing on the ridge and scuttled off back to his camp.

Kono heard the corporal move in the darkness and went to shout out again but stopped himself. He did not want to provoke Tanaka again; he would keep quiet this time and keep his fears to himself. He felt odd now, though. His skin was bristling and his hair was dampening; he thought he felt a little colder. He too looked up to the sky but, not being used to the conditions, saw nothing, only the vast emptiness of the universe overhead.

Suddenly, it happened: the rains came. They came like a river, pouring on the jungle in sheets of cold, clear water. Every inch of every tree was soon glistening and heavy and the noise of the insects and the animals ceased almost in an instant, as if someone had flicked a switch. On the ridge, Kono and Tanaka felt the full force of the storm and ran for cover under one of the trees but found that it was useless; in the jungle when it rains there are no hiding places. They huddled together, pulling their shirts over their heads and desperately trying to secure as much warmth as possible. The thunder roared and the lightning flashed across the sky like some angry god.

In their clearing Joe, the professor and Fraser too had been party to the full force of the storm. Joe had been quietly sleeping and was rudely awoken to the feeling of a rain cloud bursting on to his skin. He cursed as his eyes opened and he ran for cover under the shelter they had built two days before. The professor and Fraser were already under it.

'It looks like it is going to be long storm,' the professor said, pointing to the sky. His face seemed to light up like a child's as he watched the streaks of sheet lightning burst across the sky and felt the peals of rolling thunder hit him in the chest and set his insides churning. Ever since he was a boy he had loved the feeling of a storm. It was Nature at her wildest – it swept away the old dust and debris and created new life and new opportunities for life. Beside him, however, Fraser was not so romantic. He could feel the rain seeping in through the holes of the hastily fashioned shelter. He was examining its roof and wondering to himself if they should not have spent more

191

time on it. He managed to speak above the sound of the rain relentlessly falling. 'Professor? How long do these storms last around here? How long can we expect this to go on for?'

The professor leaned over, a grin spreading across his face. 'Hours, perhaps even days,' he said gleefully. 'Isn't it marvellous?'

Fraser did not think so. He was busy pulling the collar of his shirt tighter around his neck and wishing that he were somewhere else.

The rain continued to come as if it was the end of the world. All night it came down and each minute, each hour brought down more upon the heads of those that sat, heads bowed, in the jungle waiting for it to pass. In the village, Winthrope had moved Lisa to his hut while the storm was at its highest and sat watching her sleep, still bound but free of the cage. He passed a hand over her head and was reminded, suddenly, of a distant memory that he had almost forgotten – someone as beautiful as her who had touched him once and had then disappeared. Someone who had entered his life briefly and then gone without a trace.

The rain fell on the roof of the hut and caused ripples of sound to emanate around its circular walls like the sides and skin of a drum. He knew he would blame this on the gods, use this incident to get what he wanted. He would explain to his wives and to his daughters that the rain was a sign of the anger of the gods, brought about by the presence of a foreigner in the village and that they must find the others to assuage them. He knew this but did not like it, momentarily, as he looked upon Lisa.

The river was beginning to swell. Hour after hour of the downpour had turned its already flowing rapids into a torrent that was unstoppable. It rushed onward like a speeding herd, taking everything in its path – animals,

192

trees, the land that once formed its bank. Nothing was safe if it got in its way.

The more the rain came the more the river ran, sweeping away the dry ground around its edges, making itself wider and stronger with each passing minute until the banks could hold it no longer and it gushed over the floor of the jungle, sending animals scurrying and crushing plants and vegetation. In his shelter, the corporal had been watching the river. He knew every part of this jungle, but had never known a storm like this. He had never seen the sky so dark or the river so fearsome. With horror he saw that water had begun to seep under the sides of his shelter. He tried to stem it, to block the holes but to no avail. It came anyway. Nothing could stop it. The corporal began to panic. If only his general were here to tell him what to do; if only there were someone who could formulate a plan and get him out.

The rain made its way under the walls of the corporal's shelter and formed pools on his floor. He stood on the bed to avoid wetting his feet, cursing the river. The water relentlessly poured into the shelter, lifting his meagre possessions and making them float around the room. His chest spilled its contents and the small bookcase, fashioned out of local material, fell into the steadily rising pool of water. The corporal quickly gathered together some of his things into a bundle and made his way out of the shelter. The rain hit him hard as he ran for the ridge that he had seen earlier. He grabbed the tarpaulin that was covering the shelter and placed it over his head. At least now he was dry. He made his way through the jungle at great speed, never tripping over the undergrowth that seemed to spring up underfoot for everyone else, never unsure of where to go but darting this way and that in the way a city dweller might traverse a network of streets.

All the time the rain fell, it drummed on the leaves

overhead and made a curious rhythm that seemed to get louder and louder. The corporal pulled the tarpaulin tighter around his neck as he spied the ridge in the distance. Quickly he made his way over to it. He was a few steps from its edge when he felt a hand pulling him backwards. It was Kono, who had recognised the small but swift steps as those he had heard earlier. The larger man wrestled the tarpaulin out of the smaller man's hands and then stretched it across himself and Tanaka. The corporal could not quite believe what he was seeing. He blinked as the rain fell in rivulets down his forehead and into his eyes. The sky cracked and the clouds boomed out a warning of yet another increase in the downpour and in the light of the storm the corporal squeezed his small frame in between the bodies of Kono and Tanaka; the three men sat not saying a word to each other.

All night it fell, minute upon minute, hour upon hour until it seemed as if the jungle could hold no more water. The skies opened and the heavens poured forth hundreds and hundreds of gallons of water, replenishing the ground with moisture and giving life to the foliage and the vegetation. The humans of the jungle did not appreciate it as much. They sat for the most part under cover, wishing it would stop, wishing that the gods would take pity on them and cease the relentless drumming that after a time seemed to be the very sound of the world turning.

As the sun came up it stopped, almost as if the one had caused the other. As if being born again, the jungle shone like a treasure chest full of jewels, every leaf turned magically into a reflective surface, every tree turned into a host of mirrors, each one shining in the rays of the new sun. The professor was the first to poke a head out from underneath the shelter. He breathed in the air and it coursed through his veins like alcohol, waking him and giving him life. Beside him Joe lay sleeping.

The professor walked into the open air and stretched. He noticed how fresh the jungle seemed, how beautiful and how much like a friend now instead of an enemy. He walked over to the fire and kicked its useless embers, then steeled himself for the attempt at trying to find some small piece of dry wood in this sparkling, water-laden jungle.

Joe opened an eye and stared out of the shelter. The light hit him and made him wince. He rubbed his face and slowly stretched out his legs, kicking Fraser in the process.

The professor came back with a few dry twigs and branches and set about arranging them in the hearth.

'I've found some dry wood, by a miracle,' he said and attempted to light the fire.

Joe and Fraser extricated themselves from the shelter and sat blinking in the daylight.

'Today we search for Lisa,' the professor said. 'We'll find her, I'm sure of that.'

All three sat round the hearth and breathed a collective sigh of relief as the wood burst into flames. Although they tried to convince each other of the likelihood of finding Lisa none of them quite believed it. Each of them knew that it was a huge jungle and they were three very small men.

'Shall we have some tea?' the professor said, pulling a few bags out of his pocket. He carefully dropped one into their only cup and poured some rainwater into it. He smacked his lips as the steam was sent spinning into the air.

'There's nothing like tea in the open air, eh?'

Joe, Fraser and the professor sat and shared the tea, each one in turn taking a small sip of the boiling liquid and feeling it gradually heating their insides.

'Which way will we go?' Fraser asked suddenly. 'Which way do we even start?'

Joe pointed ahead of him. 'I say we follow the river again. I'm sure she was taken along by it while swimming. I mean, I tried yesterday to get along the bank, but these paths are murderous – you can't tell where you're going from one moment to the next.' Joe began to pack what little he had into his pockets. 'And I say we get going as soon as possible. The sooner we start the more chance we have of finding her.'

The professor finished the tea, burning his mouth. He looked forlornly into the cup as he drained its last dregs and wished he were at home, where a kettle and a shop could make his life a lot easier. He knew the trip had been his idea; he knew that if he had not talked to Anderson he would still be alive; he knew that if he had only ignored the dreams that came to him in the night, he would be in Hong Kong now, getting ready for the summer vacation. He knew all of these things and knew that the situation they were in was his fault.

He thought of Lisa and wished with all his heart that they would find her, although secretly he believed they would not. It was an easy thing, to lose one's footing while swimming, to be swept along on the current and never be seen again. She was a beautiful girl and kind; she did not deserve to die like this, alone, afraid and far from home.

He washed out the cup and attached it to his shirt with a piece of string.

'Shall we go then?' he said, and doused the flames of the fire.

Grabbing some dry firewood and the matches, Fraser pushed on into the jungle followed by the other two. Every few steps, they would drop a stone so that they could make their way back to the camp if necessary.

Already they found it hard going. The rain had made the jungle fresh and alive but it was also laden with water

196

so that each step they took, each branch they brushed against would cover them in icy cold moisture until they were soaked to the skin again, wishing for the dryness of the day before. An hour into their journey, they stopped and took their bearings; the sun was just visible overhead but it was useless to navigate by. All they had was their sense of direction and the sound of the river that they always kept to their right. It was an inaccurate way to navigate and they knew it.

Hour after hour they walked, getting wetter and wetter and more and more tired. Each took a turn to lead and the last man always dropped a grey stone on the ground every few steps. Joe was impatient to find Lisa. Whenever he was in front the pace would suddenly quicken, one step would become two and those behind would have a job to keep up. The quick pace, however, meant that more branches were brushed against and more water sent into the air in showers. Once or twice Fraser shouted at him to slow down but Joe could not or would not hear – he just pushed ahead regardless.

It was Fraser who had taken the front and the pace had slowed down to a sedate walk. Joe was at the back. Suddenly Fraser lifted a hand and stopped dead, almost causing the professor and Joe to crash into his back. Fraser turned and looked at them, his face suffused with a deadly pallor. Fraser's eyes seemed to dim as he looked at the others and his lids drooped. He bent down, scrambled around in the undergrowth for a second and then stood up, holding out his hand. Slowly he opened his fingers to reveal a clean granite grey stone. The others knew what it meant as soon as they saw it.

Joe almost fell to his knees with exhaustion and the professor just stood and stared.

Fraser was the first to speak. 'We've been walking in a circle,' he said. 'How could that be? How could we have walked in a circle? We kept the river to our right at all times, how could it be? I can hear it even now.'

Fraser craned his ears but as he did so he heard many sounds: the sound of the river mixed with the sound of water running from the trees, and the sound of the animals and birds overhead. He was not sure now where the river was. He did not know if it was behind him, in front of him, to the left or to the right. He closed his eyes. The jungle had become one big circus of noise and the sounds he thought he was hearing became lost in a cacophony of other world sounds.

'I don't know which way the river is now,' he said at last. 'I can't tell which way it is. Professor, how about you? Tell me I'm not the only one.'

Fraser knew that he should have been following his ears. He knew he had led the other two back on themselves. He knew they blamed him. The professor just shrugged his shoulders.

'I was following you,' he said and slumped down to the ground. Suddenly the jungle seemed a bigger place than they had first imagined. Suddenly the possibility of finding Lisa began to fade. Each of them started to imagine her face and saw it disappearing from view. Suddenly everything had changed.

In their makeshift shelter, Kono and Tanaka had begun to talk with the corporal. The three men had begun gingerly at first, exchanging glances, then non-committal noises, then brief words until, by the end of the night, they were engaging each other in conversation. Unlike Kono, Tanaka had guessed pretty early on that the corporal was unaware of the end of the war and had also judged that he could use this to his advantage; he also understood that the corporal knew every square inch of the island.

'Have you seen anyone else arrive?' Tanaka asked him, to which the corporal nodded.

'Four, one of them was wearing an American cap. I don't know what they want, but I guessed they were spies. Two were Japanese – one a woman! I have heard they send spies to convince strongholds to surrender. I thought you were spies when I first saw you. That's why I watched you and did not make contact.'

Tanaka nodded. 'Yes,' he said. 'They are spies. They have been sent by the Americans to flush you out. How else would they do it? They know they could not beat you in hand-to-hand fighting so they come to tempt you out with beautiful women.'

The corporal laughed. 'What do I want with beautiful women? I only serve Yamashita!'

Kono went to speak was but stopped in his tracks by a touch on the shoulder.

'Yes,' Tanaka replied. 'And General Yamashita is very grateful for all you have done.'

The corporal's eyes widened suddenly and his face lit up. 'You have spoken to the general about me?' he asked.

Tanaka nodded. 'Of course. He is very proud of what you have done here and he asks me to give you his thanks.'

The corporal bowed a generous bow and smiled.

'But ... he also gave me orders for you. He said he wanted you to show me where the gold is buried.'

The corporal looked blankly at Tanaka. 'The gold?' he replied.

'Yes, the gold. The gold buried in the mines by Yamashita. The gold that you are here to protect, the gold...'

The corporal smiled. 'I know of no gold,' he said. 'I was sent here after the general left. I have heard of the gold, but know nothing of it.'

Tanaka's heart sank. At least, he thought to himself, he knew the others were here now and he also knew they could be found with the corporal's knowledge. Why should he muddy his hands digging for the gold when he could wait until the others had found it and dug it out themselves? Tanaka smiled to himself; all he had to do was wait now, wait and watch. He patted the corporal on the back and handed him a cigarette.

'I think the general will be very pleased with you,' he said. 'Very pleased indeed.'

15

After about half an hour, Joe stood up. 'OK, so we've been walking in circles but we can't give up the search just like that. We are looking for Lisa after all – we are doing it for her.'

He wrung the water out of the bottom of his shirt and dragged Fraser by the arm. Fraser moaned and shouted but eventually allowed himself to be dragged to his feet.

'Come on. Come, this time we'll all listen out for the river. All we need to do is concentrate and we'll find our way, I'm sure of it. All we need to do is keep a constant course.'

The three men, tired and downcast, made their way again into the jungle, pushing aside large ferns and foliage as they went. The professor was finding it hard going. He let his mind wander to his classroom, to the bright faces of the students and the easy life of the university lecturer. He tripped over a tree root and cursed his luck.

Joe kept up a good pace for an hour and then let a reluctant Fraser take the lead. The speed slowed somewhat but with all three men craning their ears every second they kept a good course. They always heard the river. No matter what other noises polluted the air, they always heard the river.

Joe saw the clearing up ahead that he had visited the day before. He pointed it out to Fraser and the three men headed for it, bursting through the dense trees to rest in its spacious, empty environment. The professor sighed with relief as he flopped down upon a log which, unbeknownst to him, had held his niece only a few hours before.

'Do you think we'll ever find her?' he asked, pulling a handkerchief out of his back pocket and wiping his forehead with it.

Joe looked at him, not wanting to say no, but unable to say yes. He made to speak but was gripped by a sudden, all-powerful feeling of being watched again. He looked around. Damn this jungle, he thought, there are more eyes here than any street in Hong Kong. The aswang were watching him, their eyes peering out of every leaf, their hot breath steaming in the close air of the jungle. Wherever he went the aswang were there beside him, goading him onwards, taunting him, making him go where he did not want to go.

He spoke to no one in particular. 'I think this jungle is playing with my mind. Every step I take, every time I turn around I think I'm being watched.'

Fraser peered nervously into the undergrowth. 'Well, if you are paranoid,' he said, 'Then I must be too because for the last half an hour I've been having the same feeling, as if there are eyes peering at me from behind every tree.'

The professor shuddered. He too had been feeling the same but had failed, or had not dared to mention it. He stroked the three-day-old stubble on his chin and looked up to the tall canopy of the trees. Everything was strange here, he thought to himself, nothing was what it seemed.

Then from out of the trees there came a great blackness, something unexplainable that flew through the air and hit all three like an explosion. They reeled from the force and fell to the ground, moaning and screaming more from surprise and shock than pain. The world for Joe went black. One moment he was standing, staring through the trees, the next he was on his back fighting some

202

invisible enemy. He shouted to the air, 'The aswang! It's the aswang!'

The professor and Fraser, though, realised this was a far more mortal foe. They scrabbled at the net that covered them and tried to free themselves but it was no use. The more they struggled the tighter the net seemed to entwine itself around their limbs and catch itself around their necks and torsos. For ten minutes the three struggled but to no avail – the net had completely covered them. Joe finally opened his eyes and the first thing he saw was the legs of a young woman. They were slender legs, legs that he might have gazed upon with lust once; legs that he might have encountered in a bar in Hong Kong, in one of the back streets where love was cheap and lasted a night if you could pay. Joe followed the line of the legs upwards until he caught sight of a beautiful young girl, about fifteen or sixteen. Her skin was brown and soft and her hair flowed in long waves around her shoulders but she had the hard face of a warrior, the look of someone who had known pain and suffering.

Joe implored her to let them go but it was no good. The girl just stared and said nothing. She was joined in time by four or five others, all with the same slender brown legs and hard, almost aggressive look. Joe started to wonder whether this was his idea of paradise or his idea of hell. Each new woman that arrived carried a different and increasingly deadly-looking weapon – a knife at first, then a dagger, then a club, then a spear. Joe gulped. If there was a time to be surrounded by beautiful half-naked women, he thought to himself, this wasn't it.

Beside him, in the net, the professor and Fraser were having similar thoughts. Fraser called out to one of the women, in his best pathetic tone.

'Hello, hello! Could you free us? We are caught in your net. I'm sure you meant to trap an animal or two but you seemed to have caught us.' He laughed a little but the women were not laughing. They just looked at him and occasionally jabbed him with a stick.

The professor was a little more sedate. He had assumed that this entrapment was no accident. Suddenly it all became clear to him: he remembered the feeling of being watched and the noises in the jungle that seemed a little too human to be anything other than a voyeur.

'What do you want?' he asked, but still the women said nothing. They just stared at the bundle of netting and the men struggling on the floor for breath and space. Suddenly the trees parted and Winthrope appeared, looking odd against the green of the jungle.

'Greetings!' he intoned. 'Please relax. You will come to no harm.'

'Who the hell are you?' Joe asked.

'I will introduce myself presently. For the moment all you need to know is that I am a friend and a friend that intends to make your stay as comfortable as possible.'

'I'm not going anywhere until you tell me who you are,' Fraser shouted.

Winthrope laughed. 'I think you will not be going anywhere until I say so ... Fraser, isn't it?'

Fraser was stopped in his tracks by the mention of his name. He stammered out an incomprehensible sentence before falling into silence amid the netting. The professor, however, was not so easily placated. 'I wonder if you know you are dealing with Hong Kong citizens,' he said. 'We have the right to be treated with dignity and respect, especially by someone who is from Her Majesty's realm.'

Winthrope laughed again. He threw his head back and revealed a set of blackened and filled teeth and his belly wobbled. 'Professor, I know all about your brilliant mind. I have heard everything about you – why you are here, where you are going, what you are looking for and, let me tell you this, if you play right by me (which by the way you have very little choice but to do) you will be rewarded with what you came here for. Remember, you are strangers here, my friends, but this is my home.'

Winthrope nodded to the young women and they set about unfastening the net. They then removed each of the three men from its clutches and tied them to wooden stakes that they heaved over their shoulders. Joe, the professor and Fraser were carried, upside down, through the jungle along the exact route that Lisa had the day before. They felt every bump in the trail, every stumble that the women made as they carried them, each scratch from the branches that brushed their faces and the bare skin of their arms and legs.

Winthrope followed along behind, whistling merrily and beating the trees as he passed with a stick. Every now and then he would gently pat the behind of one of the girls that walked along with him, smiling lasciviously. After about half an hour Joe lifted his head up and saw, upside down in the distance, the village. It looked bright and sparkling in the freshness of the morning. There were children running about and women here and there seeing to everyday tasks and duties. Winthrope behind them called out, 'There she is, men, home, for a while anyway. There can be paradise or there can be hell.'

He swiped at a tree with the stick and sent leaves and branches flying up into the air. Joe wondered what the hell was going to happen to him. The rope that the women had used to tie him to the stake was beginning to bite into his flesh and he felt as if he might pass out at any moment due to the blood rushing to his head; his eyes felt fit to burst and his face was hotter than a frying pan.

Joe took a deep breath and willed himself to carry on. He thought to himself that, still, this was all for Lisa.

Once they had released him he would continue his search. He did not care any more if he found her alive, he would search and search until he found her body if need be. He wanted to do his best for her, to do right by her, he wanted her to know that, wherever she was, he was thinking about her.

Behind him the professor was conversing to his carriers. 'So, tell me,' he was saying, 'Do you speak English? Japanese? Filipino? None of these it would seem. Well, it has been nice to be carried for a while, I must say, especially by such lovely ladies.'

'Save it for later,' Winthrope offered. 'You may need it with these.'

The party made their way through the edge of the clearing and out into the village. Everyone, it seemed, came out to look at the strange procession, to gawp and to stare at the line of weird humanity that passed before their eyes. Some of the women laughed and pointed, at the professor especially; some of them remained silent, but most chatted idly to each other, weighing up the situation with a removed indifference.

Eventually the three men were taken to the biggest hut in the village and dumped, unceremoniously, by the door. Winthrope strolled up to them. 'Now, gentlemen, let me introduce myself. I am W.G. Winthrope, MD (retired) and I welcome you to my village.'

He spread out his arms and turned around on the spot to highlight the circumference of his land. 'Here you will be well looked after and you may even come to like it. Of course ... you cannot stay here forever ... but your time here will be a pleasant one, I would imagine, that is if...' He paused for a while. 'You are of use to us.' He looked the professor over and sniffed at the air dismissively. The professor did not know what that signified but somehow he knew it was not a compliment.

'I think, perhaps, before we go on we should extricate you from your stakes. Girls, would you?'

Five young women from the crowd that had gathered round ran forward and began to cut Joe, the professor and Fraser away from the stakes upon which they had been carried for the last half an hour.

'You'll understand that until we get better acquainted, I cannot permit you to be totally free of your bonds; however that will come later, do not worry.'

Joe rubbed his shins with hands that were still tied together. He noticed the rope had bitten into them so much that blood had pooled on the tops of his boots and begun to run down their sides.

'I think perhaps we should offer you some refreshments,' Winthrope said, and snapped his fingers, whereupon a number of women appeared carrying jugs of water and milk, fruit and honeyed chicken. Joe, the professor and Fraser fell upon the food hungrily and started cramming it in their mouths. The women standing around began to laugh as if they had never seen hungry men before. Joe smiled at one and felt a line of grease running down his chin. Fraser nodded to Winthrope to pour some of the milk into a waiting bowl and Winthrope obliged. Fraser lapped greedily, like a dog drinking from a bowl. Every now and then one of the men would let out a belch that sent the crowd into a paroxysm of laughter. They rocked their shoulders and shook their breasts, throwing their mouths open in a display of unadulterated joy that made the professor himself begin to giggle and smile.

Joe knocked over the bowl of water with his forehead as he tried to drink out of it, another action that seemed to gain favour with the crowd who, again, laughed long and loud. Joe smiled and when the bowl was righted deliberately knocked it over again to achieve the same results. Each of the women was clamouring for a better place to see the spectacle that had dropped into their village and Joe played up to being the clown. He wriggled his way over to one of the older women and started biting at her toes as if it were the food that now lay strewn over the floor. The woman skipped and danced, trying to get her feet out of the way of Joe's snapping mouth but the more she moved them the more Joe tried to catch them. If she moved to the left, Joe wriggled that way; if she moved backwards he would shunt forwards, licking at her toes and biting at her ankles.

After a while, the entire crowd, including Winthrope, was laughing and shaking in a raucous way. Joe wriggled on his belly like a snake to entertain them and made noises like a pig that made the women hop and skip in delight. Every now and then one of the women would summon up the courage to move forward and would offer a naked foot to Joe who would try to butt it or to gnaw at it with his flashing teeth. The woman screamed with laughter, clearly enjoying the joking attention of this man who seemed so young and fresh compared to the others.

Fraser and the professor sat together smiling but trying their best not to join in the frivolity. They were too busy trying to work out why they had been brought there and why Winthrope had insisted that they were tied. Fraser whispered in the professor's ear. 'What is this all about?'

But the professor just shrugged and rolled his eyes. There was nothing in his textbooks about any of this and he was content to let Joe take the lead where women were concerned. Joe larked and played a little more, pulling himself up on all fours and moving around the circle with difficulty. He would nose the legs of the women who stood at the front, pushing his head up against their shins until they lifted each leg with a hoot of laughter. He liked to be the centre of attention, especially the attention of young, pretty girls. He moved from girl to girl, butting their knees, pretending to bite their shins until, eventually, he came to a pair of legs that were different. Where the others had been a deep brown, these were lighter; where the others had been hard and rough, these were soft and smooth, and where the others had been excited and jumpy these were still.

Joe followed the line of the legs up until eventually he came to a face that he recognised. 'Lisa!' he exclaimed. 'What ... the...?'

He could barely form the words that came out of his mouth. He wasn't sure whether this was due to the surprise of seeing her, the happiness of finding her or the guilt that the look on her face made him feel. He smiled the best smile he could manage.

'It's nice to see you're missing me,' she said, and crossed her arms. Joe felt lower than he had ever felt. Lisa looked across at the professor and Fraser and gave a huge smile. She skipped over Joe and crossed over the circle to where they sat.

'We thought you were lost,' the professor said. 'We were looking for you. Joe was out all day yesterday trying to find you. We were captured by these – who *are* these people, Lisa?'

'I'll tell you everything, later, uncle. You have to know, though, you will be all right...' She looked at him. 'Well, I think you will be.'

Fraser piped up. 'I don't suppose you will be able to get us out of these ropes, would you, Lisa? They hurt. I think I'm losing the feeling in my hands.'

Lisa shook her head. 'They've only just let me out of mine. They don't allow strangers to wander the village alone. You'll understand why later on when they explain why you're here.'

The professor looked imploringly at her. 'Why *are* we here Lisa? Has it got something to do with the gold?'

209

Lisa hushed him and looked around suspiciously. 'You'd do well to forget the gold for a while, uncle, and concentrate on getting out of here.'

'That's if we can,' said Fraser.

Lisa laughed. 'Oh, I think the problem will be wanting to.'

She felt a tapping on her back and turned to see Joe smiling at her, his face covered in the dirt from the floor. Lisa stood, pushed her way through the crowd and disappeared into Winthrope's hut. Joe looked longingly at her, then back at the professor, who could only offer a shrug in explanation. Winthrope beside him clapped his hands together and the circle of women closed in around the three men. They were taken roughly by the hands and led to a hut that was being built in the middle of the village.

It was then that Fraser started noticing that none of the villagers were men. At first he had not thought about it but as time went on he slowly began to realise that, other than Winthrope and the few small boys he saw running about, the only three men were himself, Joe and the professor. He tried to get the latter alone to mention this but it was proving difficult. The women had prepared small beds for the men in the sunshine, so they could sit and watch the building of their hut. Some of the girls mopped the professor's brow or rubbed Joe hands until they could feel themselves being lulled into a deep sleep. Beside them, however, Fraser was vigilant. He began to take a keen interest in what was happening around him.

He noticed that Winthrope seemed to control the operation. Everything he wanted, the girls would run and get for him. Whether it was food, water or just company they seemed eager to get him everything he desired. He wondered what relationship he was to them. He was obviously English, from some part of the south, he guessed, so what was he doing here? What hold did he have over these women?

One of the older women sidled up to his bed and sat beside him. Fraser did not want to engage her at all so he remained motionless, looking straight ahead, not meeting her gaze. The woman reached across and took his hand but Fraser snatched it back; from the corner of his eye, he could see that she looked hurt but he did nothing.

After a few seconds she reached out a hand and tried to stroke his head but Fraser lifted her arm and placed it back on her lap. He swiped at the air as a fly buzzed around his face. There was silence in the village. Next to him Fraser heard the woman gently crying. He turned and looked at her. She bowed her head, either in deference or embarrassment, and let her tears fall onto her knees. Fraser felt his heart softening but he knew he must not let himself be taken in by all of this until he knew what was going on. He waved the woman away and reluctantly, after a few minutes, she went.

Fraser sat back on his bed and watched the clouds scudding across the sky. The sky looked so blue after the rains and the clouds were a brilliant white. He closed his eyes but would not let himself drift off to sleep. He knew he must keep alert whatever happened. However much they tried to relax him, he knew he must keep his mind aware at all times. Beside him, the professor snored as a young girl played with his hair. For the first time Fraser thought how ridiculous the professor was, how odd he seemed here, miles away from his classroom and his schoolbooks. The snores seemed to get louder and louder until the girl had to hold his nose causing him to start and to cough back phlegm.

Fraser was aware of a shadow crossing him. Suddenly things got darker and colder – something was blocking out the sun. He opened his eyes and saw Winthrope

211

standing over him, and beside him, cowering, was the woman who had left moments ago. 'You do not like our hospitality?' Winthrope asked.

Fraser was taken aback for a moment. There was something in the tone of voice that he did not like, something that made him wary. 'It's fine...' he managed after a while. 'I just need some time on my own.'

'Perhaps,' Winthrope continued, 'You don't like the women?'

'No, they're fine, fine ... I just need to be on my...'

Winthrope interrupted him. 'No, you misunderstand me, perhaps you don't *like* THE women?'

Fraser thought he realised what he was insinuating. 'Well, I've never had any problems before.'

He felt a sharp pain around his jaw. Winthrope had struck him and Fraser fell to the ground. He clutched his mouth and tasted the sharp, iron tang of blood on his tongue. 'You will like our women, or you will regret it!' Winthrope said menacingly. Fraser looked up and saw that he had a small club in his hands. Suddenly the pain in his jaw seemed a hell of a lot more understandable. He got up off his knees and swung his fist but Winthrope was too quick and Fraser was never much of a fighter. Again he landed in the mud, the force of his missed punch sending him off balance.

Joe and the professor awoke sleepily at the noise and stared in amazement as Fraser, for the second time in as many minutes, tried to pick himself up off the floor. He spat a mouthful of blood into the dirt and shook the grogginess out of his head.

'You will enjoy yourself, while you're here, or you will feel that again, do you understand?'

Fraser nodded. He was not about to try and hit out again. He figured you had to admit if you weren't a fighter. Winthrope raised his hat to the professor and Joe and left, leaving the woman to pick Fraser up and wipe the blood from his chin.

'What the hell was that about?' Joe asked.

'Do yourself a favour,' Fraser told him. 'If they ask you if you want anything, say yes.'

The women of the village busied themselves making the hut. Some carried wood from the jungle on their backs, some wove leaves and ferns around the struts that made the side of the building and still others daubed its walls in mud made in small pits around the hut's perimeter. Within a few hours it was made and the whole village, it seemed, gathered at its opening. Winthrope was there and beside him Lisa. Winthrope cleared his throat and began to speak.

'It gives me great pleasure to declare this new building open. It's not often that we are lucky enough to welcome four visitors into our village, three of them strong and virile men...' He gave a quick glance at the professor and corrected himself. 'Two of them strong and virile men. We have seen, over the years a sharp decline in our fortunes. These people have known tragedy and they have known pain but, hopefully, this is behind us now. Now we can start again, a new beginning for mankind – out of the ashes of the past a new dawn will arise. With the help of our friends we can make a better life for these people and, who knows, we might even be able to forge a new life for the whole world. If we show the way, perhaps they will follow. When the rest of the world has gone to rack and ruin we will be here with our bright faces and our strong hearts, right here on this island, a glorious paradise, a little piece of heaven right here on earth.'

He bowed his head and there was silence. Fraser did not know whether to laugh or to cry. The speech, although beautiful, had made a curious impression on him. He felt, suddenly, as if he knew what Winthrope had been talking about. He looked around himself at the bright smiling faces of the villagers and thought of the streets of Hong Kong, or the streets of London or the streets of New York; he remembered the scowls and the growls and the pushing and shoving; he remembered how he had hated every moment of shopping at Christmas or trying to get home in the rush hour. He could feel his heart melting.

Winthrope raised his head and made his way inside. He motioned to the older women to join him and for the younger ones to lift Joe, the professor and Fraser inside. Lisa followed on behind, feeling forgotten and ignored. She had realised that now they had found the men she was largely redundant. As she made her way through the doorway she met Joe's eyes. He smiled at her and she smiled back, feeling as if a bridge had been crossed somewhere and there was no going back to the relationship they had once had.

Inside it was dark but Winthrope lit the fire and it roared into life. The girls put the men down so that they formed a circle around the fire. One of them offered a pipe to each of the men, who refused, but accepted the milk that another offered; Winthrope took a pipe and smoked it with his legs crossed looking for all the world like a village chief.

Joe looked at him and laughed. 'You're no more a villager here than me, Winthrope,' he said.

'What is a villager and what not?' Winthrope asked. 'I live here, that makes me a villager, whatever colour my skin is, whatever my facial features are. I am here so here is me.'

Joe thought for a moment. 'But why are *we* here?'

Winthrope laughed a little. 'All in good time. Are you comfortable, gentlemen? I can bring some more cushions if you want. I had to show the girls how to fashion them from leaves and interlaced vines myself; however, they're only comfortable up to a point.' He shifted his buttocks to get comfortable. 'Can I offer you more milk? Water? I would offer you wine, a nice Merlot perhaps, but as you can appreciate it is a little difficult to get out here. I have heard of a drink the men used to drink here but I have yet to try it. Perhaps I will this year.'

Fraser took the opportunity to ask Winthrope about the village. 'Where are the men? Did they all drink their drink and die? Were they poisoned?'

Winthrope shot a glance at Lisa. 'The men are dead,' he said. 'They all contracted flu, common or garden flu. The virus was too much for their systems and they all died while on a trip looking for Yamashita's gold.'

Suddenly the professor's ears pricked up, his eyes opened wide and his face was a picture of intensity. 'You know of Yamashita's gold?'

Winthrope laughed. 'My dear professor, that's why I'm here, that's why you're here, that's why anyone is here. Except these lovely creatures; they had the misfortune to be born here.'

The professor's eyes narrowed as his brain clicked into gear. 'Do you know where it is?' he asked

'The gold? If I did, do you think I'd be sitting here, professor? No, I'd be lying in a mansion built with the proceeds. The general was a clever old stick, he knew how to hide things from the rest of the world – the Americans especially. I have been over most of the island and have never even had a sniff of the treasure. I have heard tales of it, though.'

'Tales?' Joe asked.

'Yes, of the kinds of artefacts there, and the kinds of fate that await those that find it. I came here, you see, with a party such as yours. We were ready and willing to hunt for the treasure wherever we thought it might lie.

215

However, we did not count on the belief in the spirits of the jungle.'

Joe felt his heart grow cold suddenly. He too believed in the spirits of the jungle; he had seen them and felt their presence.

'You don't believe in them?' he asked, whereupon Winthrope looked guiltily around him.

'I believe as much as I allow myself to, which is to say to the extent that it benefits me. I am a man of science, I was a doctor in another life, a medical man, how could I let myself believe in ghosts and spirits? The aswang, the dwendi, they are all names to me, not entities.'

'The dwendi?' Joe enquired, not wanting to hear the answer to his question.

'Little people, can be good or mischievous, the locals leave food out for them, just to keep on their good side'

Joe swallowed hard. He would have said the same himself until a few days ago.

'However, it's the aswang that come to me at night,' Winthrope added.

Joe and the professor looked at each other with fear in their eyes.

'They come to me in dreams. Oh, I dare say it's because I spend so much time thinking about them, you know what Freud said about dreams – they are the royal road to the unconscious and all that. I suppose they might have some deeper significance but they come to me at night.'

'What do they say?' Joe queried.

'Say? Oh, nothing much. They show me a tunnel, a dark tunnel that reeks of death, people, bodies. They make me feel its claustrophobia – no doubt the effect of the jungle on a man's mind. Then they show me...' He hesitated for a second. 'The golden Buddha.'

The professor almost fell backwards from his bed. He

gathered himself quickly and sat intently looking at Winthrope. 'You must tell us about the golden Buddha,' the professor exclaimed. 'You simply must.'

Winthrope rocked back on his haunches. His face grew cold and uninviting. His eyes closed momentarily and then opened, to reveal their full, shocking colour. 'You seemed interested in the golden Buddha professor. I wonder if *that* is why you are here.'

The professor was taken aback and stammered out an answer. 'I, well, *we* are here to find the golden Buddha, yes, and the rest of the contents of Yamashita's gold. For the past and for the future, for the sake of history and knowledge.'

Winthrope laughed and the women that surrounded him followed suit. 'History and knowledge won't get you very far out here, professor. There is no history in the jungle. To have history is to progress and there is no progress here, only life, day after day, year after year, life. That's the beauty of it.'

The professor shot a hard look at the man opposite him. 'I'm not from here, Winthrope. I'm from Hong Kong, where history is more important than anything else, perhaps even the day to day.'

'The golden Buddha, as you probably know, professor, is only the outer casing for what lies inside. Hundreds upon hundreds of years of wealth, collected by the monks of temples throughout Asia, stolen from them and brought here. It was so revered by the men who carried it that they were not allowed to look at it as their bent backs ached and broke under the weight. It is said to be so beautiful that to look upon it is to render the rest of your life useless. These people, these simple people, are not Buddhists. They know nothing of Buddhism's teaching or its creed but even they speak in hushed tones about the golden Buddha, the giver of riches and the taker of lives.'

'The taker of lives?' the professor asked.

'Yes, professor. How many men died carrying it here? How many men died burying it underground in the tunnel designed by Yamashita? How many men are still down there somewhere, clutching it, praying to it maybe?'

The professor grew agitated. 'It was not the Buddha that killed them. It was the general, the army.'

'That is as may be, professor, but superstition is a powerful thing. And so they visit me at night to tell me these things, to make me aware of the situation. The aswang come to me and make sure I am thinking about them and the Buddha – or is it my thoughts telling me about the aswang? I don't know, I don't suppose it matters in the long run. The gold will never be found.'

There was silence in the hut. The women were hushed and the men had downcast eyes. Lisa looked at the professor and the professor at Lisa. Neither knew what to do. They knew that they would probably never find the gold without Winthrope's knowledge but doing that meant opening themselves up to him. Could they trust him? Could they rely on him? Lisa thought not but could see, in the face of the professor, that he thought otherwise. She tried to communicate a message of procrastination to her uncle, who merely nodded wisely – there was nothing said but everything had been understood.

Fraser suddenly found his voice. 'So why are we here, Winthrope? And why won't you free us?'

Winthrope smiled and rocked backwards. He placed his hands on his knees. 'There is one thing that we need more than anything here, and that is men. As I explained, the men were all killed, the women think by the aswang, I know by the flu. Which puts us in the unfortunate position of, shall we say, having the birds without the bees.'

The professor was startled. 'You don't mean what I think you mean?' he asked.

'It's simple biology, professor, think nothing of it. We have good stock here. Good breeding, intelligence, fine muscles, strong backs; everything we need to start again.'

'But you're mad! This is no way to repopulate a village. What will happen in a few years' time? You need variation in stock, genes, you can't populate a village with such a limited gene pool.'

'But professor, I have no choice, and I'm afraid, *you* have no choice.'

The professor was suddenly aware of the door to the hut being closed. There was a click and he turned to see a gun being trained upon him. The young woman who held the gun looked no more than sixteen years old and she looked more scared than the professor, but held the rifle as if her life depended upon it. Across the other side of the hut, Winthrope smiled.

'It is awful to be so heavy-handed, professor. I was hoping that you might agree to my little plan without me having to exert force. The gun is a leftover from my original party. I have never had recourse to use it but it's in perfect working order and I'm sure could still do considerable damage should the need arise. You see, professor, this issue is bigger than both of us. It is bigger than our petty wants and desires. It concerns the regeneration of a beautiful people. After all, professor, when would you have the chance again to be with such young, beautiful women?'

The professor grew suddenly red and flustered. 'I don't know, it's something I've never really thought about before, something that...'

'Professor, do not be afraid, these women are house-trained.'

Winthrope laughed and the women laughed too. The

219

professor grew redder and redder. All the while Lisa was staring at Joe. She had noticed how suddenly he seemed interested in everything Winthrope was saying. Suddenly he was listening with rapt attention. Not for the first time that day she felt the pang of jealousy. It had surprised her at first but it was definitely there, like an itch that refused to go away. For his part, Joe began looking around the hut and casting his eye over the women. He saw their beautiful round faces, their deep brown eyes, their burnt umber skin. Then his eyes fell upon Lisa and they were the only two people in the world. All the pain and the fear of the last few days disappeared when he looked at her, the loneliness he had known for his entire life seemed to fade and he felt touched by her beauty and her intelligence. When she looked at him there was no jungle, no Winthrope, no women of the village.

Fraser, for his part, had begun to resemble a thirsty dog on a hot day; his initial reticence had given way to an almost evangelical persuasion by Winthrope's arguments. Once again he let his mind wander to cities he had known, their grey grubby surfaces, their stupid, mindless people; he knew suddenly what he had been looking for through all of his wandering. He knew why he had been brought here. The others may have been brought by the aswang or greed or for the love of a girl from Hong Kong but he had been brought here to help these women.

He lay on his back. 'You have my vote.' he said, and nuzzled up against the thigh of the woman sitting next to him.

16

Night was drawing in but inside the hut the revellers still ate and drank and talked. The warm orange glow of the fire made patterns on the wall of the hut and on the faces of those that sat round it. Every now and then, Lisa and Joe would exchange glances and wordless communication would pass between them, each knowing what the other was thinking. After a while, Joe shuffled forward and spoke to Winthrope.

'So,' he said. 'How about letting us out of these ropes, eh? I mean, we're hardly going to run away now, are we? The jungle is so dark out there I wouldn't even get past three feet of this place, and beside, all this water and milk, you know – I gotta go use the bathroom.'

Winthrope thought for a moment. 'OK, and you're right – you try to run away from the village and you won't get far. Your only hope is to stay here with us.'

Joe nodded as one of the women set about loosening and then untying his bonds. He made his way out of the hut. As he passed Lisa he reached down and gave her arm a squeeze. Lisa stroked his hand and smiled up at him but he was gone before she could catch his eye.

The night was cool and clear. Above him the stars shone brighter than he had ever seen them before. It was beautiful here, he thought to himself; the sky was clear, the air was clean and the jungle let you know you were part of something bigger, something that needed you as much as you needed it. He knew, though, that it wasn't home; there was none of the magic of the city, the excitement. He had smog for blood, he knew that, and here he was a stranger. He couldn't stay; they could never make him stay.

He passed a young girl sleeping by the hut, obviously too young to enter. Her long black hair trailed over her shoulders, a blanket was wrapped around her legs and she shivered a little in the cold night air. Carefully Joe unwound the blanket and placed it over the girl's shoulders, patting it down gently. They were a beautiful people, he thought to himself. Perhaps he was too ugly for them; perhaps he had too much of the city in him, perhaps he had always had too much of the city in him. He stroked the hair of the girl. 'Gun or no gun,' he said, 'Tomorrow, we have to leave.'

When Joe returned to the hut, he realised things had begun to go with a swing. He approached the door and heard raucous laughter from inside. He gathered from listening for a while that Winthrope had begun to elaborate on the plan he had for the professor, Fraser and himself. He gently eased open the door and made his way in. The air in the hut was stifling. He coughed as it hit his lungs, an action that made everyone turn around and stare at him. Winthrope was busy smoking in the corner, a strange heady mixture that Joe had vaguely smelt somewhere before, in the back streets of Hong Kong. The pipe from which Winthrope smoked was handed to his left, to Fraser, who took a long drag from it. Joe noticed the blood drain from Fraser's face as the smoke was shot out of his nose. Fraser coughed and spluttered, causing hoots and giggles to fill the inside of the little hut.

Winthrope took the pipe and laid a hand on Fraser's chest. Together they breathed slowly and rhythmically, then Fraser's eyes rolled back into his head and he seemed to lose consciousness. His legs started twitching and his arms flapping by his side, like a fish. Joe had seen this once before, one early morning long ago by the harbour. The boy who had smoked the pipe that day did not return from wherever he had gone. That was different, however – the smoke that he had inhaled was cut with chemicals and other man-made poisons while this was fresh from Nature, in all her benevolent glory.

Fraser started dribbling slightly and sweating. One of the women in the hut shuffled over and began to wipe his chin. Joe could tell Lisa was getting concerned. She knew Fraser was not even used to strong liquor let alone whatever it was that was in the pipe. She kneeled and leaned across to the professor, then whispered in his ear. The professor glanced over at Fraser but merely nodded, sagely; whatever it was he was thinking, he was not about to let the rest of the village know.

Joe rushed over to where Fraser lay and placed a hand on his forehead. 'Is he OK?' Lisa asked and he could hear the worry in her voice.

'I think so. He shouldn't have been given this, whatever it is. He faints at the smell of whiskey.'

The girl beside Fraser gently leaned over and kissed his lips and the change was miraculous. Without fuss, the girl's breath had calmed Fraser. First his eyes flickered, then his legs and arms stopped twitching and then, as if waking from some strange sleep, he opened his eyes and smiled around the hut. Joe and Lisa sighed. Fraser could say only one word.

'Wow!'

The look on his face told Joe that wherever he had been, Fraser liked it and wanted more. He gazed upon Lisa, who slouched back against the wall of the hut, the sparks from the fire dancing around her hair, causing her to take on a holy glow. Joe realised he didn't care where he was or what he was doing as long as he could do it with Lisa. He thought back over his life in an instant and realised that, out of all the women he had known, the only name he could remember was Lisa's. Hers was the only face he ever wanted to see again. He wanted to do all those stupid things with her that he had never even considered with anyone else before, engagement, marriage ... he gulped a little and felt his heart beat faster ... kids.

No matter how stupid he told himself he was being, he could not bring himself to do what Winthrope was asking of him. This was not the way to start something big and pure, perhaps the purest thing he had ever embarked upon. He didn't care if it meant he would be shot, he was not going to aid in the repopulation of the village. He was not going to jeopardise his relationship with Lisa, possibly the only thing worth having in the world now. More precious even than the golden Buddha.

Lisa looked nervous. She had been watching Joe and had finally admitted to herself that the feelings she had for him were deeper than just the casual attraction she thought she had felt at first. As his eyes looked into the fire, she thought she saw all the pain and hurt he had ever suffered in his life mirrored on his face. He was such a boy really – but such a charming, brave, funny one that she knew she had fallen for him.

Beside her Winthrope clapped his hands. 'In an hour or so, gentlemen, I will retire to my hut and I will allocate you each a number of women for the night. However, this will be just the first of many nights. You can think of yourselves as Adams, ensuring that the human race continues in this small island of beautiful people. One day, there will be a whole village of happy smiling faces, just like Fraser's here. One day the island will be thriving again. I have ensured that you each have a hut. Joe, you can stay here; Fraser, you can go in the hut next to mine and, professor ... well, there is a small one on the outskirts, you can use that. Use these wisely, my friends, for I do think of you as friends now, and most of all...' He smiled a glinting smile that seemed to speak of many things. 'Have fun.'

Fraser leered, the professor looked nervous and Joe looked at Lisa and suddenly time slowed. He looked into her eyes and noticed for the first time that one was a slightly deeper brown than the other. It was hardly discernable and could perhaps have been put down to a trick of the light, but Joe noticed it and in noticing was made to wish for more things to know about Lisa. He wanted to know everything about her, every step she had ever made, every thought she had ever thought, every dream she had ever dreamed. He leaned over, pretending to feed the fire, and touched her foot. At first she recoiled but then, as if some current had passed between them, something unsaid but palpable, she relaxed and pushed her legs nearer his hand.

In the crowded hut, full of strangers and smoke, Lisa and Joe shared a moment of intimacy few could boast of in a lifetime. It was merely a touch, the briefest of glances, but it said more about human warmth and fragility than if they had been free to express their thoughts till dawn. As if the fire had connected them with its heat, they both sat back against their respective walls and breathed deeply, knowing that something important had been said without words.

At the allotted time, Winthrope snapped his fingers and the hut was emptied of everyone except Joe, Fraser, the professor and Lisa. Winthrope began to speak.

'You have made a very wise decision in accepting the hospitality of the village. I have known people who have merely wanted to take what they could get and be on the first plane out, but you have shown courage and respect, my friends. Thank you.'

225

The professor eased himself forward. 'Do you know this area well?' he asked.

'Do you know the streets where you live well? Do you know your house well, or your apartment? Well, that is how I know the jungle. I have been over most of it in my time, walking here and there, fishing, gathering food and water.'

The professor felt a little light-headed from the smoke he had inhaled earlier. He reached into his pocket. Lisa, realising what he was about to do, tried to stop him but he was insistent.

'I have here an important document,' the professor began, 'That I thought you might like to take a look at.'

The professor pulled the map from his pocket and handed it to Winthrope, who examined it casually. 'Yes, a map,' he said. 'I have seen many maps of this kind.'

The professor smiled. 'But it is a map of peculiar importance. It is a map of the island. Do you recognise any part of it?'

Winthrope studied it more closely. 'Perhaps,' he said. 'Whose map is it?'

There was silence in the hut for a moment, while the professor debated how much to tell him. Finally after what seemed like hours he spoke.

'Yamashita's. We think it was drawn for him by a man called Amichi. I knew, or at least had dealings with, his granddaughter. She wanted me to have it. She knew that I would look after it and serve her well.'

The professor bowed his head. Winthrope's eyes widened. He traced a line with his finger and with each inch it passed his face grew lighter and his smile broader. 'Yes, I think I do know this. I can't be sure – it has probably changed since this was written, but I am almost sure I recognise this high ground here. I'd say it was about two and a half miles away.'

The professor was suddenly energised. He shrugged the hazy feeling from his brain and sat bolt upright. 'Then, we must go,' he said. 'Right away, we must leave. There may not be much time to waste.'

Winthrope held his arm. 'It's night time, professor, we can't go now. Besides, you have an obligation to fulfil.'

The professor gulped. He had been hoping that Winthrope would forget about the deal that he had agreed to. It was not that he was scared of women, but he had never had much dealing with them before. Women to him were like mountain climbing: he could see the attraction and he knew why other men did it but, somehow, he could never be bothered. He smiled politely and sat back down. 'Of course,' he said. 'The deal.'

Winthrope looked around and caught sight of Joe; he reached across and squeezed one of Joe's biceps. 'We need muscle too, eh, Joe? We need the brains of the professor here, your muscle and Fraser's gentlemanliness, eh?'

Winthrope laughed. Joe turned to look at Lisa but she was looking away. He thought he saw a tear in her eye but it could have been the way the light hit her.

'Of course, there are rules that need to be obeyed here, the same as anywhere else; you must of course be respectful to the girl and to her successor, in order that the two don't meet. The door to the hut must remain closed while you are with a wife. If any of the wives see a closed door they will not enter and as soon as they have finished they will leave, making sure the door is left open for the next girl. You see how all these things have their own little rules that make them go swimmingly? Once you have mated with the girls you are free to do whatever you wish. Tomorrow we will test your map and seek out the tunnels but for now please, gentlemen, enjoy yourselves and be proud of your status as founding fathers. Professor, Fraser?

227

Would you like to follow me? Lisa, you can sleep in my hut tonight. You will be all right.'

Lisa followed the others out, leaving Joe alone in the hut. He flicked idly at the fire and watched as the flames sent up tiny sparks of light into the smoky air. Every thought in his head revolved around Lisa; not a second passed without it being filled with images of her. He would not have thought it of himself three weeks ago, he would not have it thought it possible but, there it was, it was true. Joe was in love.

He also hated what he was being asked to do. He knew that Lisa would never forgive him, and why should she? It was a poor way to show the woman you love what you felt about her. It was a strange way to declare your feelings for someone. He told himself, however, that it was not his fault. He was being made to do these things, he had no choice – his hands were tied. He doused the fire with some water from the bucket, hoping that this would stop him feeling quite so low. Perhaps if he could not see their faces it meant he was not as guilty, perhaps...

Outside he heard the sound of the village preparing itself for sleep. The occasional child let a cry go out that shook the jungle and caused it a moment's panic but eventually all was quiet. Joe got on his bed and lay there looking at the ceiling. He laughed to himself and thought what he would have made of this situation a month ago. It would, perhaps, have been the one thing he wished for, but meeting Lisa had changed him. He no longer felt as if he was alone, no longer felt the need to fight. He just wanted to see her, to be able to touch her, to be with her.

He closed his eyes. Perhaps if he could fall asleep they would never come. They would pass by his door on the way to the professor's or to Fraser's. The irony of the situation crashed in on him as he rolled over and stared into the darkness. He heard a sound outside his hut that he assumed was his first 'wife'. It was a nervous shuffling, as if eager to get in but afraid to do so. Joe rolled over to face the door but it was too dark to see. He called out but there was no reply. Slowly, the feet moved inside the hut; Joe steadied himself. He thought perhaps he could communicate with her, try and get her to say that they had done what was asked of them. After all, Joe thought, he was sure it was equally as uncomfortable for her. The shape in the darkness closed the door and moved over to his bed.

'Look,' Joe said to it. 'I think you are very nice and everything but I just don't think it's right for me to be doing this. I've been thinking a lot about someone else lately and I am sure that anything we could do might get in the way of that. I mean, I know it doesn't mean anything between us and that if I don't do whatever it is we are about to do, I'll get a bullet, but I think that maybe it's worth it. I mean, I have been a rogue in my life, phew, yeah, I have been with some women, but she's something else, you know? Pure and innocent, like no one else I have met and I don't want to ruin things. You see what I mean, don't you? Don't you?'

A hand slowly reached out in the darkness and touched Joe's lips, quietening them for a second. He began to lie back on the bed. 'Well, I think we should stop this, before it ... er ... starts.'

Joe felt a face next to his. It was soft and warm and he thought to himself that he should just close his eyes and think about Lisa, pretend it was Lisa. After all, she was a strong girl with a good head, she would understand the position he was in. He could tell her the next day that he had been thinking about her, that would be sure to make things better. He did not know if his reasoning was correct but it was all he had.

He felt a pair of lips kissing his ear and a voice began to speak. 'Quiet,' it said. Joe recognised it as Lisa's. 'I haven't got much time. I understand. We must keep Winthrope happy in order to get out, to find the gold. Do as he wants.'

Joe stammered a reply but was cut short by a kiss on his lips that seemed to take every breath he could ever have out of his body. He wanted this moment to go on forever, to never get dim and die. He made himself fully aware of everything that was happening, every sound he could hear, every feeling he was experiencing, every taste. Everything, so that in years to come he would be able to recall this moment exactly as it was.

Lisa drew back and passed a hand across Joe's face. Joe took it and held it to his lips. It felt so smooth and inviting. He just wanted to be near her now, to be with her.

'I have to go,' Lisa said with a giggle. 'Your first wife will be here any minute.'

There was a nervous laugh between the two for a moment, Joe went to speak but thought better of it; there would be time enough later, he thought, to tell her everything that was on his mind.

Joe was woken by the sound of screaming. Something was happening in the village. He rubbed his eyes and realised that it was still dark, but he could hear the sound of shouts and feet running outside his hut. Quickly he dressed and stuck his head out of the door. In the dim light of the village he saw flames being carried this way and that, and women waving their arms and screaming as if trying to chase an animal away.

Joe realised that something terrible and strange was happening. The looks on the women's faces as they passed his door were as if they had seen the devil himself and they ran as if they were being driven from hell. Every now and then a shot from the village's only gun would sound in the night, sending the animals of the jungle into a panic and waking everything and everyone within a five mile radius. Joe ventured out of his hut and joined a moving group of women as they shuffled to a hut on the furthest outskirts of the village.

There was a strange low murmuring and shuffling as the women made their way over the hard dry dirt to the hut that was clearly illuminated now by a number of torches, all of which jutted out of the walls. Joe was surrounded by women chanting and moaning gently to themselves. In the distance he saw others running and patting their heads in frustration. He didn't know what was going on but he knew that something was wrong – something was horrifically wrong.

Suddenly he saw Winthrope in the throng standing by the door of the hut. Joe pushed his way through the crowd and grabbed him by the arm. 'What the hell's going on?' Joe asked, and Winthrope turned. Joe had never seen a man so white. His face had been completely drained of blood and his eyes stared like those of a madman. Joe shook him. 'What's the matter? What's happening?'

Winthrope could only raise an arm and point at the hut in a manner that seemed all the more terrifying for its restraint, and Joe made his way to the door. Pushing through the crowd, Joe looked into the hut, and the sight that met his eyes made him gasp. He had seen a few things in the back streets of Hong Kong. He had seen his fair share of death and blood before – some of it had even been his – but as his eyes adjusted to the dim light of the hut and he began to make out the shapes in the darkness he could not believe that what he was witnessing could have been human once.

Blood stained the walls of the hut and sparkled slightly as more torches were brought in to illuminate the scene. Now Joe could quite clearly see the body of a young girl, no more than sixteen, lying on the floor, completely covered in blood and lying beside her what looked like a mass of intestines and organs. Her face, eyes wide open, stared at the ceiling as one of the other women knelt beside her cradling the foetus of an unborn child that could have been of no more than three months' gestation. The kneeling woman rocked gently and wiped the blood from the dead baby's face, kissed its head and passed a hand along the shoulder of its mother, who was alive but dying. The hut smelt of iron and bodily fluids or like the abattoir that Joe had visited once on the docks in Hong Kong. No animal has ever died in such pain or fear as the woman who lay on the floor in front of Joe, he could tell that from her face as she looked at him one last time, closed her eyes and breathed a deep sigh. Her chest stopped rising and falling and her arm by her side fell slightly as she died.

The kneeling woman began to cry, a loud wailing cry that sent shivers down the spine of every living thing in the area. In the quiet of the night the wail seemed to speak for everyone who had lost and who had known death, and Joe too wanted to cry, not perhaps for the girl or for her baby but for the sheer inhumanity of a life that had ended in this way. He staggered out of the doorway and grasped Winthrope by the arm. 'What the hell happened in there?' he asked, barely able to catch his breath.

The blood had returned to Winthrope's face and the two sat down under the warm glow of the torches. 'The manananggal,' Winthrope said. 'The villagers talk about it but I have never seen it until tonight. They come out at night and only when there is a pregnant woman near the perimeter of the village. Usually this girl sleeps with me, in my hut, but because of Lisa ... well ... she slept here. It starts with the sound, the flapping of wings, the others say they heard it over an hour ago, going from hut to hut looking for victims.'

'Is it an aswang?'

'A variety, yes. A shape shifter. Most of the time it resembles a legless woman and flies like the wind.'

Joe thought back to his vision of the aswang a few days earlier. He remembered how it had flown around the group, encircling them, paying special attention to Lisa.

'It has a long tube like tongue,' Winthrope continued, 'that it uses to enter the stomach of its victim and suck out the intestines and the foetus of the unborn child. It is an angry demon that does not stop until it gets what it wants. It drinks the blood and then eats the flesh if it is not driven off in time.'

Winthrope pushed a hand through his hair and Joe thought he saw what looked like blood on the sleeve of his shirt. 'Rumour has it that it can only be killed if you find its lower half, and put salt or garlic on it to stop it rejoining, but that's virtually impossible. You saw the power of the thing. You saw what it can do.'

Winthrope's head fell onto his knees and he began to weep silently. Joe noticed how the blood on Winthrope's shirt had stained only the underside of the arms. He wondered whether he perhaps he had been one of the first to examine the girl and had picked up the stains then – but why only the underside? Why so little blood anywhere else?

'If only I could have been near her,' Winthrope moaned. 'If only I could have saved her. She was my wife, after all.'

Joe placed a hand on Winthrope's shoulder and tried to comfort him the best he could. Beside him, the women of the village began to disperse, each one casting suspicious glances at Winthrope and Joe.

Winthrope began to pull himself together. He wiped his nose with his sleeve and realised that it was stained with blood. He quickly lowered his arm to his side and began to wipe it on the side of the hut that he sat against.

'You believe in the manananggal?' Joe asked.

'Of course. Do you think you could not believe after tonight? You have to believe. We all have to believe after tonight.'

'But most of all, these people believe?' Joe said, and Winthrope knew exactly what he was implying.

'Yes, they believe, why wouldn't they? They believe, their mothers did, their fathers did and their children will.'

'Yes, their children, they believe for their children.'

Winthrope was silent. Joe sensed a change in the balance of the world – suddenly everything was a little stranger, suddenly things were not as they seemed. As much as he told himself that the blood on Winthrope's shirt was from the woman as she lay dying, as much as he told himself that the spirits of the jungle really had killed her and taken her baby, and as much as he told himself that the village treated Winthrope as a god because he offered them wisdom and not fear, he still could not rid himself of the feeling that this was not the first time the aswang had visited this village at a time of crisis. He decided however to keep quiet, for the moment anyway. There was the gold to consider and Lisa and the rest of the party. He would watch, though, and listen, and see how things panned out.

Patting Winthrope on the back, Joe made his way back to his hut, opened the door and flopped down the bed. Every time he closed his eyes all he saw was the face of the woman staring at him as if she were imploring him to realise something, as if she were asking him one final question. He told himself that he had heard her, had understood what she was saying. The night was going to be long now and the morning seemed far off.

17

Dawn came fast in the jungle and life began early in the day. Joe was awoken by the sound of the village waking up and going about its everyday business, preparing bread, feeding children, watering animals and seeing to the myriad daily chores. His last 'wife' had left some hours before and Joe lay on his bed smiling to himself, thinking about the few brief moments he had spent alone with Lisa. There was a knock on the door and it burst open revealing Winthrope, smiling and holding a jug of water.

'How's my fine bull this morning?' he shouted, to which Joe smiled, saying nothing.

Winthrope acted as if the night before had not happened. In fact, as he woke up and felt the sunlight on his face, Joe wondered if it had.

'Here, have some water. The sun is up and breakfast is being prepared. We can go as soon as we're ready.'

Joe took the water and poured himself some into a cup as Winthrope exited. Through the muffled noises of the village Joe heard Winthrope knocking on the door of a hut he assumed to be either Fraser's or the professor's, for he heard the same jaunty greeting being given to another 'fine bull'. There was something about Winthrope that Joe did not like. It wasn't the threats or the sudden changes of mood that disturbed him or even the strange look that came over his face whenever he talked about his plan for a new Eden in the jungles of the island – it was something subtler, a hunch that just would not go away. He had met men like Winthrope before, men who had been given too much power, who had taken more than they were due and did not realise that, eventually, everything has to be paid for. Men like Winthrope always had one more card to play, always one more surprise to give.

He drank more of the water – it felt good and cold against the back of his throat – and, then, Lisa appeared at the door. The sunlight caused a halo of gold to be formed around her. She smiled a knowing smile that seemed half regretful.

'Thanks for last night,' Joe said. Lisa hung her head demurely.

'It's nothing,' she replied. 'Did you have a good time?'

Joe shrugged his shoulders. He hadn't. He felt lower than the bed he sat on but he wasn't going to bleat about it now; why change the habit of a lifetime and, after all, Lisa would never believe him anyway.

'What was all the noise about?' Lisa asked.

'I don't know, I stayed in the hut,' Joe lied. 'I guess there was some animal loose in the village or something. What time are we going?'

Lisa shrugged. 'Don't know, when everyone is ready, I guess. I just saw Winthrope going into my uncle's hut.' Lisa let out a sudden giggle. 'I think he may be in need of more than water this morning.'

Joe liked to see Lisa laugh. It made him feel good inside, as if the world was how it should be. He put an arm around her and she nestled her head on his shoulder. Just the feel of her allowed him to forget the events of the night before. As he closed his eyes and breathed in her smell he realised that he was not thinking about the face of the poor woman who lay in the hut but Lisa, in a better place than this, in Hong Kong or one of the other islands, laughing and smiling.

'I think...' he began, but Lisa put a finger to his lips.

'Let's just sit for a while,' she said.

In his hut Fraser was getting himself ready while his third 'wife' sat on the bed combing her hair. He looked around for his belt and could find it nowhere. He searched under the bed, in the small wooden box by the door, under his shirt, but it was missing. When he had almost given up, the girl on the bed shifted her thigh and produced it from beneath her leg, smiling. Fraser laughed and took it. It was still warm. He realised how comfortable he felt here, how he liked the women's sense of easy pleasure and fun. He had been pretty straight-laced most of life but here – here was different. There was nothing to hold you back, no conventions, no discernable regulations; nothing to stop you from doing what you felt was right, intrinsically, inside.

He took the comb from the girl, sat behind her and began to comb her hair. She was little surprised at first; this was the first time any male had combed her hair, but after a while she seemed to get used to it. She leaned back into Fraser's lap and lay there for what seemed like hours although it was in reality only a matter of minutes.

For his part, in his hut, the professor was grilling Winthrope as to the whereabouts of the gold. 'You say you know this place?' he asked, to which Winthrope nodded and said that he did but he could not be sure until he got there.

The professor nodded sagely. 'Yes,' he said. 'I see, I am like that in Hong Kong. I know it so well and yet only by sight. Once I get my bearings I am fine. You say we can go this morning.'

'Yes, when everyone is ready.'

There was an awkward silence for a moment.

'So how was your night?' Winthrope asked, whereupon the professor's face turned a brilliant shade of scarlet and he began to mumble and stutter.

'Well,' he said, 'I think ... er ... I think it was ... oh dear ... well, nice.'

Winthrope laughed a loud and hearty laugh, then slapped the professor on the back.

'Well, a few more nights of this and you'll get the hang of it, professor.'

The professor looked at Winthrope. 'A few more nights?'

'Yes.'

'I thought, I thought that was it.'

'Oh no, professor – you think our bargain was that one-sided? I need you here for at least – what do you think? Six months? Eden is not started in a day.'

Winthrope flung open the door of the hut and stormed outside in ebullient mood; the sunlight streamed into the hut, causing tiny flecks of dust to be illuminated. The professor saw Lisa walking towards him. He quickly drank the water left for him and joined her in the open air.

'We need to speak, Lisa,' he said in a hurry, and pulled her into the closest hut. 'I have just been talking to Winthrope. He insists that we stay here for months. He is determined to carry out his crazy plan to restock the village. Lisa, we can't stay here for months. We need to find the gold and then go.'

Lisa nodded in agreement. 'But the gun, uncle. I wouldn't trust Winthrope not to use it and Joe says the same thing. We need to be careful. We must not upset him.'

The professor thought for a while. 'We need to – how do they say it? Play it by ear for a while. We need to see how things progress. We are looking for the gold today. He seems to think he will be able to get his bearings once he is in the jungle, and I have no reason not to believe him. So, we'll just see how it goes. What do you think, Lisa?'

Lisa kissed her uncle's forehead. 'Yes, you're right. And how was last night?'

The professor turned red again and stammered. 'Well ... shall we go? I think the others may be ready by now.'

As they exited the hut, they realised that Fraser was arm-in-arm with one of the women and that he had taken his boots off. He strolled through the village looking for all the world like a younger version of Winthrope. Lisa waved to him and he raised a hand lazily in greeting.

'What's up with him?' the professor asked.

'I don't know, perhaps he likes it here,' Lisa offered.

The expedition party was organised. There were ten in all: Joe, Lisa, the professor, Fraser and Winthrope and five of the village women. They packed water and food into baskets and carried them on their backs, ready for the trip into the jungle. Before they left, Winthrope addressed the village in his usual manner, telling of his plans to come back in a few days and that until then they should keep him in their hearts. The women and children seemed to take this all in as if Winthrope had some special power over them. Fraser, beside him, nodded every now and then and clapped when he had finished.

Eventually, the party started to make their way into the jungle, tramping over its dense undergrowth and pushing their way through the grasping arms of the trees which snatched at their faces and pulled at their hair. The light streamed through the leaves and painted everything a golden green that seemed to transform the world, making it look as if it were being viewed through stained glass. The group moved in single file, being led all the way by Winthrope, who maintained a blistering pace. Very soon, Joe and Lisa began to lag behind. Every now and then they would assert themselves and catch up to the group but after a while they would find themselves slowing down again.

After about an hour, Winthrope raised his hand and the party stopped walking. He motioned to the professor to let him look at the map. Winthrope turned the piece of paper over in his hands, looking this way and that, scratching his head, turning the paper over and looking at the other side and squinting his eyes.

'Are we there?' the professor asked excitedly.

'No,' Winthrope replied. 'A little further.'

This happened five or six times more. Every time Winthrope would raise an arm calling for the map, then he would look at it intently, turning it over and over in his hands, then he would declare that this was not the place and begin to move off. It happened so often that Joe and Lisa began to think that Winthrope did not know where he was going at all.

The air was getting thick as it was nearing midday. Above them the sun beat through the leaves and made them perspire, draining their limbs of energy. Each step they took seemed to sap them of life as the group slowed down to a snail's pace. Even the women from the village were struggling. Winthrope began to consult the women around him. He would point in all directions and ask them questions but they would just shake their heads or shrug their shoulders.

This continued for almost an hour and all the while the sun beat down on their heads, causing the blood to pound in their temples and the sweat to pour from their skin. Joe and Lisa remained at the back of the group, content to let the others move on ahead, but Fraser stuck behind Winthrope, remembering the way they had come, etching it into his mind in case he should need it later. As they walked, Lisa felt her head began to get lighter and lighter. The events of the past few days began to catch up with her and she felt the world begin to spin. She tripped slightly and fell onto Joe's shoulders causing them both to stumble into the nearby trees.

Joe propped Lisa up and gave her some water from

the bottle that he wore around his waist. 'Are you OK?' he asked and Lisa nodded faintly, but she clearly wasn't.

'I think it might be the heat,' she said. 'I could do with a rest.'

Gently Joe sat her on the ground and ran after Winthrope and the others, but by the time he caught them up they were examining the map again.

'We need a rest,' Joe puffed. 'Lisa is really tired and needs to sit and rest for a while.'

'Hmmmm,' Winthrope murmured. 'I don't know, we're almost there, I think. Perhaps just over this ridge.'

He looked around self-importantly, barely being able to disguise the fact that he had no idea of where he was going, but eventually he agreed that it was high time the party had a rest, so a fire was made in a small clearing and some water was boiled. Joe fetched Lisa and sat her near the fire, stroking her hair and making sure she drank the tea that had been freshly made; the professor studied the map. Slowly he turned it in his hands, examining the landscape as he did so. He squinted and placed a hand over his eyes so he could see, then studied the map again.

Eventually he folded up the map and deposited it back into the pocket of his shirt. 'This may be my imagination,' the professor said to no one, 'But the ridge over there looks remarkably similar to the ridge on the map.'

Suddenly everyone turned. The professor was pointing to a ridge on the skyline that housed five trees.

'I mean, I could be wrong but it does look remarkably similar.'

Fraser jumped up and covered his eyes from the sun. 'You know,' he said, 'I think you may be right. Those trees – it's obviously different from the map but, looking at it, it looks so familiar it must be it.'

Fraser lunged forward only to upset the kettle into the fire to hoots of laughter from the women around his feet.

The professor jumped up and picked up one of the baskets at his feet.

'Come on,' he said, 'Before the sun starts to go down.'

Quickly the whole group packed up their meagre possessions and followed the professor through the jungle to the ridge that he had seen from the clearing and all the while Winthrope kept saying, 'I told you we were nearly there, I knew I had seen this place. Yes, this is the place, you can tell by the trees.'

Joe watched him intently. Every footstep he took, every word he said, Joe noticed. He had not forgotten the events of the night before, even if Winthrope had. He had not forgotten the look on the girl's face as she lay dying and the blood on Winthrope's shirt. Neither had he forgotten the fear and suspicion in the eyes of the women that had gathered around the dead girl's hut as they walked away – afraid, but not sure of what or of whom.

As they reached the top of the ridge, all the members of the group could feel their pulse and their heart rates rise; of course, they could not be sure that this was really the place depicted on the map but all those who had seen it agreed that if this wasn't the place it was somewhere very like it. One by one they helped each other up the sharp incline. Fraser strode up first, taking with him a basket under each arm and seeming re-energised by his stay in the jungle; the professor came after him, being helped up by three of the women, two of whom pulled him by the arms while another pushed him from behind. Winthrope followed, being helped up by the other women, and Joe and Lisa brought up the rear.

The jungle suddenly became quiet. It was as if the animals and the birds shared in the group's anticipation as they rounded the top of the ridge, placed their hands on its apex and gazed with open eyes and open mouths at what was on the other side.

'Well, where is it?' Joe asked, pushing his way through. 'All I see is more damn jungle.'

But the professor was studying the map. He raised his hands and shielded his eyes from the sun that was now beating down into his face. He scratched his head. 'I don't know,' he said finally. 'I'm not sure it's here.'

Fraser snatched the map away from him and examined it himself. 'We could try over there by that small clearing – you see where the earth's a little darker than anywhere else?'

'Yes, of course, the soil would be darker where it was less impacted, even after sixty years. You may be right Fraser.'

The group moved off; they slowly made their way down the ridge, passing the baskets to each other and helping each other down. Winthrope made sure he was right at the head of the group by Fraser as they moved towards the clearing. By the time they got there the sun had sent a pure shaft of light through the trees to where they were standing and it felt as if the sky were guiding their way.

Fraser dropped his basket and pulled at a small sapling that grew from the ground; he began to poke it into the earth, testing it for solidity. Joe too began to scratch around, moving the undergrowth out of the way and thumping at the jungle floor with his fist.

'I don't even know what I'm looking for, professor,' he said after a while.

The professor thought for a moment. 'I have seen another tunnel, in Thailand,' he began. 'The entrance was set into what looked like a sheer face, like a hill or small mountain. The years had put trees and moss on it so it looked like part of the surrounding environment. I doubt very much whether we will find it in the ground – it's much more likely to be...' He stopped for a moment and slowly turned. 'In a ridge.'

As one, the whole group turned and looked at the ridge that they had just so diligently traversed. Slowly, as if not wanting to deny his suspicions, the professor removed the map from his pocket. He unfolded it and held it up to his eye. When it was at the correct height the professor could see that the small intricate drawing exactly matched the landscape of the ridge and its immediate environment. He checked the map again, noting the highlighted area which spelled out Sakura Sakura. He knew that this meant cherry blossom but there were no cherry trees in the area. He had heard the rumour that one of the Japanese royal family, Prince Takeda, had been involved with Yamashita, and that one of his favourite songs was *cherry blossoms*. He could feel his heart pound and his breath get quicker. Small beads of sweat began to form on his neck and he could sense his legs growing weak.

'I think we have it,' he said, and as he did so a wind which sounded like a million wings flapping in the air blew through the jungle and encircled the group. The trees swayed silently and wisps of grey smoke fluttered like butterflies through the leaves; some of the women villagers grew afraid and tried to leave but Winthrope held them by the arm and pinned them to the spot. The group suddenly felt the earth tremble and the sky blacken. All around them the air grew colder and seemed to enclose them. Joe began to feel his skin tighten and the hairs on the back of his neck stand on end. He looked around him and through the dim light of the jungle saw an old woman floating through the trees. She raced up to him at breakneck speed and then disappeared, leaving only her scent and thin traces of hair wrapped around his shoulders.

As quickly as it came, the darkness and the breeze disappeared and the group found themselves in the bright sunlight again. For a moment they stood in silence, not daring to move or look at each other, but eventually the professor made his way to the ridge and began to search its surface with his bare hands.

'Come on,' he said. 'Come on, help me. We need to feel our way along it. Look for something, anything.'

The rest of group began to feel their way along the ridge. They laid their hands flat on its surface and, one by one, made their way along its entire length but they found nothing. Thinking that perhaps they had missed something the first time round, once they had finished they turned round and did the same in the opposite direction, but still after an hour there was nothing to be found. Almost as one they fell to the floor, their backs against the ridge and let out a collective sigh of disappointment.

Above their heads, they could tell that the sun was going down. They knew that pretty soon it was would be dark and there would be no chance of finding the entrance to the tunnel, so Lisa and Joe were sent to gather wood for a fire while the others set up what little camp they had.

Away from the group Lisa and Joe felt as though they could breathe properly at last.

'Do you think there's something up with Fraser?' Lisa asked in a quiet moment.

Joe thought for a minute. 'Yeah, I think he's fallen in with this life. I think he's fallen under the spell of Winthrope – a dangerous thing to do in my opinion.'

'Ah, he's not so bad.'

'Did you hear that screaming last night?'

'Yeah.'

'That was no animal.'

'What do you mean?' Lisa asked incredulously.

'Well, I'm not one to speak out of turn but, let's just put it this way, Winthrope had blood on his shirt and I am sure it didn't come from any animal bite.'

Lisa was shocked. 'He didn't kill someone?'

Joe shrugged his shoulders. 'Hey, look at that dead tree sticking out over there. Do you think we should get that? It's a big one but it will probably last all night.'

The two walked absent-mindedly over to the trees that jutted out of the ridge at a sharp right angle. Joe placed a hand upon its trunk and began to pull but it wouldn't budge.

'I think maybe it's more alive than I think,' he laughed. 'Probably more alive than me right now.'

Lisa grabbed him by the waist and began to pull also. They tugged and tugged at the branch until all four of their hands began to burn and tear. Joe placed a foot on the ridge to give him better leverage and arched his back, straining every muscle. Eventually with a pop, the tree came out of the ridge and sent them both flying backwards. Joe landed on Lisa with a thump, knocking the wind out of her body and covering her in loose divots of earth. Joe began to laugh out loud. Suddenly all of the tension he had been feeling for the last week or so was let loose and he let out a manic screaming laugh that Lisa thought would go on forever. His eyes bulged and his chest puffed out in crazy giggles as he picked himself up and stood over Lisa watching her brush the last of the ridge off her clothes.

Lisa, however, wasn't laughing. She was staring at the ground open-mouthed, her eyes wide with horror. On the end of the small sapling tree that Joe held in his hand, forming part of the roots that had grown around and inside it, was a human skull, turned a strange yellow by the earth and the vegetation. Lisa pointed at it, hardly able to speak until Joe, realising something was wrong, glanced down.

18

Joe raced to the others who were by now setting up camp. 'Come! Come!' he shouted, hardly able to say the words. Luckily, Lisa had followed behind him and managed to explain the situation in a clear and concise manner. The professor dropped his water flask and rushed over to where the tree now lay on the ground.

He picked up the skull and examined it closely. 'I would say this was buried in the last sixty years or so,' he announced after a while. 'Certainly in the last hundred. I'd say the person was a man and probably Asian. He could well have been part of Yamashita's group.'

He handed the skull to Winthrope, who held the skull up to the fading light. 'There's no sign of any damage, but there is slight marking to the bone, as if something has been growing in and around it.'

'The tree had grown into it,' Lisa explained. 'Just a small tree – look.'

She held up the tree for the others to see.

Winthrope began to look at the sky.

'There's absolutely no point in trying to search for anything in this fading light. We have to set up camp and start tomorrow.'

The professor looked heartbroken and began to speak but thought better of it. 'Yes, you're right,' he concluded. 'The gold has been there for over sixty years now. One more night won't make any difference.'

* * *

That night the aswang were busy in the jungle. As Joe and the professor closed their eyes to sleep they made their way silently through the trees and entered their heads where they made them dream of dark deep tunnels that led nowhere but had to be walked down.

Joe found himself in a small room with no doors and no windows. It was cold and the ground was hard underfoot. He reached up and touched his chest and felt blood there but there was no pain, just a freezing cold that seemed as if it might go on forever. He began to search around the room but found nothing. Then he heard a voice, it was a sweet voice and familiar – Lisa's voice. She was calling to him from outside the room and he could barely hear her. He moved over to the wall and placed an ear against it. Yes, it was her, he could hear her, she was calling him. He shouted to her but he knew she could not hear. He shouted again but still knew that it was useless.

His voice began to fade and he called out 'No!' – he did not want her to go. He wanted her here beside him. He wanted to touch her and to hold her and to tell her that everything was going to be all right, but her voice just got dimmer and dimmer, softer and softer until he could hear it no longer.

He began to bang on the wall with his fists and shout to her until his throat and hands ached. If it was the last thing that he did, he wanted to see Lisa again. He kicked the wall and pounded it again and again but no matter what he did, no matter how hard he tried the wall would not budge. He was trapped inside and she was outside.

Joe woke up to find that the rest of the group were still asleep. The first thing he did was to glance over at Lisa and was relieved to see her breathing gently, her soft breaths making wisps in the cold night air. He leaned over, tucked the blanket that covered her over her shoulders and began to gather wood for the fire. He looked up and saw the first rays of the sun dancing over the trees, sending scudding waves of light into his eyes. He thought to himself that never before had he experienced a place so beautiful and yet so utterly isolating, where one minute he felt like a king and the next he felt like nothing.

He stoked the fire and watched as one by the one the party began to wake.

When everyone had woken they made their way along the ridge to where Joe had pulled out the tree the night before. They stood in a circle and examined the hole. It was about as big as a dinner plate and looked as though it might collapse at any minute. The professor moved closer and looked further in. 'There's not much there,' he said. 'Looks like we might have to move some of the earth and ... er ... the rest of our friend here.'

Joe and Fraser set about digging into the hole with their bare hands and it wasn't long before the rest of the body, which was nothing but bones and rags, came out of the tunnel entrance. Winthrope kicked at the skeleton with his boot.

'Yes, looks like Imperial Army to me. I've seen that uniform before,' he said, and squatted down to shake some of the dirt away from the scraps of material that still clung to the bones like some eerie woven skin. Winthrope motioned to two of the women and they ran forward, picked up the skeleton and moved it away. Joe and Fraser were grasping at handfuls of earth and passing them through their legs. With each handful the smell got worse. It was clearly the smell of death and stale air. It hit everyone's noses and turned their stomachs.

'There's an entrance,' Joe said, and furiously scrambled at the earth with every last drop of energy he had in his body. After about five minutes of digging, they had fought their way through to a small wooden door set into the ridge. Its surface was covered in earth and insects and the roots of plants that had attached themselves to it over the years. Joe brushed it clean.

'Is there anything on it?' Lisa asked. Fraser looked at it closely but decided that the door was just a door – a bit damp, a bit dark but just a door.

'Let's get it open,' the professor said, and barged his way through.

'Hang on a minute,' Winthrope said. 'You have no idea what is on the other side. There could be anything. I have heard they booby-trapped all of these tunnels, with bombs, with sharpened staffs, with anything. We'd better be careful.'

The professor thought for a moment and then agreed wholeheartedly. Quickly Lisa ran into the jungle, to return a few minutes later with a long green vine. She tied one end to the door and carefully walked backwards until she was well out of range. 'All we need to do now,' she said, 'Is pull, then if anything happens we'll be all the way over here.'

So Joe, the professor and Fraser grabbed hold of the vine and started to pull. Suddenly there was a crack and the whole door came off its hinges. Moving closer to it they could see that its reverse side had been almost stripped of its surface patina by what looked like fingernail marks; someone had been desperately trying to get out. Gingerly, the professor put his head through the doorway then recoiled sharply. He clutched his throat and clawed at his face, his skin began to turn purple as he gasped for air and his eyes became bloodshot.

'Gas!' he managed to shout through the pain. 'Gas, in the tunnel.'

Joe quickly pulled out a handkerchief and placed it over his face. He then tore a piece of his shirt off, grabbed a water flask from one of the villagers and started to wipe the professor's face. Gradually, he calmed down. Joe

251

encouraged him to breathe easily until finally the professor lay on the jungle floor looking up at the sky, breathing deeply in and out and feeling the colour return to his face.

'Was that a trap?' Winthrope asked.

'Could have been,' the professor said. 'Or could be just natural gas. There are a lot of bodies in there. We'd better wait a while before we go in there with torches, just in case.'

The group made masks from their clothing and any other scraps of material they could find and busied themselves while they were waiting by making torches from short thick branches and dry twisted leaves. After an hour or so, the professor once again put his head into the tunnel, this time readying himself for a quick exit if need be. It was not necessary, however, as after thirty seconds of sniffing and breathing he turned round and smiled at the rest of the group. It was OK.

Slowly and with caution, the group all entered the tunnel. The professor went first, followed by Fraser, then Joe and Lisa, then Winthrope, then the village women. As they moved, each one of them felt the sides of the tunnel with their hands and noticed how cold it was and how it felt like nowhere on earth. About three metres in the light suddenly faded and the professor decided it was time to try to light one of the torches. Joe was passed one by the villagers and he carefully raised a lighter to its end. Thankfully after a few sparks, the torch burst into flames and illuminated the inside of the tunnel and the group could look around them.

Joe and the professor shuddered. Only they knew that it was exactly what they had seen in their dreams. The walls of the tunnel rose up and met at an apex just above their heads and their surface was covered in small gnarls and pick marks. The floor was uneven and littered with bones that looked as though they might have been scattered by some animal at some point in the past. From the way they had come, a thin shaft of light shone in through the door. From the way that they had to go there was only blackness. Lisa reached out and clutched Joe's hand. This was what she had wished for for weeks and now it was here she wished she were somewhere else.

They continued to walk along the tunnel until they came to an intersection that was being guarded by another dead soldier. Fraser examined him.

'Looks like he's been shot. Look – there's a bullet hole in the back of his skull.'

'Possibly killed by his commanding officer,' the professor said, 'Who may well have been who we met by the door.'

Joe suddenly said with a start, 'Professor, look at this! This tunnel looks as though it has been bricked up. Now, why do you think they did that?'

The professor moved over to where Joe stood and shone a torch over it. 'To hide something?' he said and the two looked at each other for a moment. 'This must have been their last act before they were themselves shut in. Look, the last brick at the top has still to be put in.'

The professor was right. Towards the top of the tunnel, in amongst the bricks there was a single gap the size of the last one that had yet to be put in its place.

'We can use that as a starting point,' Joe said, and began to pull at the wall. Fraser darted forward and began to help and together the two of them started to dismantle the wall. They pulled and pulled, occasionally turning round and depositing bricks onto the floor of the tunnel until the wall that blocked their path was nothing but a heap of broken rubble.

The group made their way through the hole in the wall and found themselves in a large underground room that had a huge stone block in its centre.

'The gold must be inside that block,' Fraser said to no one.

He moved closer to the block and gently tapped at it. The professor stepped forward and touched it, feeling nothing. Winthrope did the same and for a while each member of the group had their hands on the block, assessing it, testing it, trying it out. Suddenly there was an explosion and the world seemed to erupt in light. Two of the village women recoiled in horror as they realised their flesh had been ripped open and their limbs severed by its force.

'Mines!' Joe shouted and rushed over to the woman who had been thrown back against the wall of the room and sat moaning and dying. 'Jesus, everyone else watch out.'

Quickly Winthrope organised for the two women to be taken out of the tunnel by the other villagers although he could see that they would not even make it to the entrance. For a moment the group watched them disappear and it began to dawn on them exactly what they were up against here. This was a place of death and pain, a place from which none of them would escape entirely unscathed.

Lisa suddenly shouted in excitement. 'Look – the explosion has blown a hole in the block. There are steps leading downwards. We must be going in the right direction.'

Joe stopped her from getting closer to the block. 'You'd better be careful,' he said, holding her by the arm. 'I don't want any more accidents.'

Carefully the professor stuck his head into the hole and asserted that it was safe for everyone to clamber into the hole and move carefully down the steps. The steps led them downward for only a few metres into another darkened room, this time a lot smaller and a lot colder. Lisa shuddered as she breathed the stale air. Fraser flashed the torch around the room and realised they were surrounded by wooden crates, stacked right up against the ceiling.

'This could be it,' Fraser said and the professor dropped to his knees. He had never fully believed he would get here – he had thought that this day would never come. He closed his eyes and gave a prayer to whatever god was watching over him at this moment.

Winthrope lunged forward and began to scrabble at the boxes with his fingernails. 'Come on, then!' he said. 'This is Yamashita's gold. Let's get it and get out of this place.'

Winthrope ripped open the lid of the nearest box and the sight that greeted him took his breath away. As if illuminated by some magical internal radiance the whole room seemed to grow suddenly lighter. Winthrope held his breath for a moment and let the sight sink in but the professor pushed past him. He reached a hand into the box and pulled out a shining gold ingot.

'These bars come from Cambodia,' the professor said, holding one up to the torch.

'I don't care where they've come from, I know where they're going,' Winthrope replied, snatching the ingot back and throwing it into the box with the others.

'These need to go to their rightful owners,' the professor said, but Winthrope began to pull boxes out from the pile and stack them by the steps.

'Well, you can do what you like with your share, professor, I know what I'm doing with mine.'

'Your share!' Joe shouted. 'Who said you had a share! You struck a bargain with us.'

'I'm not greedy,' Winthrope said. 'Just an equal share like the rest of you.'

'He might be right,' Fraser interjected.

'But he's been useless the whole way through,' Joe said. 'Why the hell does he get a share?'

Lisa tried to calm him down but it was no use. Joe began to pull back the boxes that Winthrope was stacking. There was sudden animosity in the tunnel and Lisa could feel the temperature begin to rise. She would have been grateful for more warmth, but not this hostility, not here.

The professor put himself between Winthrope and Joe. 'Gentlemen, gentlemen, remember where you are. This is a place of deep sadness. Do not make it more so. There is bargaining to done later but first we must get this to the outside.'

Joe and Winthrope agreed and one by one the group hauled the boxes back up the stairs, through the tunnels and out into the open. When all but one of the boxes had been removed Joe stood in the empty room, alone, and a strange sensation came over him. In the dim light of the room he saw shapes appearing. They were barely discernible at first but after a while they began to manifest themselves into recognisable forms. All of a sudden he made out the boy in his dreams.

'You!' he said to the shape, but it could not hear him. It took him by the arm and led him across the room to where the last box stood. The shape knelt down beside it and beckoned to Joe to push it to one side. As he did so he saw a hole behind it – a hole barely big enough to get his shoulders through but somehow, for some reason, Joe squeezed through.

As he did so Joe came out into a small alcove that was pitch black. He quickly lit a match and saw in front of him the golden Buddha sitting with legs crossed and with its hands placed peacefully on its knees. Suddenly Joe knew why he had been brought here and he understood the visions in his dreams. He knew everything. He turned, expecting to see the boy who shown him the way but was instead alone in the room, the silence only broken by the sounds of the others returning to the room behind him.

Joe broke through the wall and made the hole big enough to drag the statue through with Fraser's help. The professor stood and stared in awe at the statue.

'It's beautiful,' he said. 'I think it comes from one of the Hong Kong islands, perhaps Lantau. I have a feeling it is from the Po Lin monastery. I don't know why but ... I just seem to know. It must have been stolen by the Japanese and brought here.'

'How much is it worth?' Winthrope asked, but Joe declared suddenly and with venom, 'It's not for sale! I'm taking it back.'

'You're joking! Think of the money you could make.'

'It goes back to Hong Kong!' Joe shouted.

'Well, what about my share?'

Joe took Winthrope by the collar and brought their faces close together. 'You can have whatever you want of the rest,' he sneered. 'You can keep my share. I only want this and it goes back to the monastery.'

'Well, if you do, they won't reward you for it.'

'Maybe not.'

'Well,' Winthrope said with a shrug. 'It's your life.'

Joe began to haul the golden Buddha up the stairs alone until Lisa ran forward, took a corner of the base and helped him. Together they slowly inched it up the stairs, along the tunnel and out into the open air. Once out it looked more beautiful than ever and Joe could not take his eyes from it as they stood it gently on the green of the jungle undergrowth.

Behind them the others were exiting with the last of the gold. They were sweating and puffing but smiling as they dumped the boxes on the ground near to the Buddha.

'All my life I've chased money,' Joe said. 'It's never got me anywhere. I'm still as poor and stupid as I ever was.'

Lisa laid an arm around his shoulder and rested her head upon it.

'I need to do this thing to make amends,' he told her. 'To try to do something good for once, to try and set things straight and put things right.'

He stepped up to the Buddha and placed a hand on his head. He noticed that it rocked a little as if loose so inquisitively he pushed it, then rocked it, then pushed it some more. Eventually the head of the Buddha came loose revealing a hollow space inside that was filled with precious stones and gold coins. Joe darted a hand in and pulled out a fistful of them, letting them run through his fingers and fall back into the cavity. 'There must be a million dollars worth in here,' he said to Lisa. 'And it's beautiful, it's all beautiful.'

There was a snap in the trees that seemed to reverberate around the whole island and the group looked round in unison. There, standing above their heads on the ridge that they had climbed over the day before, stood three figures: Tanaka, Kono and the Japanese corporal.

'It is indeed beautiful,' Tanaka said, smiling and aiming his gun at the group. His eyes were flashing widely and the yellow of his teeth was clearly visible in the strong light of the early morning. 'I do thank you for finding it for me and I thank you even more for bringing out into the open.'

The professor began to lunge forward but Joe grabbed him by the arm and stopped him.

'Yes, it would be very unwise to do that, professor,' Tanaka said. 'After all, you are not a young man any more but you still have a lot to live for.'

'Why are you doing this?' Lisa implored. 'At least allow us to take some of these things back to the museum or back to the monastery where they belong.'

'Your words are admirable, my dear, but I'm afraid they are a little romantic for me. I am a simple fellow, you see, and I like to wrap things up cleanly and neatly.'

The group was stunned into silence. Lisa began to speak to the two men standing either side of Tanaka. 'All we want is to take this back to the rightful owners. They come from poor communities that were raped and plundered by the Japanese army. It may have been war but it is a war that is over. There are no sides any more. There are no winners and losers, there is only right and wrong now.'

The corporal beside Tanaka turned his head at this. He looked at Lisa. 'There are still orders to be carried out,' he said brusquely.

'There are no more orders,' Lisa said.

'Yamashita ordered,' the corporal said.

'Yamashita's dead,' the professor replied. 'He died after the war. The war is over, time has passed and there is no fighting any more.'

The corporal looked stunned and opened and closed his mouth trying to find words.

'There are no American planes any more – you must have noticed. There are no uniforms here, no spies.'

Suddenly the truth of the situation hit the corporal and he fell to his knees. All of a sudden the one thing that had kept him alive now came crashing down around his ears. He began to weep softly into his hands, sniffing loudly and breathing more and more deeply as the tears stained his uniform a deep dark beige.

'Get up, fool!' Tanaka shouted and kicked him like a dog, but the corporal was a broken man. He rolled over and lay face down on the ridge, weeping into the ground.

Joe went to pick up the jewels that flowed out of the golden Buddha, but Tanaka spun round and stopped him in his tracks. 'I wouldn't touch that if I were you. It could be very, very bad for your health.'

Joe froze. He had been in this position a number of times in his life and he knew there were only two things you can do: you either stand still and hope that the other

doesn't kill you or you lunge at them ... and still hope
that the other guy doesn't kill you. Either way there was
a chance you would end up with a bullet in you. The
ratio was three to two. Three times in his life he had
lunged, twice he had stood still; he decided to make it
three all and did not move.

Tanaka was enjoying the power he had over the group.
He shot into the ground near one of the village women
and sent her running into the undergrowth. Tanaka laughed
to see her run and gave her a final shot in the back
dropping her to the floor.

'That was a warning to you all,' he said. 'We are in the
middle of nowhere, are we not? There is no law out here.'

'Who the hell is this?' Winthrope asked, but there was
silence. Everyone was waiting for Tanaka to speak. They
knew that he was in control now; they knew that he gave
the orders.

He nodded to Kono. 'Go and pick up the gold.'

Kono shrugged and sighed wearily then trudged down
the ridge to where the boxes lay. As he got to the bottom
his eyes met Lisa's.

'You don't have to do this,' she said to him, sensing
the trepidation in his demeanour. 'This gold should go
back to the people it rightfully belongs to. You don't have
to go along with this.'

Kono turned his face away as if her words were painful
to hear, as if they spoke to something very fundamental
within him. He picked up a box of gold and heaved it
to the top of the ridge. As he got to the top Lisa shouted
out to him, 'You don't have to do this.'

Tanaka pointed his gun at Lisa. 'Shut up!' he shouted.

Lisa stepped forward, all the time feeling the gun trained
upon her. Joe clutched at her arm and tried to pull her
back but she moved forward anyway, not caring for Tanaka
or the weapon that he held in his hand.

'You don't have to rob the people of their history again. It was done once, don't let it happen again. This is our chance to put right the wrong that was done to them. This is our chance to give something back and to make sure history is not repeated.'

Tanaka scowled at her. 'Shut up! Shut up or I'll damn well shoot. Do you think I care who or what you are? Do you think I won't shoot the whole lot of you?'

Kono was making his way down the ridge again for more boxes of gold as Lisa implored him. 'Take the gold if you want. Take it all but leave the Buddha. The Buddha is a sacred object, someone's image of eternity; it should not be bought and sold on the market to the highest bidder. It belongs to the people who made it, who invested it with their thoughts and their prayers.'

Tanaka spat on the ground. 'Take the Buddha!' he ordered. 'Take the Buddha!'

Kono closed his eyes momentarily and he was in the tunnel again; there was pain all around him and he wanted it gone. He didn't care any more about the money, about the respect of his father, about Tanaka – he just wanted the pain to be gone. Then he saw her, the girl in the temple, her face as he had killed her. She was nothing to him, she hadn't harmed him or done him any wrong and yet he had killed her because of an order.

Kono heard a shot hit the ground near his feet.

'Get the Buddha!' Tanaka barked through gritted teeth and Kono bent down slowly to pick it up.

'You don't have to do this,' Lisa shouted, and made a move towards him. Tanaka fired a shot over her head and sent her tumbling to the ground; seeing this Joe leaped forward and made a grab for the gun, only to hear the sound of it firing and feel the sting of hot metal hit him. He recoiled with the shock and suddenly everything was happening in slow motion. The clouds stopped moving in the sky, the jungle stopped breathing and the only sound that could be heard was the echo from the crack of the bullet that had struck him in the chest.

He landed on the ground with a thud and the first thing he felt was Lisa's hand on his head, stroking his hair and the whispering of her voice as it played gently in his ear. 'Don't die, Joe, don't die.'

The world was growing colder and seemed to be getting further away. In his head he saw the woman from his dreams motioning to him; he didn't want to go with her but he knew he must. Everything in him wanted to stay with Lisa but he knew she was somewhere else now. She was outside of the room and he was inside – there was a wall between them now.

Lisa was trying to stem the blood that pumped from Joe's chest. She frantically held a piece of her own clothing over it to stem the bleeding but it was no good – the more she tried the harder it got until her hands were stained red and felt warm.

Tanaka grinned and aimed his gun at Lisa. 'I hate to see two people divided. Perhaps you should join your boyfriend.' He pulled the trigger. But it slammed down to silence – the chamber was empty. In frustration he threw it away and barked an order at Kono.

'Kill the bitch!' he shouted. 'Let her go with her boyfriend.'

Kono dropped the golden Buddha and moved towards Lisa. As he looked up, he saw her kneeling by Joe's body, covered in Joe's blood, and for an instant was transported back to the temple and the girl. He closed his eyes, but the image would not go away. No matter how hard he tried the face of the girl came back to him – her eyes looking at him, her mouth opening as the last breath left her body and she died. He would not let it happen again. He could not let it happen again. There had been too many deaths, too much suffering, and now it was time to end it.

Kono felt a strange revelation taking place in his mind; the spirits of the jungle were in him. With fire in his eyes, he ran up the ridge and grabbed Tanaka, who struggled lamely in his grasp. Kono cried out like an animal in pain as he lifted Tanaka off his feet and held him in the air; Tanaka kicked but found he was no longer able to reach the ground. He desperately struggled as he felt the last vestiges of air being squeezed from his body and his face turned a deep shade of purple. Tanaka made a last lunge at Kono's neck but it was no use. Kono shook the other man and, with a crack that was clearly audible from several feet away, broke his back and let his body fall, like a crumpled pile of clothing to the earth.

Joe felt himself in some other place, a place where he had been before. He recognised it from a dream he had once had. He knew he was safe here, he knew that he would be safe for ever. All the running he had done in his life was coming to an end and he knew that here was where he wanted to be more than anywhere else in the world.

'We need to get him to the village quickly,' Winthrope said. 'We need to get him to the holy woman.'

'The holy woman?' the professor said. 'What this man needs is a hospital and a doctor.'

'Fine,' Winthrope said mockingly. 'You just call for one and I'll stay here. Come on, help me with him, we need to get him there quickly.'

Fraser and Kono picked Joe up and began to carry him to the village while the other members of the team sadly collected the bodies of the three unlucky women or hoisted some of the gold upon their shoulders and followed them. The rest would have to be collected later.

The hut of the holy woman was a little way from the

rest of the village and as they approached it the whole group began to feel nervous and afraid. Joe was still conscious and murmured to himself as they hoisted him over the threshold and lay him on the floor. The woman lit a pipe and began to chant. She blew smoke over Joe's body and passed a hand just above his chest, intoning as she did so. Without taking her eyes off him, she spilled hot wax from a candle on to a silver dish plate. The drying wax seemed to take the shape of Joe's face agonising in his battle between worlds, as the smoke seemed to engulf him and enter into his every pore, transforming his corporeal body into something dreamlike and magical. Lisa thought she could see his spirit desperately trying to free itself only to be caught by the smoke that surrounded him.

It was a fight between life and death, between the forces that want to snatch a soul away and those that want to keep it on earth to feel, to breathe and to live. Lisa could see that Joe was fighting for all he was worth. She knew that he did not want to leave her now they had found each other; she knew he was desperately battling not for his sake but for hers.

The holy woman blew more smoke and Joe began to feel a warmth around him. Suddenly there was a light behind his eyes and everything seemed alive again. Suddenly something was calling to him just like in his dream. The woman reached forward and placed her hand on Joe's chest; she closed her eyes, blew more smoke in his direction and violently pulled the bullet from his flesh. It was lifted up triumphantly and then dropped on to the floor where it sat, a harmless shard of metal.

Joe began to feel his legs and his arms again. Something was pulling him back to life; something was making him swim against the tide. He opened his eyes and the light streamed in. Lisa reached over and kissed his forehead and the world had begun again. The holy woman smiled and said something to Winthrope, who translated.

'She said you must rest for a few days but you will be fine. She said it was lucky it didn't go in any further, or else she wouldn't have been able to do anything at all.'

Lisa hugged Joe's head and cried a single tiny tear that fell onto his cheek and seemed to stay there.

19

After a few days' rest Joe was up and about ready for the trek homeward. He emerged from the hut where he had been sleeping under the watchful eye of Lisa only to be greeted by Fraser wearing the typical garb of he villagers. Joe could barely contain his amusement.

'You're not taking that back with you, are you?' he asked.

'No,' Fraser replied.

'That's a relief. I would not want to go walking through the streets of Hong Kong with you dressed like that.'

'I'm not coming back,' Fraser said. 'I'm tired of Hong Kong, of London, of New York. Those places are nothing to me any more. I belong here, here in the jungle with my wives and Winthrope.'

'But Winthrope's not to be trusted. There are things about him that you don't know.'

Joe longed to tell Fraser about his experience of a few nights before but thought better of it. 'Just be careful is all I am saying. Jesus!'

Joe suddenly ducked behind Fraser. He had caught sight of Kono striding through the village looking for all the world like a giant. He strode up to Fraser and shook his hand.

'The plane's already packed with the bars and the Buddha.'

Joe came out from his hiding place. 'The plane?'

'Yes,' Fraser explained. 'The plane Kono and Tanaka came in on; it's over the other side of the island. They've been waiting for you to get well enough to be able to fly it back. You have Kono to thank that you're still here at all. If it wasn't for him you'd be dead out in the jungle.'

Kono extended his hand but Joe, wary, recoiled. Fraser grabbed Joe's arm and forced his hand into Kono's, whereupon they both shook.

'I guess I should say thanks.'

Kono seemed a little embarrassed at this. 'It's nothing,' he said. 'Let's just say it was all part of the service.'

After packing what little things they had, the group prepared to say farewell to the village. Lisa hugged Fraser as they were about to leave.

'Are you sure you're doing the right thing?' she asked, to which Fraser shrugged his shoulders.

'Who knows?' he said, and smiled.

The corporal led the way through the jungle to where the plane was moored just off the beach. Joe climbed in and began to check the instruments. He noticed there was a thin sheen of blood on some of them.

'Tanaka's doing,' Kono explained.

'He was some guy, that boss of yours,' Joe said.

It was a squeeze getting the professor, Lisa, Kono and the gold into the plane but they managed it and the corporal shut the door, happy with the group's promise to send another in a few days to pick him up and take him back to Japan. Joe started the engine and it started first time. They taxied along the water for a few metres and then began to pick up speed.

'I have no idea if this tub is going to take off with all this weight,' he said,

'You'd better hold your breath.'

The plane coasted faster and faster until, with one mighty push it was launched into the air and flew up off into the early morning sky.

The trip out was, as is often the case, easier than the

trip to the island. Kono kept everyone fascinated with tales of Tanaka and they laughed when they heard how they had all been tailed for weeks before they had set off. As they landed at the small Hong Kong airport they breathed a collective sigh of relief; their trip was finally over and they were looking forward to getting back to what they thought of as their nice simple lives.

Once they had taxied into the hangar that less than two weeks before had been the scene of their daring escape, they alighted and began to unload the plane. Kono disappeared and returned a minute later in the car that had once belonged to Tanaka and they busied themselves filling it with gold from the boxes and then gently placing the golden Buddha into the boot.

'We should get that to the University first,' the professor said. 'Where we can conduct some research on it to find out exactly where it came from.'

Joe looked concerned.

'We'll find them, Joe. Don't worry, we'll find them.'

They all clambered into the back of the car and moved off into the airfield and then into the streets of Hong Kong. Kono drove at a steady pace, the first time he had done so in twenty years, and looked at the sights and the sounds of the city. He thought to himself how busy it seemed but also, somehow, how peaceful. The people here were just getting on with their own business, not harming anyone and – for the first time in many years – he had no desire to either. He glanced around, at the shops and the people, revelling in the sights and sounds of ordinary life. His thoughts were interrupted by a huge crash that made him instinctively look into his rear-view mirror. In it he saw a black Mercedes car with three men inside toting guns and grinning like devils. Every now and then they would ram them making them swerve and weave in the road.

Joe looked round and sighed. 'Oh, they're with me. You'd better lose them,' he said and he felt the full force of acceleration take him, once again, into the streets of Hong Kong.